NIGHTBORN

NEXT IN THE
THRONES & BONES SERIES . . .
SKYBORN

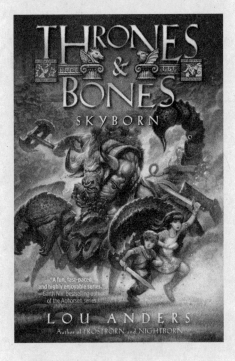

NIGHTBORN

❖ BOOK 2 ❖

LOU ANDERS

illustrations by JUSTIN GERARD

A YEARLING BOOK

This is a work of fiction. Names, characters, places, and incidents either are the product of the author's imagination or are used fictitiously. Any resemblance to actual persons, living or dead, events, or locales is entirely coincidental.

Text copyright © 2015 by Lou Anders
Cover art and interior illustrations copyright © 2015 by Justin Gerard
Maps by Robert Lazzaretti copyright © 2015 by Lou Anders
Rules of Charioteers board game copyright © 2015 by Lou Anders

All rights reserved. Published in the United States by Yearling, an imprint of Random House Children's Books, a division of Penguin Random House LLC, New York. Originally published in hardcover in the United States by Crown Books for Young Readers, an imprint of Random House Children's Books, New York, in 2015.

Yearling and the jumping horse design are registered trademarks of Penguin Random House LLC.

Visit us on the Web! randomhousekids.com

Educators and librarians, for a variety of teaching tools, visit us at RHTeachersLibrarians.com

The Library of Congress has cataloged the hardcover edition of this work as follows:
Anders, Lou.
Nightborn / Lou Anders ; illustrations by Justin Gerard. — First edition.
pages cm. — (Thrones and Bones ; book 2)
Summary: Karn Korlundsson must travel to the faraway city of Castlebriar, learn to play a new board game called Charioteers, decipher the Riddle of the Horn, and tangle with mysterious elves in order to rescue his best friend, Thianna Frostborn, facing great dangers at every step. Includes directions for playing Charioteers.
ISBN 978-0-385-39036-1 (trade) — ISBN 978-0-385-39038-5 (ebook)
[1. Adventure and adventurers—Fiction. 2. Dragons—Fiction. 3. Animals, Mythical—Fiction. 4. Mythology, Norse—Fiction. 5. Board games—Fiction. 6. Fantasy.] I. Gerard, Justin, illustrator. II. Title.
PZ7.A518855Nig 2015 [Fic]—dc23 2014042921

ISBN 978-0-385-39039-2 (pbk.)

Printed in the United States of America
10 9 8 7 6 5 4 3 2 1
First Yearling Edition 2016

FOR XIN

WILDERNESS
OF THE
BEAR FOLK

NORRØNGARD

YMIRIA

PLAINS
OF THE
MASTODONS

Dvergrian
Mountains

SWITHENMARK

Red (
Mountain

NELENIA

The Cold Sea

ARALAND

UNGLAND

SAISLAND

TH
BOV

ESCORAINE

The Glistening
Isles

TALVEDRA

BRUJALANDIA

N

SAEALFHEIMER COAST

WASTELANDS
OF CHIXMAL

Ophidian Mo

W

E

The Stormsea
Isles

IXTUN
TRIPLE
ALLIANCE

S

Sea of Moira

OMMERIKE

The Continent of Katernia

0   100   500   1000

Miles

THE TOWN OF CASTLEBRIAR

Westwater River

0 100   400   800

feet

CONTENTS

NIGHTBORN

CHAPTER ONE

Dangerous Games

The outside world was the best kind of terrifying.

Small and quick, Desstra darted from shadow to shadow under the light of the moons. Her teammates crept silently through the trees on either side. She felt exposed in the open air. So vulnerable without tons of rock overhead. But the unfamiliar night sky excited her, and the smell of victory kept her focused. They could win this.

Desstra sensed a pressure against her leg and froze. The trip wire was stretched taut across her shin. An ounce more force and it would snap.

She knelt carefully. She caught the thin wire between thumb and forefinger, holding it still as she moved her leg away. Her gaze followed the line to a bent tree limb.

A small cluster of spider egg sacs balanced on the branch. The sacs were the size and shape of rotten fruit. No baby spiders here. They would be filled with poison, acid, gas, or something equally nasty. Breaking the wire would send them hurling her way.

It was a crude trap, hastily constructed. The ones she'd set showed more finesse. Hard to detect, harder to disarm.

"What's the delay?" growled a voice to her right— Tanthal. Of all the dark elves who lived in the caverns of Deep Shadow, she liked him the absolute least. Couldn't he see that she had narrowly avoided a trap? Probably saw and didn't care. Tanthal was always critical of her. He was snide and superior. She hated that they were teammates, even if he was one of the two best students in the school.

Tanthal came up to her, a sneer on his pale face. She indicated the trip wire.

"We are in something of a hurry," he said.

"How very helpful of you to point out the obvious."

"If you're done wasting time here—"

"Don't get your tips in a twist," Desstra taunted, but then her own sharp ears twitched. Tanthal noticed and stopped speaking. He was arrogant but far from stupid. The Wyrdwood held worse dangers than rival classmates.

There—a shadow in the tree ahead.

Desstra's right arm whipped forward even as her left shoved Tanthal aside. He rolled gracefully and came to his feet. Then his lips parted in surprise when he saw the dart buried in the ground where he had stood.

A grunt of pain, then a dark elf dropped heavily out of the foliage. Desstra's own slender dart gleamed where it stuck in the elf's neck. He lay facedown.

"Is he—?" Tanthal began.

"Paralysis," Desstra answered. "Diluted hemlock. He'll be okay when it wears off in a few hours."

Tanthal looked as if he might kick the unfortunate elf. She pushed Tanthal aside and rolled her stricken opponent over so he wouldn't suffocate in the last of the winter snow.

"You're too soft," said Tanthal. "Leave him. We have a game to win."

He stepped over their fallen rival. Desstra gritted her teeth and followed. Tanthal was right on both counts. A stronger poison would have been within the rules. And the stakes were too high not to play to win.

Tonight was the final exam, the culmination of two years of training. The classes had been sent into the Wyrdwood and pitted against each other in a contest that would test all their skills—stealth, sabotage, speed, combat, strategy. And an ability to operate on the surface. Only the winning team would graduate and join the elite members of the Underhand, the secret order that protected the people of Deep Shadow and acted as their eyes and ears in the world above. It was the highest honor, not to be cheaply earned.

Desstra, Tanthal, and a female elf named Velsa were all that remained of their team. They slowed as they approached the enemy camp. Desstra flattened herself against the trunk of a tree and peered through its branches. She saw the black banner where it fluttered atop a spear standing alone in a glade. There was no one around. No one she could see. Guards would be hidden nearby, and the area would be rigged with snares and other hazards.

She caught Tanthal's eye, then pointed overhead and hoisted herself into the branches. When she was high enough, she climbed slowly out upon a limb. Balancing on her heels, she reached in her satchel for a spool of spider's silk. The thread was amazingly thin but strong as steel. Her specially treated gloves could handle the web without it sticking to her fingers. She let it spool out, dangling the web level with the banner. The wind caught it and carried it toward her target. When the line brushed the banner, it adhered instantly.

Desstra waited while her teammates readied their weapons. Then she gave a quick jerk on the spider silk, yanking the banner, spear and all, from the ground. She caught it in one hand, then leapt from the tree. Around her, three rival elves broke from cover. Time to run.

Tanthal's mace collided with one opponent's skull. The student fell, sprawling, and didn't move. But another elf was directly in front of Desstra, arms spread wide and wicked stilettos in each hand. His smile told her just how easily he expected to subdue her.

Desstra planted the spear in the snow, using it to vault into the air. As she soared over the surprised elf, she let something fall from her satchel.

The egg sac broke at her opponent's feet, spattering a sticky fungal paste all over him. The paste swelled rapidly, turning into a nasty yellow foam that would hold him tight until it dissolved.

Desstra allowed herself a moment of pride. The object now was to get the stolen banner back to their own base camp. Her classmate Velsa would run interference for her. Desstra would carry the prize. Tanthal had balked at that—he'd wanted that honor for himself—but she was unquestionably the fastest runner in their class.

Unfortunately, the remaining opponent was almost as fast, and he outdistanced Velsa easily. Desstra skipped aside from his slashing knives. Then Velsa was there, grasping but failing to slow the rival elf. Something whipped through the air between them. Tanthal's mace. But it didn't hit anyone. What had he been aiming at?

The trip wire snapped under the force of the projectile. The bent branch hurled its cluster of egg sacs. Enemy and teammate were both showered in an explosion of choking gas. They went down together, clutching their throats and gasping.

It was all Desstra could do not to lob her own egg sac at Tanthal.

"Don't just stand there after I saved you," he said, bending to retrieve his mace. "We need to keep moving."

Desstra hesitated, reaching into her satchel. She might have an antidote for Velsa.

"Leave her," barked Tanthal. "She'd rather bear the pain now than fail to graduate due to your misplaced kindness."

Now they were two. They ran on.

"You sacrificed one of us!" Desstra spat, unable to keep the shock from her voice.

"As long as our team wins, what does it matter?" Tanthal replied. "We'll all graduate. Velsa will thank me when we do. They all will."

Desstra wasn't so sure. While it was true that every member of the winning team would automatically graduate, they would also be evaluated separately. Their individual placement in the Underhand depended on it. It occurred to Desstra that in eliminating one of their own teammates, Tanthal was improving his own chances of being given a higher-ranked position. It was a cold move but not an illegal one. One that benefited the team some but Tanthal more.

They slowed as they drew near their own base camp. Desstra had set all the traps here personally. A complex series of trip wires and hidden spikes made the area nearly impassable to anyone who didn't know the design.

For Desstra, sure-footed as she was, dancing across the obstacles was child's play.

But there was a problem. Three rival students had fanned apart to block their approach. Their own guards had been overcome, though Desstra's traps still protected the camp.

"What would you say the chances are you'd let me carry that?" said Tanthal, indicating the banner.

"I'd say, 'not good,'" Desstra replied. She was suspicious of his motives. When the arrogant elf frowned, she said, "Don't ask questions when you think you won't like the answers."

"We need to get past those three. Give me the spear. I'll make sure I have their attention. When they come for me, you can navigate your traps. When you're across, I'll toss the spear to you. Unless you can't catch it."

"I can catch," she growled, though she wasn't ready to agree to his plan.

"Good, then you can run it home."

The strategy made sense. But it seemed unusually selfless of Tanthal. Desstra couldn't see a hole in it, however, so she passed the banner across.

Tanthal broke from cover.

"Looking for this?" he yelled, waving the banner back and forth in the air.

The three rival students converged on him instantly.

Desstra gave them a wide berth, swinging around to head for their base camp. They didn't spare her a glance, all eyes on the banner. If they let it slip by, their chances of graduation were over.

Desstra reached the first trip wire and leapt across.

"Desstra, catch!" came Tanthal's shout.

But that was all wrong. She wasn't anywhere near across.

She turned just in time to see the spear hurling her way. She caught it by instinct, not understanding why Tanthal had the plan so wrong.

All three dark elves ran straight at her. Then she saw what Tanthal had done. She had the spear. Only the spear. He had removed the black banner.

But the other team didn't know that. They were heading straight for her. She turned to run, leaping her many trip wires. But the elves in her wake didn't see the traps. They cut right across the wires, each elf snagging several.

Chaos erupted in every direction.

Gas, darts, foam, webbing. They were all engulfed, Desstra included. Her right foot was stuck fast in a vicious glue of her own design, while her left arm was wrapped in a net of spiderwebs that would take some work to untangle.

Fortunately, she had avoided setting any traps with deadly acids or poisons, but the mess she was in now was bad enough. Neither she nor her three rivals were going anywhere soon.

Tanthal chuckled as he strode casually by, nimbly picking his way across the ground. He waved the black banner at them as he passed.

"You—you—the banner—" Desstra couldn't talk. She was choking on her indignation, as well as on an unpleasant purple gas. Her eyes stung and her throat burned.

"Nothing about the rules says the banner has to stay on the spear," he laughed.

"You betrayed me!" she yelled back.

"And we won. Relax, Desstra. I just made sure you graduated."

He gave a short bow, then marched into their camp.

Desstra slumped to the ground, with nothing to do but wait for her traps to dissolve. Her opponents grumbled and cursed, but she was deaf to their complaints. She would graduate, true, but how would her evaluation go? Surely her instructors would see that she had been instrumental in the win—would have won for her team, in fact, had Tanthal not betrayed her. Stuck in the bonds of her own traps, she wasn't sure. Results were what mattered. Not excuses about what could have or should have been. One thing was clear: Tanthal had played both sides expertly, and Tanthal had won.

"I win," said Karn, sliding his Jarl off the edge of the board with a grin. "That's two barrels of fish you owe me for my one ox."

Bandulfr's hairy face loomed over the Thrones and Bones set. His bloodshot eyes studied all the pieces, looking for something to which he could object. Then he spat in defeat and sat back, a wide smile stretching open to show his many missing teeth.

"It's a fine game you play, young Karn Korlundsson," the fisherman said. "But would you make it best two out of three?"

"Wish I could," replied Karn truthfully. "But I've got to get to the fur market to unload some arctic fox pelts. Pack up the barrels for me, will you? I'll send Pofnir along to collect them later."

Bandulfr's disappointment showed in his face. Then he leaned into Karn's own. Karn could smell the sea all over the man.

"Your father's letting you do all the trading this year, is he? Thinks parading the young hero around gets him a better deal?"

"It's time I learned," said Karn.

"And you have. And well. Too well," said Bandulfr. "But I guess the chance to haggle with a local legend takes the sting out of the hard bargains you drive, eh, boy? Not many Norrønir have done what you've done. Beat old Helltoppr in his barrow and faced down the dragon Orm in his den? Can I see it, then? Just for a moment?"

Karn sighed. Everyone wanted a glimpse.

He withdrew Whitestorm from its sheath and held

the sword up. The blade had a red-gold sheen from something unusual mixed in with its steel, and it was lighter than it should be for its size. But it didn't have any fancy engraving. No magic jewels in its oval guard or round pommel; no mystic runes running down its length. It was just an ordinary spatha-style sword, actually a bit too long for him. Better suited for a taller warrior or someone mounted on horseback.

Korlundr had insisted his famous son wear the sword on this trip. Karn had to admit he was enjoying all the attention. Everywhere he went, folks slapped his back and asked him what it had been like when his uncle had betrayed his father and sent Karn fleeing alone into the northern wastes. They wanted to hear how Karn had stood up to a dragon, how he'd faced an undead draug warrior in his barrow and restored his father to life. But mostly they wanted to hear about Thianna, the half-giant girl from the Ymirian mountain range whom Karn had met in the snows. Thianna, who had been fleeing from her own family problems and who had become his companion in adventure, then his best friend in the world. He wouldn't have survived without her.

"Was she really as big as all that?" asked Bandulfr. "What was she, this big?" He held a hand over his head.

"Bigger," replied Karn, grinning. "In every way."

He left the fisherman's stall and took the street east from the docks, heading to the fur market. Life in

Norrøngard was good, but he missed the enormous girl, the excitement of having her in his life. That sort of wild adventuring belonged in the past now.

Lost in thought, Karn didn't notice the shadow falling over him until the beat of wings kicked up dust clouds and people started screaming and pointing and running away.

Sharp-taloned claws caught him under the armpits. Then, the ground falling away fast, Karn was rising into the sky.

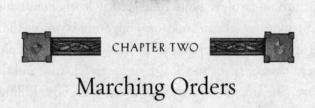

CHAPTER TWO

Marching Orders

The stone was hard and unforgiving. Desstra's knees ached. Even so, she shouted the school slogan as loud as any of her classmates.

"Swift as the great wolf." She yelled at the top of her lungs, but kept her eyes lowered. "Silent as the shadow."

The students' combined voices echoed off the vaulted walls and ceiling. The natural rock of the cavern had been carved long ago into an ornate auditorium. Huge columns flanked the stage, with sculptures on the walls depicting important moments in the history of Deep Shadow. It was every dark elf's dream to see their own deeds recorded in the eternal stone.

"Deadly as the serpent," chanted the class. "Strong as the rock of our home."

It was all quite thrilling. For the winners, anyway.

Moments earlier the losing team had been stripped of their student uniforms and dismissed in disgrace. Never again would they be allowed into this hall or any of the Underhand's private caverns. Desstra had stolen a glance at their retreating backs and bowed heads. The former students would have to seek other professions— mushroom farmers, household guards, leather craftsmen, stonemasons. It didn't matter. They would console them- selves that these were all respectable means of employ- ment necessary for the health of Deep Shadow, and they were. She imagined such jobs could even be fulfilling— to someone who hadn't set hopes on being one of the Underhand. But these professions weren't glorious. Glory belonged only to Desstra and her fellows.

One by one, her classmates were called by name— Soren, Ulami, Urven, Velsa, Dindrel. One by one, they rose and approached the stone altar, where an elder presented them with their new gear. New armor, and Underhand cloaks and hoods—all crafted from black leather. Now they were full Underhand agents, ready to give their lives for the city. As each student left, Desstra's anticipation grew. Finally, only she and one other elf re- mained. Predictably, it was *him*.

"Tanthal," called senior instructor Orysa. Tanthal rose and approached the altar. "You have done well. We are exceedingly pleased." Desstra heard the rustle of some- thing changing hands, heard Tanthal gasp.

She couldn't help but glance up. Her classmate held a long leather coat. Rather than the plain black given to the other graduates, Tanthal's coat was black with yellow patterns. Its leather was made from the mottled skin of the giant fire salamander. The leather was strong and supple and, like the creature from which it came, resistant to flame.

Desstra's breath caught in her throat. Such skin was only used for an officer's cloak!

And her own name was still to be called. She ducked her head quickly, but her ears were burning with pride. Tanthal had been called first. Was she to be ranked even higher? The instructors had seen her performance. They knew her class's victory in the Wyrdwood was due to her ability, whatever treachery Tanthal might have committed at the end.

She heard her untrustworthy classmate's footsteps retreating as he was led from the hall. And then it was Desstra's turn. She was alone with the senior instructor. She waited, head bowed, for her name to be called.

And waited.

And waited.

Desstra couldn't help herself. She looked up.

"I suppose you think that you deserve to be congratulated."

Senior instructor Orysa was as stern as they came. Eyes hard as obsidian. Face like chiseled granite. Her black hair was shorn away, leaving a pale white skull bald and naked except for a web pattern of tattoos.

"I suppose I do," quipped Desstra, then bit her tongue when she saw that Orysa's expression hadn't changed. "Don't I?"

"Your performance in the Wyrdwood. How do you rate it?"

"Highly. I mean, we did win," Desstra stammered, confused by the instructor's tone.

"Tanthal won," Orysa corrected. "The rest of you were carried by his victory."

"But," Desstra protested, "I set the defensive traps. I retrieved the banner. I—"

"Desstra," said Orysa, cutting her off. "Your tactical, camouflage, and weapon skills are excellent. No one disputes that. Your potions are potent. Your traps, elegant and efficient. You have quick reflexes, and you exhibit a deadly accuracy with your darts."

"No argument here," said Desstra. Despite her bravado, she was starting to get concerned. If they agreed on her skills, where was her uniform? Why was she the only one left if not to be ranked the highest? "But?" she asked tentatively.

"But it is felt that you lack a certain, shall we say, ruthlessness. A willingness to do whatever it takes."

"Wait a minute. I won . . . for us. I won."

Orysa shook her bald head.

"You are soft-hearted. Not stone-hearted. You may be silent as the shadow, but you are hardly strong as the rock of our home. Stand up."

Desstra rose, dizzy with confusion. How could she be the last to graduate in the class if she was being reprimanded? As she stood, her eyes came to rest upon what was laid atop the stone altar—a most unusual outfit.

A sleeveless leather jerkin. It was patterned like Tanthal's coat, but rather than being black and yellow, the mottling was of a different color.

"Orange?" said Desstra. Orange-patterned salamanders were few and far between. In a society that stressed conformity, they were generally held to be harbingers of bad luck.

"An aberration," said Orysa. "A rare specimen that doesn't fit in with the others. Like you."

"I don't understand," Desstra said. Orysa sighed.

"You present us with a problem, little elf," said the senior instructor. "Like this reptile skin, you, too, are an aberration. Your skills are too valuable to fail you outright. And yet—yet we don't feel that you are ready to move on. And so you are going to be given another chance. It has been decided that you will be held back. You will remain at the student level."

"I'm to be put with another class?" Her head swam. She'd expected to graduate with honors, and instead she wasn't graduating at all. To start over, with fresh recruits, would be humiliating.

"No," said Orysa. "You don't need more training. That is clear. What you need is the urgency of real stakes, real work to harden your spirit. You need to face that which is deadly as the serpent, and overcome it. Danger and the threat of death. You are to be assigned to an officer and sent on assignment into the field."

Into the field, but not as a graduate. Desstra had never heard of such a thing. She looked down at her strange orange-and-black leather armor. How could she face her classmates when her very clothing marked her as different?

"A few months ago," Orysa continued, "the Keeper of the Wings reported great agitation among his colony. They heard something, disturbing them in their roost. A sound too shrill for even elfin ears. Agents were sent to the surface world, traveling overland to the northeast of Norrøngard to investigate the sound. They have failed to return. However, our spies elsewhere have confirmed that an object of power lost long ago has resurfaced. It is beyond our reach at present. But more such objects are being sought, and a mission in the south has reported an interesting development. You and an officer will join this mission in progress, and your graduation will be conditional on his favorable assessment of your performance. Desstra, you are being given a second chance. Do you understand? Do not squander this opportunity."

Desstra nodded, shame and regret burning on her pale cheeks. Her weak heart had cost her graduation. How could she face her family—or anyone—ever again? It was better that she was being sent out of Deep Shadow, where she wouldn't have to confront their disappointment.

"You are to prepare for your mission immediately. We expect you to obey your superior in all things."

"Yes, senior instructor," said Desstra. She heard someone approach from behind her.

"Don't look so glum, my sad apprentice," said a smug voice. "Things could always be worse."

That was a lie. Desstra knew the minute the officer spoke that things were as bad as they could ever be. She turned slowly, feeling as if the roof of the cavern were collapsing on her in that moment. If only it would!

The officer who stood before her in his newly donned yellow-and-black leather long coat looking so sickeningly pleased with himself—the officer she was assigned to, the one she must obey, who would decide her fate and determine the course of her life—the officer was Tanthal.

Karn dangled in the cold, thin air. The ground was unnervingly far below. Mile after mile raced by beneath his feet. It was frightening to look down, but he had to crane his neck painfully to look up. The creature that carried him was a wyvern, like those he and Thianna had faced last winter. The wyverns had come from a faraway country, carrying olive-skinned warrior women with armor of bronze and lances that spouted flame. They had been seeking Thianna, or rather, the magical horn that she carried. But Karn and Thianna had defeated them, and the horn had been destroyed. Swallowed, in fact.

This wyvern was without a rider. Karn was fairly certain it was the same one that had helped Thianna before. When he'd last seen the creature, it had told the giant girl that it was leaving, flying away from the problems of humans and their struggles. Karn wished he could speak to the wyvern mind to mind as Thianna had done, but that was a gift of the horn and a talent of Thianna's mother's culture. It wasn't something he could do. He had no idea why this wyvern had captured him, and no idea where they were heading.

Curiosity mounting, Karn studied the terrain. They seemed to be heading east and north. They flew over water that would eventually flow to the fjord by his home. But they were miles north of Korlundr's Farm. They were nearer Dragon's Dance, where he'd first met Thianna, where his adventure had begun. Karn caught a glimpse of the ancient campsite as it passed underneath. He made a mental calculation, sketching a line in his mind from the town of Bense to Dragon's Dance and continuing on. When he realized where the line pointed, he began to struggle.

The wyvern snarled and gave him a shake. Karn knew his efforts were pointless. After all, he didn't want the reptile to drop him—though a fall wasn't much worse than what might be in store for him when they reached their destination. They were headed to Sardeth, to the Blasted City. The home of the great dragon Orm.

Karn and Thianna had faced the dragon before. They

had even come to an understanding with him. Orm had let them go, on the promise that they destroy the Horn of Osius. And Thianna had, orchestrating events so that the dragon had actually swallowed both the horn and the mysterious woman who'd sought it. Karn thought the dragon had been satisfied with that outcome. Had Orm experienced a change of heart? Maybe the enormous linnorm regretted letting them go. Worse, maybe Orm had somehow heard of Karn's bragging in the city of Bense. Was he angry that a mere boy was claiming to have bested him? Karn wished he had kept his big mouth shut. The admiration of a few Norrønir fishmongers and fur traders was hardly worth becoming a dragon's dinner.

The ruins of Sardeth appeared directly below them. Karn looked glumly at the scorched trees, the crumbled buildings that had once been a proud outpost of the Gordion Empire. The dilapidated coliseum that was Orm's den was dead ahead. The wyvern dipped, bringing Karn down to deposit the boy around the midsection of the tiered seating. The coliseum floor had collapsed, exposing the warren of tunnels and rooms that was the underground hypogeum where animals and gladiators had once awaited their turn in the arena. As Karn watched, something moved in the shadows. Then Orm Hinn Langi, the Doom of Sardeth, rose up into the air.

"Greetings, Mouse," said the dragon with a smile.

Karn's hand instinctively dropped to the pommel of his sword. Orm's large eyes followed the motion. The dragon's pupils narrowed. Karn realized how useless Whitestorm would be against the enormous creature. Orm could roast him alive or swallow him whole before his blade even cleared its sheath. He forced his fingers to relax, staring back at the dragon and waiting to see what would happen next. The dragon's response was the last thing he'd expected.

Orm laughed.

"Your pardon, Karn Korlundsson," the great linnorm said, the rumble of his humor echoing off the coliseum walls and setting all the stonework vibrating, "but you should see your face."

"My face? What?" stammered Karn. His cheeks burned as he realized the dragon was having him on. He felt both relieved and embarrassed. "You mean you're not—?"

"Hungry?" said Orm with a wicked smile. He laughed again. "No, why would I go through the bother of fetching you all the way from Bense just to eat you? Don't flatter yourself you're that appetizing a meal, young Norrønur."

"I guess I can live with not being tasty," Karn said. "But why bring me here? What do you want?"

"Why, to talk," said Orm.

This was another surprise in a day full of surprises. And while Karn was glad not to be on the dinner menu, conversations with dragons weren't exactly known for being risk free. Still, he was curious. One question presented itself immediately. He gestured to the wyvern where it perched in the coliseum stands, watching them both.

"How did you get that one to catch me? How did you even know where it was?"

"Good, good," said the dragon, clapping his foreclaws. "Intelligent questions. I expected no less, and I do hate being disappointed. I used the Horn of Osius, of course."

"You know its name now?" said Karn, who didn't recall that Orm had ever been told the name of Thianna's horn. Also, the horn had been destroyed. Thianna said that Orm had taken care of it quite permanently. "But didn't you—?"

"Swallow it? Yes." Orm shifted, showing off more of his long, snakelike body. "And I have learned a good deal about the hateful thing since I devoured it. I discovered its name, a bit of its purpose. . . . I have even absorbed a little of its power. What is it that they say? You are what you eat, after all."

"You can do that?"

Orm just flicked a tongue in response.

"Okay, you can. So you used the horn's power to call this wyvern. Then you compelled it to go after me."

Orm smiled.

"Bravo. I knew not roasting you in flame was a good idea."

"I'm glad you think so," said Karn. "But why? I don't mean about the roasting. I mean the fetching and talking bit."

For answer, the dragon ran his great tongue around inside his lips, worrying at something lodged in his enormous teeth.

Orm leaned forward—Karn jumped a little at this; he couldn't help himself—and thrust his snout close to Karn's own face. Karn felt the heat and rotten-meat smell of the dragon's breath. Then Orm curled an upper lip aside and spat something out sideways at the boy's feet.

Karn looked down at the saliva-drenched mess before him. It looked like clothing, no, armor—black leather armor with yellow patterns. He recognized it.

"That's Svartálfar armor," exclaimed Karn. "Dark elves."

The dark elves—actually they had pale white skin but dark eyes and dark hair—were a subterranean species who dwelled deep under the mountains in southwestern Norrøngard. They were rarely seen on the surface. In the past, open wars had been fought between the humans of Norrøngard and the elves of the Svartálfaheim Mountains. These days there was an uneasy truce, and encounters with the elves were rare.

"The Svartálfar came poking around my coliseum," explained Orm. "Something they haven't dared do in centuries."

"So you ate them?" said Karn, his stomach churning at the thought.

"Naturally," said the dragon. "Though not before I learned what they were after."

"The horn?" guessed Karn. "You're sure? They told you?"

The dragon smiled. "Well, as you yourself know from experience, I do so like to play with my food."

Karn gulped. He did know this was true.

"They must have been disappointed to learn you'd swallowed the only horn."

"I'm sure they were," said the dragon. "Though I supposed that in a way they found what they were looking for." Orm chuckled at his own joke. "But that's not the important bit," he continued. "What you should be paying attention to is this: they didn't believe it *was* the only one."

Karn stood straighter at this revelation.

"Not the only one? You mean there's *another* Horn of Osius? Oh no!"

"Oh no, indeed." Orm's eyes narrowed. The previous horn had allowed Thianna to get inside Orm's mind. This had made the dragon uncomfortable. But if someone were to really master the horn, they might be able to control Orm the way he compelled the wyvern. The great linnorm had destroyed a city and devoured legions of soldiers in his youth. If the dark elves—or anyone else—got their hands on another horn, they could turn Orm into a weapon of devastating, unstoppable power.

"Before it went down, my food told me that a second group of dark elves have been sent south to search for another horn."

"Where?"

Orm nosed at the gnawed armor at Karn's feet. Karn looked again and saw a metal scroll case amid the debris.

"Open it," said the dragon.

Frowning at the wet, warm spit on its surface, Karn took the scroll case and popped the lid. Reaching in, he withdrew a yellowed parchment.

"Can you read?" Orm asked.

"Yes," said Karn, irked by the question, even though literacy wasn't common among the Norrønir.

"Then do so now."

Karn squinted his eyes at the rune markings. The daylight was fast ending, and the setting sun had dipped past the edge of the high coliseum walls.

"It's a little dark."

Orm spat again, and Karn really did jump as a small fireball erupted from the dragon's mouth. The flame burned where it struck, a wad of sizzling, molten spit that cast a circle of reddish light.

"Is that adequate?" Orm asked with mock politeness.

"It'll do." Glaring first at the dragon for startling him, Karn turned his attention to the paper. Neither the parchment nor the writing was particularly old. So it wasn't ancient or valuable. Someone had copied this down recently. That meant what it said was more important than what it was. He studied the words.

"It looks like a riddle," Karn said.

"Read it aloud," Orm commanded.

Karn did so.

> *"First to a Castle in the Briars,*
> *Where ends all of life's desires.*
> *Over Oak and under Corn,*
> *There to seek the soundless Horn."*

Karn looked up.

"I don't understand," he said. "What does this mean?"

"I suspect it is a clue to the whereabouts of the second horn, a clue the dark elves are following. The opening line awakened a memory in me."

"'First to a Castle in the Briars'?"

"Yes. I suspect that is a thinly veiled reference to the city of Castlebriar. A former Gordion outpost in the country of Nelenia and now an independent city."

"Okay. Makes sense. I've heard of Nelenia—it's way south and east of us, somewhere near the middle of the continent—though I don't know the city. But what does this have to do with me?"

"What does it have to do with you?" The dragon looked surprised. "Isn't that obvious, Karn Korlundsson? I want you to go and find it."

Karn nearly dropped the parchment.

"Me? Why me?"

"Why not you? You've proved resourceful in the past.

Intelligent. Clever. You defeated Helltoppr in his barrow. Why—you've even bested a dragon." Orm narrowed his eyes menacingly. "Isn't that what they say in the markets of Bense?"

Karn slapped a palm to his forehead.

"I knew that was going to come back to bite me!"

"You want me to bite you?" teased the dragon.

"No! No!" Karn cried hastily. "It's an expression, a figure of speech."

"Very well. No biting, then. The riddle is very old, but I believe the dark elves have ascribed new meaning to it in light of recent events."

"You mean they've heard some of my story?"

"All of Norrøngard seems to have heard. It isn't unlikely their spies heard as well and came here to seek the truth."

"Um, I'm sorry about that. But I still don't know why you need me. I'm a farmer now. I don't run off on adventures. Why not ask someone else? Why not ask Thianna? She's bigger, stronger. She's much better with a sword than I am. She knows what the horn is and how to use it. After all, her own mother's people made it. And she's even going that way. Really, no matter how you look at it, she's obviously a much better choice than me."

"I thought so too," said the dragon calmly.

Karn stared into the great linnorm's eyes.

"Oh," said Karn.

"Oh, indeed," agreed the dragon. "I summoned the wyvern and fetched Thianna after the dark elves invaded my home. Yesterday, the wyvern returned without her, having missed their prearranged rendezvous. I believe she has run afoul of their schemes."

A fear worse than winding up as dragon dinner gripped Karn.

"Thianna," he said, his skin growing cold. Then another emotion burned the fear away.

Karn was shouting and shaking with rage, swinging Whitestorm back and forth in the dragon's face. He was furious that Orm had sent his friend off into obvious peril. Then he realized the danger of hurling insults at the largest dragon in this part of the world. He froze midswing and mid-insult.

"Are you quite through now?" said Orm.

"I think so," said Karn. "Um, I'm sorry."

"I should expect so."

Karn sheathed his sword and dropped his head. He went over what he knew. "So, Thianna might be in trouble. And you want me to go find her?"

Orm nodded.

"Why don't you go yourself?"

Something flickered across the dragon's face. Distaste? Could it even be fear? "I forswore the south long ago," he said.

"Why?"

"Not your business."

"Neither is tracking down magical horns."

Orm's nostrils flared. "I lost something there. Something very dear was taken from me. I left and I never looked back. Leave it at that."

"And ate several legions of Gordion soldiers when you got here. That always seemed extreme to me. Was it the Gordions who crossed you?"

"I will not discuss this with you," Orm growled. "Let it go."

Karn didn't want to, but arguing with dragons was not a wise activity. Still, he began to suspect that Orm hadn't come to Norrøngard by accident. Norrøngard was the farthest corner of the continent from the heart of the old Gordion Empire. The dragon had chosen this remote location on purpose. When he came here, he had been fleeing something. What could have happened to so rattle a creature as big as Orm? He filed it away to consider later.

"All right," said Karn.

"You will go?" asked Orm.

"I would do anything for Thianna," Karn said. "Though I'm not sure what I can do without her."

"You will have to be sufficient on your own. But perhaps I can lend you some assistance." Orm sniffed at Karn, his snout nosing at the sword at Karn's side. "That weapon isn't one of mine. But I smell its potential. Draw it from its sheath."

Ordinarily, Karn would doubt the wisdom of raising a

blade to a dragon, but he'd already threatened Orm with it once today, so what did he have to lose? He withdrew Whitestorm and held it before him.

"The sword has a more storied history than you know. Once it was a weapon of great power."

Orm readjusted his great bulk, then reached forward with both of his foreclaws. Karn squared his shoulders and kept Whitestorm steady. The dragon placed his claws to either side of the sword. Orm closed his eyes, and Karn heard a rumbling in the dragon's throat. Words he didn't recognize in a language he did not speak. It was the secret language of dragons. The skin on Karn's arm tingled. The blade seemed to pulse with energy.

Orm opened his eyes.

"It is done. I could not restore its lost magic completely, but I have lent it some of my own. You will find it easier to wield, though it will only augment your own skill, not replace it."

Karn stared at the blade. Did it seem to glow faintly in the twilight?

"Thank you."

Orm's eyelids dipped and rose in subtle acknowledgment.

"Now," he said, "how is your Common speech?" The dragon was referring to the language of the old Gordion Empire, which now served as a shared tongue amid the many countries on the continent of Katernia. Karn knew he couldn't expect his Norrønian to be understood all the way in Nelenia.

"Rusty," he admitted.

"Ah," said the dragon. "Then I am afraid you will like this next bit even less. Place your head in my mouth."

CHAPTER THREE

The Deeds of Heroes

"Men die. Cattle die. Only the deeds of heroes live on."

Bandulfr was roaring loudly in Stolki's Hall. The fisherman had heard Karn tell of his recent encounter with Orm and was overjoyed that the boy might be setting out on another quest. Others were less thrilled at the prospect.

"Nonsense," said Pofnir, the freeman who managed so much of the business of Korlundr's Farm. "Karn needs to stay and conduct the trade. He doesn't have time to go gallivanting off on some strange dragon's errand. Tell him, Karn."

"Well, I—" began Karn.

"Bah," snorted Bandulfr. "Life is brutal and short. Old age is an embarrassment."

"Um, I wouldn't really be embarrassed—" said Karn.

"Of course you are," said the fisherman, clamping an arm around his shoulder and trying to pull the boy away from the freeman. "Karn knows that songs of praise and a noble name are what matter."

"No, wait," said Karn, who wasn't appreciating the way everyone was speaking for him as if he weren't there. Also, he was looking for a polite way to point out that *Bandulfr* was hardly a noble name in Bense. Nor was the fisherman particularly young.

"Karn doesn't want to listen to this foolishness," said Pofnir, prying Bandulfr's arm off Karn and trying to lead the boy away in a different direction. "He has to go over the exchange rate for unblemished cattle hide in preparation for tomorrow's negotiations."

"Yes, but—" said Karn.

"Cattle hide?" roared Bandulfr, planting a palm in Pofnir's chest and shoving the freeman aside. "Karn, tell Pofnir how you've already outwitted trolls, beaten an undead draug, outsmarted a dragon, and saved your father's life. Tell him that you don't have time for cattle hide! This will be an adventure for the skalds to write songs about!"

"Well, I never—" hollered Pofnir, poking Bandulfr with a finger. "Karn knows you just want to pack him off on an adventure so you don't have to haggle with him anymore!"

Karn watched the two men argue—one so eager to see him rush off into danger and the other reminding him of all his responsibilities. He looked hopefully at the door to Stolki's, hoping that his father would return from the day's negotiations. He wanted Korlundr's advice. Karn didn't feel strong enough or brave enough to tackle the challenge ahead alone. And not just alone—he wouldn't have Thianna with him.

Thianna. Missing and in danger. Karn's uncertainty vanished.

"A boy is counted a man when he can swing a sword, hurl an insult—" Bandulfr was yelling.

"I'm going," said Karn loudly.

"What?" Pofnir blinked. "But the cattle hides?"

"Can wait," said Karn. "I know. And I'm sorry. But I'm going. Not for the dragon. Not for the horn. Not—I'm sorry, Bandulfr—for the songs. I'm going for Thianna. Because she needs me."

"But what can you do?" said Pofnir, still blinking at him.

"What I can."

Pofnir looked like he might object, but there was a commotion by the door. All eyes turned toward the disturbance.

Karn craned his neck for a glimpse over the crowd. He hoped Korlundr had returned. But that wasn't what he saw.

Pale-skinned people with black hair and black clothing were pushing into Stolki's Hall. Norrønir grumbled and spat at the sight of them but fell back to let them in nonetheless. Though Karn had never seen these strange folk so close before, he knew them instantly.

"Dark elves," he said under his breath.

"Be healthy, gentlefolk," said Stolki, bustling over with mugs of mead in his hands. "It's a long time since we've seen the Svartálfar in Bense. Will you be wanting food as well as drink?"

"Neither," said a haughty elf with a sneer. He wore a yellow-patterned long coat. "We're looking for a boy."

"A boy?" repeated Stolki.

"Yes," said the elf. "A local legend, this boy."

"No boys here." Bandulfr charged over, managing to somehow show off the ax swinging at his side. "Only men among the Norrønir. *Hard men.*"

"Busy men," added Pofnir, stepping up. "Men with work to do." Karn felt a rush of gratitude. Both of them were protecting him. Others in the crowd placed themselves between Karn and the dark elves.

He felt a hand on his shoulder.

"This way." It was his sister Nyra. "Keep your head down," she said, taking his hand. She led him through the crowded hall. When they came to the back door, she turned to face him.

"Go and rescue your friend," she said. Then she pushed something into his palm. Karn saw that it was her coin pouch.

"I can't take—"

"Of course you can," said Nyra. "Now, go be a hero."

"Will you . . . ?"

"I'll tell Father. He'll understand. And Mother. She won't like it. But she'll understand too."

Karn gripped his sister tight.

"Take care of them," he whispered.

"Take care of yourself," she said.

Then she shoved him out into the night.

I really thought I was done with being chased, thought Karn. He was moving as swiftly as he could while still being cautious.

For the most part, he was avoiding the city streets, creeping over fences and through backyards instead. Unfortunately, stepping off the wooden planks that formed Bense's main thoroughfares meant that his boots were now thoroughly caked in mud. They squelched as he ran.

Karn was heading for the center of town, to a spot where several streets came together to form the large Trickster's Market, where everything that wasn't fish, fur, or steel could be bought. It was mostly deserted at this time of night, everyone having retired to a tavern or hall for the evening.

He slipped from the shadows and stepped into the market. Stalls and tents ringed the area, which was dominated by a heap of stones piled roughly at its center. The stones were known as a hörgr, a shrine to one of the Nor-rønir gods. This one was to Lothar, the god of trickery and mischief. Karn was heading for the stones now.

Unfortunately, a dark elf stood between Karn and his destination. The elf was dressed in black with orange markings. Hooded. Slight of build. Possibly female, but he wasn't sure. Standing with back to the hörgr and seemingly alone. Good. Karn sized up the situation and decided how to play it.

"Looking for someone?" he said, stepping deliberately into the elf's line of sight.

A pale hand dipped to a leather satchel. Karn would bet there were weapons stashed inside. Nasty ones.

"I haven't seen you around. New to Bense?" he asked. "Then you may not know that this is called Trickster's Market. Care to guess why?"

The hand by the satchel hesitated. The elf was trying to work out what Karn was on about. Time to bring him (her?) up to speed.

"Let me show you."

Karn let out a loud, long whistle.

The wyvern reared from behind the stones of the hörgr, screeching horribly and spreading its wings to their full extent.

Startled, the elf jumped clear of the stones. Karn almost laughed as he (she?) dove to the ground and threw his (her?) body into a roll. Instead, he seized the opportunity and raced past. Bounding from stone to stone, Karn reached the wyvern and swung into the saddle.

"Let's go," he said.

The wyvern took to the air.

Below them, the elf hurled something that burst against the reptile's belly in a noisome purple cloud, but it dissipated quickly in the beat of the wyvern's wings. Then the town of Bense dropped away and Karn was heading over the waters of Serpent's Gulf. He allowed himself a last look behind as the shores of Norrøngard receded. Then he turned his face to the south and the excitement of the adventure to come.

Once again, Desstra was both terrified and exultant under the open sky. Only this time, she was a part of it. Here, above the clouds, Desstra felt like she was one of a hundred thousand points of light, a shooting star hurtling across the world. The cold air whipped through her hair as she flew through the night. Her pale white skin positively glowed in the moonlight. She gripped the ruff around her wing's neck and bent to rub her face in the soft brown fur. It squeaked in pleasure and wriggled its head.

"I don't know why you two are so happy," said Tanthal, who rode slightly ahead of her. "After all, we lost the Norrønur."

Desstra's ears twitched angrily. Did Tanthal have to spoil every good moment? Probably so. It was what he lived for.

"Yes," she replied. "Your rather unsubtle plan to barge in and nab him worked brilliantly."

Another elf riding nearby chuckled at that. Tanthal's expression darkened. He didn't like to lose any face in front of the team.

"You were the one he got by in the market," he said. "He was alone then. Just one boy."

"He wasn't completely alone, now, was he?" objected Desstra, thinking of the enormous reptile that had so startled her. Yes, it irritated her that Karn had gotten away, but she wasn't going to take responsibility for such a poorly planned operation and a surprise wyvern. "Anyway, how was I to know he could fly too? Norrønir don't fly. Not like this." Thoughts of flying lifted her spirits again. She patted the head of her wing. "Nothing is as good as this, is it, boy?"

Flittermouse squeaked again. Desstra was amazed by how quickly she had formed a bond with the giant bat. When the Keeper of the Wings had brought them into the roost, Flittermouse had dropped from his perch and flown down to her immediately. Some of her classmates had shied away from the sharp-fanged creatures, unsure and intimidated by them, but Desstra had run to Flittermouse and flung her arms about his neck.

"You're too soft on your wing," Tanthal said. "It will

run right over you if you don't show it who's boss from the start."

"Flittermouse will do no such thing," said Desstra. "We understand each other just fine."

Tanthal snorted.

"Anyway," he said, "Bense wasn't a total loss. I only thought that the boy could tell us something of his recent experiences with the horn. Instead, the presence of the wyvern means we now know he seeks it too. And that he does so because Orm has most certainly enlisted him. Our paths will cross again, and we'll know not to underestimate him next time."

He watched Desstra stroke Flittermouse's fur. Irritated by her affectionate treatment, he made a course correction by cruelly jerking on his own wing's sensitive ear. The bat squeaked in pain, but it flew where it was told.

"Stone-hearted, Desstra," he said. He fished in a pocket and tossed something to her. She caught it. It was a round rock.

"What's this?"

"A reminder," he replied.

"Of what's in your head?" she mocked.

"Of where we come from," Tanthal snapped. "I expect you to be strong as the rock of our home. And I'm watching you. If I don't like what I see . . ." He let the rest hang in the air, unspoken. As if she needed reminding of who held the reins of her future. "Maybe we should start by teaching you to stop pampering that bat. It's a beast of burden, not a pet, and it only responds to force and authority." He tweaked his wing's ear again, as if to demonstrate what he meant, but this time the giant bat buckled under him. Tanthal was nearly thrown from the saddle. He cried out and clutched tightly to keep from falling.

"Force and authority?" laughed Desstra. "If that's what you were aiming for, I'd say you missed." Several other elves chuckled at this. Tanthal swatted the bat's neck in irritation.

"Sometimes a soft touch works best," Desstra continued. "You should think of it like setting traps. Or mixing poisons. Maybe when we get to Castlebriar, I'll show you what I mean."

CHAPTER FOUR

Barbarian at the Gate

Karn left the wyvern hidden in the woods. They had arrived during the night, when their descent wouldn't be noticed. He had worried that his lack of camping gear would make a night in the forest uncomfortable, but he needn't have been concerned. After his time in the wilderness of Ymiria, this mild southern climate was nothing. And if there were any wild animals in the forests, the presence of an enormous, cranky reptile that hissed loudly when it snored certainly kept them away.

"I'll be back as soon as I can," he told the wyvern, which snorted indifferently and went back to sleep.

Nelenia. Araland, Ungland, Saisland—all had zipped by as he traveled halfway across the continent to Nelenia. He saw towns, villages, castles, mountains, lakes, rivers, roads. Even though he'd grown up hungry for stories and maps of other places, nothing could really prepare him for the sheer scale of the lands.

Now the city of Castlebriar was before him. And what a sight it was! Ancient Gordion walls still surrounded the city on all sides except for the docks, but nearly half the population had spilled out into dwellings beyond these walls. He followed a road now—a real road, not the dirt paths of Norrøngard. It was stone-paved and flanked by footpaths and drainage ditches. Karn marveled that something as simple as a nice road could make him feel out of his depth.

Ahead loomed an ancient bridge, complete with guard towers on both ends. He saw a lumber mill on the opposite bank. To his right were row upon row of half-timbered houses, white plaster visible between the exposed framing. It was nothing like the longhouses and wattle-and-daub cabins of Bense. Karn felt rustic and unsophisticated, a barbarian boy from the edge of the world. A long, long way from home.

There was a line at the city gates, where two guards stood, questioning each traveler before letting him or her in.

After a short but smelly wait behind a flatulent donkey, it was his turn. The guards looked at him expectantly.

"Um," said Karn. "My name is Karn Korlundsson. I'm here to find—"

"Look, boy," replied one of the guards. "We don't

speak Norrønian. You want to be understood, you talk Nelenian or Common."

Karn blinked at the man. He understood everything perfectly. So why couldn't the man understand him? He tried again.

"My name is Karn Korlundsson." Karn's words died in his throat.

"That's better," said the guard. "Go on."

But Karn was trying to stare down at his own mouth. He ran his tongue around the inside of his teeth and stretched out his lips.

"I think there is something wrong with this one," said the second guard.

Listening carefully to his own words, Karn spoke again.

"My. Name. Is. Karn. Korlundsson," he said, drawing out each word to listen to the sound. He *was* speaking Common. And speaking it very well. Karn grinned. Sticking his head in a dragon's mouth had been a terrifying experience, but what a result! He was fascinated by Orm's gift of tongues. He wondered how many languages he could speak.

"My name is Karn Korlundsson," he said again, this time in Nelenian.

"So you keep saying," said the first guard.

"Turn him away," said the second guard. "He seems touched in the head."

"What? Wait!" said Karn, snapping out of it. "I'm sorry,

really. I was just getting my bearings. I need to come into the city. Really, I do."

"Yeah, well," said the first guard, "everybody *needs* to come into the city. What are you bringing that the *city* needs?"

"I don't understand."

"Your business here, boy. What is it? If you are a merchant, where are your wares?"

"I'm not a merchant. I'm a farmer, actually, but I'm here to find a friend. Her name is Thianna Frostborn. Dark-haired, olive-skinned, she's quite tall." Karn held a hand up over his head to indicate Thianna's height. Guard number two whistled, but guard number one wasn't impressed.

"Not a merchant, then. Just a vagabond."

"I told you, I've come to meet someone."

"Frosty the giant girl, right. Well, if you're a businessman, you won't object to us doing a little business." He held his palm out.

The second guard snorted.

"He means the entrance toll, son. It'll be three copper pieces, then."

Karn nodded and dug in his satchel for Nyra's coin pouch. He didn't have Nelenian money, but the guards didn't seem to object to the Aralish coinage he handed over.

"Hold up, boy," said the second guard, placing a hand

on Karn's chest as he made to walk past. "You can't carry that pigsticker around."

"What?"

"Your sword, son," said the second guard. "You'll have to wrap it. We'll seal the bindings in wax. Commoners are forbidden from wearing swords openly inside the city."

Karn really didn't like the idea of tying up White-storm. Then the wording the guards used struck him.

"Wait," he said. "Commoners?"

"Yes. Only nobles can carry in public."

He considered this. Norrøngard didn't have nobles the way these southern lands did. Just jarls and every-body else. And haulds, farmers whose family had possessed a farm for six generations or more, like his father. And hadn't Karn himself been conducting the trading this past week in Bense? That made him a hauld in train-ing, a kind of noble.

"I'm no commoner," he said.

The guards both snorted at this. He realized that his woolen shirt and trousers were rough by Nelenian fash-ion standards. His muddy boots certainly didn't help. He was just a crazy barbarian with no business in the big city, alone and friendless with a dragon-touched magic sword that wouldn't do him any good if it was tied up and sealed with wax.

"I'm *not* a commoner," he said again, standing as tall as he could and puffing up his chest. He reminded himself that city guards were nothing compared to draug and dragons. "I am Karn hauld Korlundsson, seventh generation of Korlundr's Farm. Do you two even know what a hauld is?"

"Of course we know what a howled, a hauled, a whatever that thing you said is," stammered the first guard.

"Then you understand why I can carry a sword." Karn glared.

"Um . . . ," floundered the first guard. "Yes, sir."

"We didn't mean no offense," said the second guard.

"If that's all, then?"

"Oh, yes, sir. Have a good day, sir," said the first guard. "And welcome to Castlebriar."

Karn smiled as he stepped through the iron portcullis of the city gates. He glanced back at the crowd of farmers waiting to enter the city. Surely plenty of their farms had been in their families for years. The guards obviously didn't know what a hauld was, and a good thing too.

"Close your trap, son. Flies will get in."

Karn realized he'd been standing and staring. Castlebriar was houses, temples, stores, and businesses crammed up against one another, many of them several stories tall. Paved streets. Bustling crowds everywhere. Street vendors. Performers. Criers. Beggars. And unlike Bense, where aside from the occasional dwarf everyone was a Norrønur, quite a few of the passersby weren't human.

48

"Wood elves," he said to himself. It was his first-ever glimpse of the forest-dwelling race. Unlike the pale, reclusive dark elves of home, the wood elves' flesh ranged from the golden color of oak to the dark brown of walnut to the near black of ebony. They were slender, graceful creatures dressed in greens and browns and reds. Woodland colors. "They're all so . . . beautiful."

"Eh, to some, maybe," grumbled the speaker at his side. Karn glanced over . . . and down.

The being beside him looked a little bit like a dwarf. But it wasn't as broad and barrel-chested as dwarves tended to be, and it had pointed ears like a tiny elf.

"Your mouth's hanging open again, son," the creature said.

"I'm sorry, it's just that . . . pardon me, but are you a dwarf?"

"A dwarf? No. I'm a gnome. Don't you know the difference?"

"Gnomes," said Karn. "I've heard of you. I didn't mean to offend—to assume . . . We only have dwarves back home."

The gnome sighed.

"I suppose it's an easy mistake, if you're not from around here. Look, gnomes dig in the dirt. Dwarves in the rock. They like jewels and we like flowers. There's a lot more to it than that, of course, but it's a good rule of thumb if you get stuck."

At that point, a crier came up and seized Karn's sleeve.

"Looking for lodgings, young master?" the crier asked. "Wulver's Catch has clean rooms, polite service, excellent seafood. No vermin under the bed."

"Thank you, I'm not sure—" Karn replied, pulling his arm away and waving off a second crier who was moving in. "I just want to get my bearings. I'm looking for a friend, actually, more than a room."

That gave him an idea. "But I should try to figure out where she might have stayed."

"A friend, eh?" said the gnome. "Well, the Lazy Fisherman is probably too rough a place for anyone sensible. Is your friend an elf?"

"No."

"That probably rules out Windy Willows. Wulver's Catch is nice if you don't mind the limited menu. Fish, fish, and more fish."

"Where would *you* stay?"

"Well, the Stane is clean and nice. You'd get the most for your money there, really, if you don't mind the walk."

"No, not where would *I* stay. Where would *you* stay?"

"Me? Well, I'd stay at Fosco's Folly, but it's not really built for big people. Fosco caters to the wee folk and others of short stature. Your friend is a dwarf or a mousekin, is she?"

"No, um, she's actually quite tall. About—" Karn held his hand up over his head to indicate Thianna's size.

The gnome whistled.

"Well, she certainly wouldn't be comfortable at Fosco's. A big girl like that wouldn't find it at all pleasant."

"You'd think that," said Karn, "and for anybody else you'd be right. But then you don't know Thianna. Fosco's it is. What direction is it?"

Direction was hard to come by. Desstra knelt before the statue of Malos Underfoot, patron of dark elves. A single forlorn candle burned at the statue's base. It looked lonely and sad.

She had been delighted to find the shrine to the five sacred elders just inside Castlebriar's east gate. Tanthal, impatient to rendezvous with their contacts and be about their mission, waited on the street outside. Didn't he want the ancestor's blessings? He probably didn't think he needed it. Too perfect to need any advice. She was glad to be free of him, if only for a moment.

Around her, local elves and travelers paid homage to the other four aspects of her people—Light, Sea, Mountains, and Forests. Not surprisingly, the statue of Nasthia Greenmother was getting the lion's share of the attention. Desstra hoped that the neglected dark elf ancestor would appreciate her attention and grant her guidance. She slipped a coin out of her pocket and placed it beside the sputtering candle. Images of poisons, traps, and various dirty tricks bubbled up in her mind. But real and useful wisdom was slow in coming.

First to a Castle in the Briars,
Where ends all of life's desires.

At least they had the city right, but what did that second line mean? The end of life's desires? For her it meant becoming a member of the Underhand—all she had ever wanted. To do that, she'd have to complete the mission. Completing the mission wasn't the only challenge she faced either. Managing Tanthal was going to be tricky. He might threaten her with the prize of graduation, but was he smart enough to realize he needed her if they were to succeed?

Karn had arrived in Castlebriar just ahead of them. The guards at the gate had confirmed it. Intelligence reports said he was fond of games, which might give him an advantage in unlocking the riddle of the poem and finding the horn before she or Tanthal did. And despite his accent and his dress, he'd blend in better than she would. She needed a way to keep tabs on him without tipping her own hand.

She looked up at the statue of Malos. Blue veins in the semitranslucent marble looked like actual blood vessels in pale flesh. She looked at her own pallid wrist. What was beautiful in the twilight looked sickly in the sunshine. Moreover, her milky skin marked her as a cavern dweller. An outsider. Dark elves were rare aboveground, rarer this far from home. She was already drawing looks, even here at the shrine to the Five with no one about but other elves.

Desstra studied her surroundings, her eyes lingering on the statue of Nasthia Greenmother. It had been worked in a lustrous golden brass. If only Desstra were a wood elf—no one would question where she went or what she did.

"Sorry," she said, picking up the coin from Malos's pedestal. She walked over to the statue of Nasthia and added her offering to a large pile. "But I should give credit where credit is due."

"Ow," hollered Karn as he bumped his head on the lintel.

"You need to watch it there, kid."

Karn grumbled—the advice was a little too late to be of use—and straightened slowly and carefully. Fosco's Folly lay in the north side of the city, where merchant estates blended with the old money of Castlebriar. Sure enough, it specialized in catering to short customers.

He took in the common room. Well-made but undersized tables and chairs were scattered about, where half a dozen customers sat dining and drinking. Karn saw gnomes, dwarves (he was learning to tell the difference), and several creatures who looked like nothing so much as large rodents dressed up in Nelenian fashion. He averted his eyes before he offended anyone by staring.

"You're the innkeeper? Fosco?" he asked the gnome who had spoken when he entered.

"Fosco Pertfingers," the owner replied. He was a stout old fellow with a heavily wrinkled face. "You sure you wouldn't be more comfortable somewhere else?" he asked, not unkindly.

"I'm sure I would," replied Karn. "But I'm not looking for a room. Actually, I'm looking for a friend who came to Castlebriar before me. I think she may have stayed here."

"She's wee folk, then, is she?" asked Fosco.

"No," said Karn, shaking his head. "She's quite the opposite of wee." He pointed up at the ceiling.

Fosco's eyes lit up.

"Young Miss Thi," he said. "Yes, she did stay here. Your name Corn?"

"Karn."

"Karn, right. You're that Norrønian boy she told me about."

"She's here!" said Karn, excitement coursing through him.

Fosco's face clouded. "She rented a room, but I haven't seen her in a while."

Of course it wouldn't be that easy.

"Could I see it?" Karn asked. "The room, I mean."

"What for?"

"I need to find her. Maybe there's a clue to where she went."

"No harm in it, I suppose. To tell the truth, I'm a little

54

worried about her. Not that I stick my nose into my customers' business, mind you."

The old gnome led Karn to a staircase at the back, where they ascended to the second floor.

"Ow," cried Karn as he smacked painfully into an exposed timber beam.

"You might want to watch your head," said Fosco unhelpfully.

"You think?" snorted Karn. But despite the sore forehead, he couldn't help but feel glad at his progress. He had guessed correctly that the low ceilings and short clientele would make Thianna feel more comfortable after growing up as the littlest giant.

"Here we are," said Fosco, opening a door to a small but clean room with a short table and chair, a nightstand, and a very short bed. There was a flower arrangement on the nightstand, next to a small gold-colored statue of some kind.

"This is where she stayed?" Karn asked. Fosco nodded.

"The ceiling's just a little higher than most of my other rooms," explained the innkeeper. "On account of the slope in my roof. Figured she'd need more head room."

Karn looked at the bed, way too small for someone of Thianna's size. He saw that the bedsheets were tightly tucked in, far too neat to be Thianna's handwork.

"Did she sleep on the floor?" he asked.

The gnome shrugged.

The room had its own washroom, just a cast-iron tub

and a bucket in a large closet, but Karn peered inside. The bathtub had a chunk of melting ice floating in chill water.

"*This* is where she slept," he said in triumph. Thianna had clearly been using her magic to freeze the water in the tub, so that she could sleep on a block of ice just as she had back home. "You can take the girl out of Ymiria," he said, "but you can't take the Ymiria out of the girl." He turned to Fosco. "I'd like to rent this room, if I could." He had to stay somewhere. The bed might be too small for him, but as he was alone in a strange city, the notion that Thianna had been in the same place recently would be comforting.

"That will be five silver scepters a day," said Fosco. Karn nodded. He didn't have scepters, but he was sure he could work out the equivalent from Nyra's coin purse. He sat on the edge of the small bed to count out the amount. His eyes fell on the statue. It was of a woman seated on a throne, a lion reclined beside her like a tame cat.

"What's that? A mother goddess?" asked Karn.

"Cybelle," said Fosco. "One of the old gods of the Gordion Empire."

"Goddess of lions?"

"Wild animals. She's the mountain mother. Also goddess of town and city walls, fertility, and corn."

"I didn't know Nelenians followed the old gods," said Karn.

"We don't. Anyway, I don't."

"Then why have it in your rooms?" Karn asked.

"It isn't mine," said Fosco. "Your friend Young Miss Thi bought it in the market."

"That doesn't make any sense." Karn picked up the statue of Cybelle. "Thianna's an Ymirian. They aren't really fond of gods."

"So what's she doing with a statue of a goddess, then?"

"Isn't that a good question?" said Karn.

"Whoever you are, you are not very good at this."

Desstra was in the Old Market. It was a rough district in the eastern corner of the city, near a still-standing ancient Gordion coliseum. She was here to acquire a few final items that she needed for her evening's performance—the plan she had persuaded Tanthal to let her put into effect. The stall before her sold cosmetics— jars of brazilwood chips soaked in rosewater, the rouge known as Lady's Red Powder, tinctures of beeswax and oil to soften the lips.

Desstra lifted a hand mirror, pretending to study herself in it. Instead, she angled the mirror so that she could see over her shoulder. "Got you," she said. There. About twenty paces away, in the shadow of a shop. Wearing a hooded robe despite the heat. Carrying some sort of staff wrapped in leather.

She'd spotted the same person several times already that afternoon. Twice might have been a coincidence, but in a place this size, more than twice meant hostile intentions. No question, she was being followed. The question was by whom. Not the city guard—the guard wouldn't need to hide their presence. Not a pickpocket or cutpurse—a thief would have struck already. Not an assassin or spy, some rival organization of the Underhand—a professional wouldn't be so easy to spot. This one hadn't the skill for subterfuge. This one was sloppy. And working alone.

Desstra set the mirror down, to the disappointment of the stall's vendor. She squared her shoulders and turned around. She marched across the market, straight toward the robed figure.

The hood swiveled back and forth, the figure pretending not to watch Desstra approach. Maybe he thought she would turn aside. He thought wrong.

Just before she closed, the figure darted away.

Desstra broke into a run.

The stranger was fast, even though an odd gait spoke to a limp or injury. But Desstra was faster.

The staff swung out, tipping a cart of potted plants over in her path. The little gnome shopkeeper ranted, shaking a fist after the robed figure. Desstra vaulted over both gnome and cart.

Her quarry headed south, into the narrow streets and dark shadows of the Castlebriar slums.

Desstra drew an egg sac from her pouch and lobbed it at the robed figure's retreating back, but her aim was off.

The sticky yellow foam dripped down the wall, useless and wasted.

Desstra reached the corner. Her ears twitched—a sixth sense warning of trouble even before she saw it. She flung herself backward, bent nearly double, the bright sky above stinging her eyes. The dagger nearly nipped her nose as it passed over her face. It clattered on the street.

When Desstra came upright, her throwing darts were in her hands. But there was no sign of her quarry.

She extended her ears, listening. Heard hurried footsteps to the right. Took the corners as fast as caution would allow.

The robed figure was just ahead.

Desstra pounded the cobbled street. Hurled a dart. It struck the robes but didn't seem to hurt the person inside. Was there armor underneath?

The staff struck a rotting support and sent an awning crashing down in her path. When Desstra managed to get clear, the robed figure was gone.

She came out of the slums on the alley of a main street. A tattered robe lay at her feet, her own dart stuck in the dirty fabric.

The street was crowded with pedestrians. Gnomes, humans, wood elves, the fur-covered rodent-like beings known as murids. Merchants, beggars, fishmongers, servants on errands, townsfolk going about their business, farmers carrying produce to market, cargo on its way to the docks, a foreign soldier in weathered bronze and leather armor. Her quarry could be any one of them. Or none of them.

Desstra bent and retrieved her dart from the folds of the discarded robe.

"There you are," said her teammate Velsa, as Desstra stood and resheathed her weapon. "Tanthal sent me to find you," the other dark elf explained. "We've spotted the boy."

"Good," said Desstra. "It's time we got this game under way."

Karn spent the rest of the day scouting Castlebriar. He tried to ask quietly in shops and inns if anybody had seen a giant girl. It was hard to do that and not draw attention, but he needn't have bothered. He got nowhere. He nosed around the docks looking for he didn't know what. He went as far into the slums as he dared. But everywhere he was coming up empty.

By late afternoon, he returned to Fosco's, tired, dejected, and bedraggled.

"Back so soon, kid?" The old gnome grinned as he wiped down dishes behind a bar in the common room. Karn nodded. "Just beating the streets?"

"I had to start somewhere," Karn replied.

"No luck?"

"None."

"I'm sorry about that." Fosco frowned and set his hands on the bar top. "You know, under the law, an innkeeper is entitled to a tenant's belongings should they turn up, well, dead."

"She isn't dead!" Karn roared. Fosco held up his hands placatingly.

"I'm not saying she is. I'm saying, don't blame me for not saying anything right off. I was waiting an appropriate time before counting her out. But now you're here. So I suppose I should just give it to you."

"Give me what?"

Fosco bent under the bar and came up with a bundle in his arms. Karn stared at the worn brown bag.

"Thianna's backpack! You have it!"

"I haven't looked in it," said Fosco defensively.

Karn snatched the pack. Unlacing the flap, he pulled it open. He saw some of Thianna's familiar gear—cooking utensils and supplies, a bedroll, a change of clothing, as well as the phosphorescent stone that she kept on a cord. He was looking for any clue that might help him figure out where she had gone. Then he found a piece of folded parchment.

He flattened it on the table. It had just one line of writing, where someone had scratched a few Norrønian runes in charcoal.

"'Leflin Greenroot,'" he read aloud. Karn looked at Fosco. "What's a Leflin Greenroot? Is that a local plant?"

Fosco chuckled. "Sounds like a wood elf name to

me. Greenroot, Brownfeet, Greentooth, Goldennose . . . They always go in for those kinds of names."

"A wood elf. Do you know him?"

Fosco's look let Karn know just how dumb the question was.

"Okay, Castlebriar is a big place. I get that. But how can I find him?"

Fosco drummed his fingers, thinking.

"Windy Willows," he said. "Upstairs off a row of shops by the west gate. It's a wood elf hangout. As good a starting place as any to find this Greenroot."

"Thank you." Karn shouldered the pack. His feet hurt from a day on the streets, but now he had new energy. He turned toward the door.

"I hope you find your friend, kid," said Fosco.

"So do I," he replied. "So do I."

The music was at once haunting and beautiful. It seemed to come from everywhere and nowhere. Karn was fairly certain it was a stringed instrument, but the rich, resonant sound was like nothing he'd ever heard.

The room before him was subtly lit with candles, the light levels low. A smell of sandalwood was strong but not overpowering. He wished he had taken a bath at Fosco's before heading out. The incense probably wasn't strong enough to cover his own stench. Nothing to be done about it now.

All the elves in the room looked his way as he entered.

"Um, be healthy," he said uncertainly to the sea of staring eyes.

"What else would we choose to be?" a woman with red-brown skin and waist-length hair replied. She laughed lightly and turned back to her conversation.

Not exactly inviting me in, thought Karn. But at least no one is trying to kill me.

"I'm looking for Leflin Greenroot," he said tentatively to the elves at one table after another. No one replied.

This wood elf tavern was nothing like the noisy, stinky chaos of Stolki's one great hall back in Bense. The arrangement of the inn felt very haphazard. Karn passed recessed nooks and curtained alcoves as he wound through the rooms. The floor wasn't even all on the same level—each time he passed through a doorway, he had to step up or step down.

Several chambers in, Karn finally found a bar—a huge, polished wooden one that curved around the room in a half circle. It appeared to have been built out of a single piece of wood, though how they got it in he had no idea. In the opposite corner of the room, on a small dais, Karn found the source of the music. He watched, fascinated, as a beautiful wood elf woman struck small hammers against strings that were stretched over a trapezoidal sounding board. The music she produced was otherworldly, but it seemed neither worshipful nor warlike. If anything, it made Karn want to dance. Preferably amid the trees and under the moonslight. He wondered what the strange instrument was called.

"You like the dulcimer?" said a tall wood elf beside him.

"Yes," replied Karn. "I guess I do."

"Good taste." The man had mahogany skin and walnut hair.

"I'm looking for someone," said Karn. "A wood elf named Leflin Greenroot."

"Are you, now?" The elf frowned. "Maybe your taste isn't as good as all that after all."

"Please, can you tell me where I can find him?"

The elf shook his head.

"You don't know where he is, then?"

"I didn't say that. I said I couldn't tell you where you can find him."

The wood elf crossed to a table, taking a chair to join a game that was being set up. Karn followed.

"It's important that I speak with him."

The wood elf ignored him, as did the others at the table. They busied themselves arranging the game.

Karn looked down at the tabletop. Colored playing tokens were placed on a board that had squares arranged in a rough curve, like a sort of race course.

"What is this?" he said.

"Never played a game of Charioteers?" the mahogany-skinned wood elf replied.

"Never even seen it."

"Then be quiet while we play," said the elf. His companions snickered.

Karn studied the board. Games fascinated him. And he knew that they often gave him insights into the gamers. Charioteers appeared to be for four players. Each controlled four playing pieces of the same color. There was a clear starting line and a clear finish line.

"It's a racing game," said Karn. The elf nodded.

"What are those spaces for?" He pointed to the star-like markings that were painted at certain points around the track.

"Safe spots," said another elf at the table. "You can't be sent back if you're on one of them. Two players can occupy a star at the same time."

"Sent back?"

"Don't encourage the foreign boy," said the first elf.

"Let me guess," said Karn. "You send an opponent back by landing on them. Unless they are on a star-marked space. The object is to get, what, all four of your own pieces to the finish line?"

"For a long game or tournament play," said the elf. "But usually you are only required to get any two across to win."

"Starting order makes a difference," said Karn, tapping the board on the far left, where the player who began there would have a longer route to the end of the track.

"Aye," said the elf. "The game is meant to simulate the chariot races of the famous Hippodromes of the old

Gordion Empire. The charioteer teams who were backed by the wealthiest patrons got the choice starting positions. We roll dice to determine the starting order."

"Are we going to talk or play?" said the second elf.

"I need to talk," said Karn.

"I told you, boy," said the elf. "Leflin Greenroot doesn't want to talk to you."

"Let him decide that."

"No."

Karn studied the elf.

"You like games, don't you?" He allowed the challenge to fill his voice. "I mean, you really like them?"

"What are you on about, boy?"

"Let me play. If I lose, I'll go away and not bother you again. But if I win, you tell me where I can find Greenroot."

"Interesting, but my friends here and I will just gang up on you and take you out immediately. Won't be much of a contest, I'm afraid."

"Then let's find someone else to play the other positions," said Karn. "Someone neutral."

"This is a wood elf inn, boy. And you're a foreign lad a long way from home. Where will you find someone willing to play against my interest?"

"I'll play," said a voice. Karn saw that a young wood elf female had entered the room. She seemed about his own age, though with elves it was hard to tell. Her skin was a lustrous golden oak, her hair the blond of yellow birch wood. "I promise not to aid either one of you unfairly. I'll play for my own interests."

The mahogany elf studied her a moment.

"Fair enough," he said. "But that still leaves us short a fourth player."

"Oh, I don't think that will be a problem." All eyes turned to see who had spoken.

"Greetings, Karn," said Tanthal, dropping nonchalantly into a vacant chair. Though Karn didn't know his name, he recognized the newcomer immediately as one of the dark elves who had burst into Stolki's Hall. "It seems I find you on the horns of a dilemma."

CHAPTER FIVE

Dicey Situations

"Absolutely not." Karn had a hand on Whitestorm's hilt. He'd pulled the sword half out of its wooden sheath but stopped when he saw the dark elf hadn't risen. Tanthal sat in the chair, stretching and lacing his fingers behind his head as if he didn't have a care in the world. His expression said that he thought Karn's reaction was childish and embarrassing. Karn let the blade slide back down but kept his hand on the pommel.

"Another young foreigner in the Willows?" said the wood elf. "Two in one night, and both from Norrøngard."

"Svartálfaheim," corrected Tanthal. "I am Tanthal of the city of Deep Shadow, which lies beneath the Svartál-faheim Mountains."

The mahogany elf snorted.

"So one's *from* Norrøngard and one's from *under* Norrøngard. You're both a long way from your tiny corner of the world."

"I came looking for a friend," said Karn.

"And you," said the wood elf, glancing at Tanthal. "Are you looking for a friend as well?"

"I don't think he has friends," said Karn.

"At least I have allies," replied the dark elf menacingly.

Ignoring the awkward exchange, the wood elf spoke to the golden-skinned female. "I don't think we've had the pleasure."

"Nesstra," she said with a slight head bow.

"You've not been in Windy Willows before."

"No, sir. I grew up in the town of Fairshadow, in the Blackfire Forest."

"I know where Fairshadow is. I have associates there. What is your family?"

"The Sunbottoms," she said. Karn thought she threw an uncertain glance at the dark elf before answering.

"Well, Nesstra Sunbottom, welcome to the table. And welcome, Karn. And welcome, Tanthal. I'm going to enjoy beating you all." He scooped up four dice, the white bone shining against his red-brown palm.

"You haven't told us your name," Karn said.

"That's correct," replied the mahogany elf. "I haven't." He let this pronouncement hang for a moment. "If you need a name to call me for this evening, you can call me Mr. Oak."

Dice were handed out.

"Highest number gets the choicest spot," Mr. Oak explained again, for the benefit of the newcomers. Unfortunately, the highest number turned out to be Tanthal's, who rolled a six. This meant that the dark elf would play the gold team, starting the game in the position that afforded the shortest number of squares around the track. Mr. Oak came in next as black. Nesstra Sunbottom was green. Karn rolled the lowest and began play in the worst position, the unenviable red team. Hoping he'd gotten his bad luck out of the way early, he said a prayer to Kvir just in case. I hope Norrøngard isn't too far away for you to hear me, he thought. But if the god of luck was out of earshot, Karn would make his own fortune.

Studying the board, he saw instantly how charging ahead wasn't necessarily the best strategy. Racing around the course meant other players could pick you off as they came up on you from behind, landing on your playing piece and returning it to the start. However, the rules said that any even number of moves could be divided among your pieces. He rolled four evens and split his moves in half to bring two pieces into play, rather than sending one racing to the lead.

"Timid," observed Tanthal.

"Smart," replied Nesstra, with a smile for Karn. This earned her a scowl from the dark elf.

The turn passed to Nesstra and then Mr. Oak, both of whom exited the starting gate without event. Then it was the dark elf's turn. Unfortunately, Tanthal's luck continued. He also rolled a three. Rather than head straight forward, he went out of his way to land on Nesstra's piece, sending her back to the beginning.

"You didn't have to do that," observed Karn. "It doesn't really accomplish much this early in the game, does it?"

"It lets my opponents know I am not to be trifled with," replied Tanthal.

The pattern for their play continued much the same. Tanthal always seemed to be playing for spite, with Nesstra suffering the brunt of his attacks. Mr. Oak played skillfully, neither taking unnecessary risks nor inflicting unnecessary pain, but not afraid to do either when it served his goal. Karn preferred to bring more pieces into play, working them as a team and taking only calculated risks. He landed on other players when they stood before him and his path, but he didn't deviate from his course to do so. He found that the dice introduced a degree of uncertainty that his favorite game, Thrones and Bones, didn't have. He preferred a game that was purely strategic, but the presence of four players instead of two did add an interesting dimension.

"Charioteers ... it seems to encourage cooperation and backstabbing both," he observed.

"You're picking this up rather fast," Mr. Oak commented with grudging admiration.

"Thank you. Games fascinate me." He glanced around. "As do other places."

"There is an old saying," said Mr. Oak. "'If you are in Gordion, live in the Gordion way; if you are elsewhere, live as they do there.'"

"That's an enlightened philosophy," said Nesstra, "realizing other peoples have something to teach you."

"It's only enlightened when you're from a pigsty," said Tanthal. "When you are from a city as grand as Deep Shadow, you know your own ways are superior."

"And yet here you are," Karn said.

"And here you are as well. Errand boy for a dragon."

"A *hungry* dragon. You should remember that."

"Mmm. Perhaps. But he is a long way away."

Karn glanced at the two wood elves. Who knew what they were making of this conversation. Nesstra smiled shyly at him. Mr. Oak studied him with calculating eyes.

As the game progressed, Tanthal kept his lead. Karn thought the dark elf was surviving on luck with the dice more than skill or cunning.

Nesstra had a chance to send him back, but she didn't take it. Karn wondered why. With Nesstra's inaction, Tanthal was the first to cross the finish line. But the dark elf hadn't brought any more pieces into play, and now had a long lap full of opponents to negotiate if he was to get a second piece through as required for a win. Unfortunately, he continued to roll well, and his second piece closed the distance in no time.

Karn found himself with a chance at stopping Tanthal, but only if he spent his whole allotment on a move that would see him colliding with Nesstra. He hoped she'd understand. He met her eye, and she gave a hint of a nod. Was it permission? He got the sense Nesstra wanted Tanthal beaten as badly as he did. Karn landed on her piece, sending her back, but this put him near enough to Tanthal to overtake him on his next turn.

After that, the dark elf was angry. Victory was likely out of his reach, so when he brought his pieces back into play, he used them vindictively. It didn't make him any friends. Karn, Nesstra, and Mr. Oak all ganged up on Tanthal at every opportunity. Tanthal swore vehemently as he was sent back to the start again.

"Good thing you have all those allies." Karn chuckled.

Finally, Karn's and Nesstra's second pieces both had a clear shot at the finish line. Nesstra was in the lead, and only Karn could stop her.

He rolled and saw that his result would let him land on her perfectly.

Karn's hand poised above his playing piece. Then he saw the disappointment written on her golden features. Beating Tanthal meant more to her than it did to him. Why that was, he didn't know.

Karn split his move between two pieces, deliberately leaving Nesstra untouched. She rolled and won on her next turn. She came in first, and he came in second.

Her eyes said "thank you," though Tanthal's said

something very different. What Mr. Oak's eyes communicated as they studied Karn, he couldn't tell. Mr. Oak came in third. Disgusted, Tanthal didn't have the grace to play his final moves. They all sat back from the table, eyeing each other.

"You had a chance to win and didn't take it?" said Mr. Oak.

"Idiotic," Tanthal sneered.

"You're the expert on that, then, are you?" Nesstra shot back.

"The move was stupid," Tanthal said.

"Refreshingly uncommon," Mr. Oak corrected. "Whether it's due to idiocy or some other motive remains to be seen."

"Well, I've had enough of this," said Tanthal. He stood up, making a show of dusting his clothing. "Enjoy your little victories. The bigger ones will elude you." With that, the dark elf strode from the room. Karn turned to Mr. Oak.

"How about our bet? Are you going to tell me how I can find this Greenroot guy?"

Mr. Oak was silent so long Karn thought he might not answer. Then he took a piece of parchment from his pocket and wrote something on it with a quill pen. He pushed it across the table at Karn but didn't take his hand off it.

"What's that?" Karn asked.

"Answers," said the elf. "But before you hear them,

decide for yourself whether you really want to ask the question."

Karn stood in the street outside the Windy Willows. He looked at the moons overhead. The Nelenians didn't call the larger one Manna's moon, as his own people did. But the satellite looked the same here as it did in Norrøngard. Everything else, though . . .

The sound of a scuffle pulled Karn's attention from the sky. He saw the golden-skinned she-elf. She was being accosted by two of the strange rodent-like beings he'd first seen at the inn. One looked like a large mouse. The other was more ratlike. Both had daggers out and were menacing Nesstra.

Whitestorm was in his hand instantly. Karn dove at the nearest of the two, the mousy one. His father's blade whipped across the mouse's face, nicking the creature's nose. It squeaked—*squeaked!*—and threw up a hand to cover its injury. But then its beady eyes narrowed. The rat-thing broke off from Nesstra and drew a second long knife from its belt. Karn wished he had a shield.

"Stay behind me," he said over his shoulder to Nesstra. He swung Whitestorm in a broad arc, forcing both assailants to step away. Whitestorm, always light for its size, practically glided through the air now, the benefit of the dragon touch. But the Norrønir had a saying, "The weapon is only as good as its wielder."

Karn wished he had a giant girl beside him. Thianna would be using one of these creatures for a Knattleikr ball right about now. Instead he had to defend himself alone while protecting a tiny elf.

The rat dove in on Karn's left, striking with both of its daggers at once. Karn brought Whitestorm around in a strong sweep, batting the weapons aside. But now his right flank was open, and the mouse leapt in. A knife bit into his right leg before he could block it.

Ignoring the sudden pain, Karn brought the pommel of Whitestorm across with two hands. He drove it hard into the mouse's injured nose. The creature shrieked and toppled back. But neither rodent was retreating far. Karn knew then that there would be no walking away from this fight.

Both rodents readjusted their grip on their weapons. The rat smiled evilly. Karn widened his stance and held Whitestorm out before him. Ready as he'd ever be. This was it.

"You might want to run," he said over his shoulder to Nesstra.

"Then again," the elf replied, "I might not."

Slender darts flew on either side of Karn's ears. Each struck home, one in the rodent's snout, the other in the mouse's neck. The rat dropped first.

"Unfair," the mouse exclaimed, then it too fell to the ground.

Karn turned to Nesstra.

"A sleeping potion," she said, chin held high. "They'll only be out for a few minutes."

"What are they?"

"Cutpurses, obviously."

"No, I mean what *are* they?"

"Oh. Murids. Rodent people. A mousekin and a ratkin." She looked at Karn's leg. "But you're wounded!"

Karn looked down to where blood was flowing through his torn pants.

"We need to see to that," Nesstra said. She glanced at the Willows and shook her head. "Let's get you home."

"Home," laughed Karn. "That may be farther than you want to go. But I'm staying at Fosco's Folly."

Nesstra slid Karn's arm over her slim shoulders. His leg didn't seem that bad, and he felt silly putting his weight on such a slender girl, but the wood elf was surprisingly strong.

"You don't need to—"

"Shh," she said. "I owe you anyway, for rushing to my rescue."

"Doesn't look like you needed rescuing."

"I usually wear my darts on my thigh, but for the Willows I had them in my satchel. I couldn't get them out in time when they accosted me. But you kept them busy long enough."

"Sleeping potion!" said Karn, amazed. "How do you know how to mix those?"

"I'm a wood elf," said Nesstra. "We're good with herbs.

77

Anyway, thank you for letting me be the one to win. The game, I mean."

"You seemed to need it. At least you were taking the worst of that dark elf's abuse. I figured it would sting him the most for you to be the one to take first place."

"Tanthal seems to know you."

"Not really. We're just getting acquainted."

"Do you always make enemies this fast?"

Karn shrugged.

"Better to know who they are upfront, believe me." Karn fell silent, thinking about his uncle Ori, who had betrayed him and his father both. Nesstra was quiet too. She saw him watching her.

"I know something of the cruelty of dark elves," she said.

Fosco hurried over when he saw Karn hobbling through the door of his inn. Together, he and Nesstra sat the Nor-rønur boy down in a chair and propped his leg up on another. The golden-skinned elf tore the pant leg away.

"Hey, that's my only pair," objected Karn.

"Quiet," she said, prodding at the cut. "You're lucky; the wound's not deep."

Nesstra opened her satchel and rummaged about in its contents, bringing out a small glass vial.

"This is going to sting, but it will prevent infection." Karn gritted his teeth while she applied an ointment.

Then she pulled out a needle and thread. "And this will probably hurt worse."

"Well, you seem to be in good hands," said Fosco, blanching at the wound. He patted Karn on the shoulder and wandered off to see to his other customers.

"So what brings you to Castlebriar?" asked Nesstra. Karn's face must have looked suspicious, because she added, "To take your mind off it." She held a needle up.

"Ah," he said. "I've come here looking for a friend." Karn grunted as Nesstra slid the needle through his lacerated skin.

"Go on," she said, pulling the thread tight.

"A good friend." Grunt. "From Ymiria." Nesstra raised an eyebrow. "She's a half giant." Grunt. "Her father's giant. Her mother human." Grunt. "She disappeared a few days ago."

"And you've come all this way to find her? She must be a good friend."

"Wouldn't you do the same for your friends?"

"I don't know," said the elf sadly. She pulled the last of the thread tight and bit it off with her neat little teeth. "But that's it for the leg. It should be fine, and my ointment will see it healed in no time."

"What about you?" said Karn. "Where did you say you were from?" Something strange flitted across Nesstra's face. "Fairshadow, wasn't it? Nesstra Sunbottom of Fairshadow."

"What a good memory you have, Karn of Norrøngard."

She paused from repacking her medical supplies. "I've lived in the 'shadow my whole life. I wanted to see more of the world. Find a way to make my family proud."

"I understand that," said Karn. "Where are you staying?"

"I was looking to stay at the Willows. But I could see about a room here. That is, if you don't mind the company."

"No," he said, glad to have a friend at last in a strange city. Someone else for whom Castlebriar was also a new experience would be welcome. He started to stand.

"Sit," she ordered. Nesstra walked to a nearby table, where Karn saw another Charioteers set. The elf picked it up and carried it back to where he sat. "While you rest your leg, we'll play another game. Just the two of us. And this time, you don't let me win. We need to find out which of us is really better."

Karn smiled.

"You're a gamer too?"

"Yes," she said, scooping up the dice. "While we play, you can tell me all about this Thianna and how we're going to find her."

"We?"

"Of course," said Nesstra. "You came to my rescue, after all. Let me help you complete your quest. Besides, I've no doubt you are going to discover what you came here for, and I want to make sure I'm right beside you when you do."

"You didn't tell me the little one had a sting."

The ratkin rubbed at his snout where the dart had struck. He seemed to be suffering an allergic reaction to the sleeping potion, causing his nose to swell up red and puffy. It looked like a rotting strawberry. His companion, the mousekin, scratched at his neck above the collar of his doublet.

"Two stings," the mouse said.

"You were warned she was armed," said Tanthal. "If you can't handle a little girl's claws, you should be embarrassed for yourself, not angry with me." They spoke amid the Castlebriar slums, where conversations between unsavory types wouldn't draw undue attention. Even so, locals gave them a wide berth.

"Armed, yes," said the ratkin. "Poisonous, no."

"You were paid," replied the dark elf.

"And you got exactly what you wanted for your coin. But we got more than we bargained for."

"That's the nature of any contract," said Tanthal. "You make the best deal you can, and you hope for a favorable outcome."

"Yeah, well, maybe the terms of the agreement weren't made clear enough for our liking," said the ratkin. "What we're saying is that maybe we should be compensated for our extra trouble."

"Lots of trouble," the mouse said.

"You want more money?"

The rodents nodded.

Tanthal sighed. "I'm disappointed. I truly am." He gestured to Velsa, who stood with another dark elf. She stepped forward, and the rodents saw that she was carrying a small wooden chest. Velsa placed the chest on the ground before the murids.

"That's it, then?" said the ratkin greedily. "Our extra compensation?"

"Extra compensation," repeated the mouse.

"It's everything you deserve," said Tanthal.

The rodents bent eagerly over the chest. The latch was complicated and didn't unfasten quickly.

"Pleasure doing business with you," said the ratkin.

"Pleasure," repeated the mouse, rubbing his paws.

"No, no," replied Tanthal as the dark elves withdrew. "The pleasure is all mine."

The ratkin frowned at this, but he had the chest unlatched. He flipped the lid open. A cloud of noxious purple smoke billowed from the otherwise empty chest.

The rodents' screams were loud, but they didn't last very long.

CHAPTER SIX

Root of the Problem

"Where do we start?"

Nesstra was waiting for Karn in the common room of Fosco's Folly when he came down, bright and early in the morning. He noticed that she was wearing her darts on a sheath on her left thigh.

"Not taking any more chances," she explained.

Together, they walked out into the Castlebriar streets.

"It's really beautiful today," Karn remarked, looking at the bright blue sky.

"Spring," said Fosco, who was sweeping the ground before his front door.

"I've heard of it," said Karn, half joking.

"You don't have spring where you're from?"

"If we do, we don't call it that. But we really only have two seasons: cold and colder."

The gnome grunted.

"So what do we know?" asked Nesstra, once they were out of earshot. "Let's go over your riddle: 'First to a Castle in the Briars, Where ends all of life's desires. Over Oak and under Corn, There to seek the soundless Horn.'"

"We only really know that we're in the right city," said Karn. "So I guess we start with the second line."

They spent the day looking for the end of life's desires. This meant a lot of time in the markets, trying to find the things that they themselves desired or things that they imagined whoever wrote the riddle might have desired. They looked at colored fabrics, fancy jewelry, fragrant perfume, well-crafted swords, and, in Karn's case especially, a large variety of game boards and playing pieces. They surveyed the multitude of rich foods and exotic spices that came into the Castlebriar markets from all over the continent. None of them quite seemed to fit the bill. Eventually Karn declared it was time to leave the markets and look elsewhere.

They stood outside wealthy homes, wondering what it would be like to live inside. Karn could see how a good many people—certainly the folks in the Castlebriar slums—would consider such a dwelling to be the absolute completion of their desires. In the religious district, they

talked to a lonely monk from a faraway land who spoke of
the necessity of separating oneself from all forms of desire and earthly attachment, but he didn't know anything
about magical horns or being over oak or under corn, and
he wasn't very helpful. Karn paused at a statue to Cybelle
and wondered again at her presence in Thianna's room.
He didn't know why an ancient Gordion goddess had in-
terested a frost giantess. He sighed.

"Don't worry," said Nesstra. "I'm sure you'll find the
horn."

"I'm not looking for the horn," Karn snapped. "I'm
looking for Thianna."

"I'm sorry," said the wood elf. "I only meant that as
Thianna was looking for it, we'd find her and it together.
That's why we're following the clues she followed."

"I know. I didn't mean to snap. I'm just worried."

Nesstra laid a hand on his shoulder.

"Tell me about her."

"Thianna?" Karn smiled. "Well, she's big. Really big.
Really, really big. She's tough. She's pretty loud. Very
loud, actually. Brash. Kind of bossy. She's sort of a hit-it-
first-and-ask-questions-later kind of girl. She won't back
down in an argument, no matter who's on the other side
of it, even a dragon. She's a little touchy about her height,
though."

"About being tall?"

"No, no. She loves being called 'tall.' Don't call her

'short,' though. Not unless you like broken noses. And if you want to get her to do something and she doesn't want to, just suggest she can't. Then stand back and watch her go."

"Is she a gamer, like you?"

"Nah. She's not much good at board games. She likes ball games better. Violent ones, particularly. She is a really good snow skier."

"Ah." Nesstra nodded. "Are you a good skier too?"

"Not particularly, no. She also likes to wrestle. And no, I'm not big on that either."

"So you two don't have a lot in common?"

"Not in terms of interests, no."

"It doesn't sound like you actually like her very much."

"Are you kidding?" Karn exclaimed. "She's my best friend in the whole world. I'd do anything for her."

Nesstra was silent again. Karn recalled how she'd reacted the previous time he'd mentioned his friendship. He didn't know much about wood elves, or elves in general. Maybe they thought about these things differently. Still, the young wood elf was certainly proving a friend to him now. Was it all gratitude? A debt for his assistance against last night's attackers? Or was she so lonely? He understood being away from home in a city of strangers. Karn put a hand in his pocket, felt the parchment that Mr. Oak had given him.

"Why don't we call it a day?" he said, feeling only slightly guilty about not trusting her completely.

"You're upset?" she asked.

"No. I just want to be alone for a bit. I can meet you back at Fosco's tomorrow."

Karn stood in the northernmost tip of the city, in the shadow of the ancient Gordion walls, a high guard tower to his back and the door of a three-story half-timbered house before him. In his hand he held the parchment. Leflin Greenroot's name was scrawled on it, with an address and the words *Come tomorrow night at sunset. Come alone.*

The words were written in the Common alphabet. He read Common better than he spoke it, but he suspected that he read it even better now thanks to the dragon's touch.

Karn waited until the sun dipped behind the wall. The first star of evening gleamed overhead.

He knocked on the door.

There was a noise inside. Karn wondered what Leflin Greenroot would look like. More important, how should he explain why a boy from Norrøngard had come so far to see the wood elf? For that matter, why had Thianna written this elf's name down at all? Was he a friend, a contact, an ally, or an enemy? Maybe knocking on the door wasn't the smart move. Maybe this was a trap. Maybe . . .

The doorknob turned. The door opened. Smart or not, the move was made.

A wood elf stood in the entranceway, and Karn gasped.

"Hello, Karn," said Mr. Oak.

"You're Leflin Greenroot!" Karn gasped.

"When I said that Leflin Greenroot didn't want to talk to you," said the mahogany-skinned wood elf from the night before, "I knew what I was talking about. Leflin Greenroot, at your service."

Mr. Oak, or rather Mr. Greenroot, stepped aside to allow Karn to enter his home.

Karn found himself ushered into the main living area of the house. A staircase presumably led up to bedrooms, and a kitchen could be seen through a doorway. The rest of the ground floor was given over to a combination den and library, with several comfortable chairs, a large table, a writing desk, and shelves and shelves of books and scrolls.

"I'm something of a historian," said Greenroot when he saw Karn's interest in his library. "Isn't that what's brought you here—delving into the past?"

"I told you before," said Karn icily, "I'm looking for my friend."

"You played an interesting game last night, I'll give you that," said Greenroot. "You were clever enough to win, but you chose to be kind. That's what you did, isn't it?"

"Beating that smug Svartálfar seemed to mean more to Nesstra than to me."

"Hmm. I doubt I would have kept my word if you had just beaten me, but what you did was unexpected."

"So you'll keep your word now?"

Greenroot considered. "I promised you answers. Are you sure you want them?"

"I have to find Thianna."

"She isn't here." The wood elf gestured around as if inviting Karn to look for a giantess hiding among the furniture.

"But she was?" asked Karn, never taking his gaze from Greenroot's.

"No. She tracked me down at the Windy Willows, just as you did, and was coming to see me, but she never arrived." Karn's expression darkened. "And so you follow her footsteps. And here you are. With dark elves for enemies. And you know what she was searching for."

Karn understood that Greenroot already knew what Thianna and Tanthal were after.

"Tell me about the Horns of Osius," he said.

Leflin Greenroot sighed. "I suspected that's why your friend was calling on me. Buried secrets should stay buried. I'd have told her that."

"Please, it's all I have to go on."

"Very well, have a seat. We're going to take a trip into the past."

"You know, of course, of the Gordion Empire that lasted for over a thousand years and fell nearly a millennium ago. But how much do you know of the empires before?"

"Before?" asked Karn.

Greenroot snorted. "I thought as much. It was not a human empire and so you aren't taught it. But there was a great civilization, greater than any that has followed it." He pulled a scroll case from the wall and unrolled a large map upon the table. Karn saw the familiar shape of the continent of Katernia, but few of the country names matched the ones he knew. Greenroot pointed to a large territory marked out in gold leaf paint. "An empire of the Light Elves ruled much of the civilized world, and you humans existed only in the shadows of that light."

Karn bristled at "you humans" but kept silent.

Greenroot continued. "But weeds grow wherever a garden is untended." Greenroot pointed again. "There was a tribe of humans living on a small island called Talsathia, south of what is now the island continent of Thica."

"Thica?" said Karn, recognizing the significance of that place. "Thianna's mother came from there."

"Interesting," mused the elf, tapping a finger on the map in thought. "Interesting to be sure. As you'll see. Now, it was in Talsathia, using a mystical forge, that a human known as Osius crafted three magical horns."

"Three? Oh no, don't tell me there are three of these?"

"That bothers you?"

"Yes, it bothers me!" exclaimed Karn. "One was trouble enough."

"I'm glad you feel that way." Greenroot studied Karn in a way that made him feel the elf was judging him. Again. "But yes," he said. "There are three and only three. These horns, as I believe you know, gave Osius mastery over serpents. Using their power, he gathered and enslaved the Great Dragons. And the rule of the Dragon King began.

"The war of the Dragon King versus the Light Elves was fought for many years, and I could tell you stories about it until the moons set and the sun rose, but that is for another time. For now, I'll just say that, though it was not destroyed, the Light Elf Empire was crippled."

"Score one for the weeds."

"Hmmm." Greenroot made a face. "Perhaps. But then, at the height of Talsathian power, the Great Dragons rebelled. The dragons struck a blow against their masters and sank the island of Talsathia, carrying the forge and its secrets beneath the waves. The reign of the Dragon King was over.

"You remember my comment about weeds and untended gardens?"

"How could I forget?" said Karn. "It's such a flattering image."

"Well, certain human tribes on the continent were now free of Talsathian dominance. They picked at the remains of the Light Elf Empire. They grew into what would eventually become the Gordion Empire. Not as fine an empire as the Light Elves, but the last great empire this continent will see. Unless you count the Uskirians, and I do not."

Karn didn't care about Greenroot's prejudice, only facts.

"But what happened to the horns?" he asked.

"Rumors of powerful artifacts from doomed Talsathia abounded.

"One horn, it was said, traveled to Thica. It was used there for a time, then lost to history and found again. And then recently lost."

"It went to Norrøngard."

Greenroot raised an eyebrow at this.

"Don't worry," Karn told him. "Believe me, it's gone."

"You are sure about this?"

"Oh yes. Thianna fed it to a dragon."

"A dragon?"

"Like you said, that's a story for another time. What about the other horns?"

"Very well." Greenroot nodded. "One horn, it is said, remained submerged at the bottom of a sea in sunken Talsathia. I think we can discount it for now.

"But one horn eventually traveled to the Gordion outpost of Castrusentis. Its bearer died without successfully mastering it. Recognized as valuable and dangerous, the horn was hidden away from the world. But a clue to its location remained. Over time, the story of the Horns of

Osius passed into legend, and the outpost of Castrusentis evolved into a proper city—the city of Castlebriar."

"*Castrusentis* was the Gordion name for Castlebriar," said Karn. "And the clue—'First to a Castle in the Briars.'"

"So you know the riddle?"

"Yes, but why leave a riddle behind if you want something hidden?"

"Because riddles both preserve a meaning across the centuries and ensure that only those qualified to understand can actually decipher them. But as to your friend Thianna, I suspect she found something."

"Found *something*?"

"Yes. Something she was bringing to me for my opinion. Do you have that something?"

"I don't have anything."

Greenroot placed a hand on Karn's shoulder. The weight of that hand didn't seem friendly.

"She didn't send you an object? Are you sure? She didn't leave it for you to find? Tell me the truth, boy. This is important."

Karn thought about the golden statue of Cybelle on the bedside table. But that was a trinket. Not an ancient artifact or mysterious map.

"Nothing. She gave me nothing. She didn't pass anything along to me. All I have is the riddle."

Greenroot seemed perturbed. Karn felt he should say something.

"Thank you," he said.

"Thank me?" replied the elf. "For what?"

"For helping."

"I'm not telling you this to help you, boy. I'm telling you the horn's story to warn you away. So that you will give up. What's hidden should stay hidden. There are those who prefer such things remain out of the world—secret organizations that exist to ensure that they do. It's possible your friend fell afoul of one of them. You have to understand, their concerns are huge in scope." He swept his arm out to indicate the map of antiquity again. "They consider the good of the world, across centuries and millennia. They don't take prisoners. If your friend fell into their hands, they would eliminate her."

Karn scowled. "She isn't dead."

"If she has been captured by the forces I speak of—or an opposing force—"

Karn hammered a fist on the table. "You don't know Thianna. If she's been captured, then you should feel sorry for her captors."

CHAPTER SEVEN

The Frost Giant's Daughter

"We're getting tired of playing games with you."

Yelor the dark elf couldn't help himself. He reached up to touch his swollen nose, wincing at the jolt of pain. The hateful girl had broken it during their last session. The Underhand senior officer assigned to Castlebriar was fairly certain that prisoner interrogations were supposed to be more painful for the prisoner. Sadly that wasn't proving to be the case here.

"Maybe if you played them better you wouldn't be so tired," snickered the frost giantess, annoying as ever.

Thianna Frostborn was standing in the middle of a dimly lit room. All the furniture had been removed and everything cleared away for several feet around her. The dark elves were taking no chances.

The ropes that she had snapped on her first escape attempt had been replaced with thick iron chains. Yelor was squinting through a blackened and puffy left eye as a result of that incident.

The chair that she had splintered into little more than kindling wood on her second escape attempt had been replaced by an actual tree trunk. The trunk was nailed securely into the floor and ceiling. Yelor's twisted ankle throbbed at the memory.

If they didn't get answers out of her soon, he was going to be black-and-blue from head to foot.

"Listen, you infuriating child," said Yelor. "All you have to do is tell us where the key is, and then this can end. I promise you."

The Underhand officer hated the pleading in his voice. He hated this assignment, hated being so long aboveground in this hot southern land, where the only elves apart from his own team were ugly tree lovers.

Yelor looked at the trunk to which Thianna's arms were bound. At least there was a certain satisfaction in his choice of hideout. It was hardly the place a wood elf would ever come, with their love of living trees.

"We will find the key eventually," he said, striving for calm. "If you help us now, you will not only spare me days of aggravation, but you will spare yourself a difficult ordeal."

Thianna appeared to consider his words. Then she

hung her head and mumbled something underneath her breath.

"What is that?" Yelor asked.

Thianna mumbled again.

"Come, girl, I can't hear you."

The mumbling continued.

Yelor exhaled in exasperation. She *was* secured with chains, after all. He shouldn't be so afraid just to approach her. She was only a girl, even if she was a big, brutish, violent, and uncouth one.

He brought his ear close to Thianna's mouth.

"Now, what is that you are saying?"

"Skapa kaldr skapa kaldr skapa kaldr skapa kaldr," she chanted.

She lifted her head, grinning triumphantly.

Crraaack!

Too late Yelor realized that the half giantess had cast some sort of frost spell on her iron manacles. Brittle with hoarfrost, they shattered like icicles, and her two oversize fists hammered painfully into either side of Yelor's slender head.

"Good night, sleep tight," the girl laughed in his face. As the floor rose up to meet him, Yelor realized that he would have two new injuries from this, Thianna's third escape attempt.

❋

Thianna didn't bother trying the door. She knew they barred it behind Yelor each time he entered the room for one of their sessions. She only had moments to batter it down, but fortunately they'd provided her with a means.

She walked around to the other side of the tree trunk and put her shoulder to it. A quick, hard heave, and the trunk tore loose from the ceiling. It crashed into the door, shattering the wood and tearing it from its frame.

The frost giantess leapt through the ruined opening. A guard lay unconscious amid the debris. She took his sword. He didn't seem to mind.

Then another elf was on her.

She didn't have time for fancy moves. She met his blade with so much force that it was knocked from his grip. The sword was flung across the room to stick, quivering, into the wall. Then she struck him in the face with the pommel of her own sword, and down he went.

The room she was in was long and rectangular. A great circular saw hung in a wooden frame over a pit. The tree trunk made sense now, as did the background sound of running water she realized had been ever present. The dark elves had hidden her in a lumber mill. This was the second floor. A doorway for the removal of sawn logs and a staircase leading down were at the far end of the room.

Unfortunately, several more dark elves were coming up those stairs.

"Come on, fellows," Thianna greeted the dark elves, flicking her sword in invitation. "Nothing easy is worth doing."

Thianna burst out into the evening air. Several dark elves trailed in her wake. Two of them were trying to grapple her to the ground. She'd left a couple more out of commission inside. An elbow shoved into a chin freed her of one of her assailants. She stomped on the other's foot.

Temporarily unencumbered, she looked around. The lumber mill had several buildings. The stumps of felled trees stretched before her. It looked as if she was south of the Westwater River, but not far from Castlebriar. She saw the city to her right, on the other side of the water.

Good, she thought. I'll be back there in no time.

Someone was approaching from the road to the city. Another elf. About her age, she judged, but hardly her size. Just a slip of a girl.

"Stop her," groaned a wounded elf from inside the mill.

The girl suddenly had weapons in her hands. Long, slender darts.

"You can't be serious," Thianna said.

For answer, a dart flew at her head.

Thianna reared back and just managed to bat it away with the flat of her sword. She almost didn't see the second dart until it was too late. She flung herself aside. It missed her by less than an inch.

"Stop that!" the giantess roared. She swung her sword at the little elf. And missed.

"You're fast, I'll give you that," said Thianna.

The elf grinned. But only for a second. Then she had two more darts in her hands. She held them like long stilettos.

The two girls circled, sizing each other up.

"You can't do much damage with those little needles," said Thianna.

"Poisoned," answered the elf. "A scratch will do it. One's diluted hemlock."

"And the other?"

"Something really nasty."

Thianna lunged, but the elf danced away, somehow managing to strike out at the giantess's forearm as she did so. Thianna shoved with her free hand, knocking the elf away. What would have been a cut only tore her sleeve.

They feinted back and forth at each other, but neither could land any real blows. They were both too quick, too sure on their feet. Despite her size advantage, Thianna realized she was facing one of the fastest and most co-ordinated opponents she'd ever met. She had nearly two feet of height on the girl, but they were evenly matched. Having grown up around frost giants who made fun of her for her own size, she could almost admire the elf for giving such a good show of it. Almost.

A dart cut another gash in her sleeve. Thianna punched

with her free hand again and clipped a shoulder. The elf staggered.

"Got you!"

"Sure you do," the elf said. "You know what they say about big trees?"

"What's that?" said Thianna, dodging out of the way of the dart the elf had just thrown.

Something else flew at Thianna's head. She struck it with her sword without thinking. But it wasn't a dart. It was small, round, vaguely egg-shaped. Her sword connected like she was batting a Knattleikr ball. But it didn't fly away.

The egg-thing stuck fast to her blade. A noxious purple gas billowed from it. Thianna's eyes instantly stung, and her throat started to seize up. Thianna hadn't been outfought; she'd been outwitted! Tricked! All the thrown darts had lulled her into a pattern. She hadn't thought when she struck the last projectile from the air in the same way as the first. The elf had wanted her sword to connect. Thianna's vision was dimming. She dropped to her knees, choking and gasping for breath.

The elf crept close to her, but now all Thianna could do was cough. She felt her consciousness receding. The elf put a hand on her chest and firmly shoved her over.

"Big trees? They hit the ground the hardest when they fall."

 CHAPTER EIGHT

Grave Matters

"You've got to be kidding me!"

Karn stood in the doorway to his room at Fosco's Folly. The table, chair, and nightstand were overturned. The sheets had been ripped off the tiny bed. The mattress was dumped on the floor, its canvas slashed open, and all the straw pulled out. The golden statue of Cybelle lay on the ground, slightly dented as though someone had struck it to see if it was hollow. It wasn't. Thianna's backpack had been opened and its contents emptied and rifled through.

His room had been thoroughly ransacked. Or at least as ransacked as a room this barren could be. But it was clear that while he was meeting with Leflin Greenroot, someone had snuck in and searched through his things. Nothing seemed missing, though, not even Thianna's cooking gear, which was about the only thing of any value.

Behind him, Fosco whistled.

"Someone had a time in here tonight," he said.

"I'll pay for the damages," Karn replied.

"What's to pay for? Stuff the straw back into the tick and stitch it up. I suppose you could pay for the thread, if you like."

Karn nodded. Mechanically he began picking up the items in the room. Despite his bluster in front of Leflin, he feared for Thianna. He wanted to go home and forget all about magic horns and dark elves.

Fosco saw his face. He touched Karn on the arm in sympathy.

"All comes of letting the big folk stay here, I suppose," he heard the innkeeper grumble as he left.

Karn stuffed the straw back into the torn mattress, then sat in the doorway with his back to the frame and restowed Thianna's possessions in her backpack. Whoever did this hadn't known Thianna had lodged here previously, or the room would have been ransacked sooner. They'd followed Karn here. Doubtless after he announced himself at the gate. He was a terrible sneak.

Karn was so lost in dejection that he banged his head on the door frame as he stood. "Oh for Neth's sake!" he swore. "You'd think someone reared in a longhouse should know better." Not for the first time, he tried to picture Thianna amid the tiny inn. Then a notion came to him.

Both Greenroot and whoever did this—dark elves, he was sure—were convinced that Thianna had given him something. Which meant that they didn't have it. And that meant she really might still be alive. She wasn't carrying whatever it was on her person or they'd have found it. She must have hidden it somewhere. But the elves, or whoever, wouldn't have supposed that Thianna would stay at an inn for wee folk. Only Karn knew her well enough for that. He looked at the ripped-up mattress. His opponents were trying to think like he thought, looking for hiding places that Karn would have selected. Not hiding places that Thianna might have chosen. Dark elves weren't necessarily short, but they weren't particularly tall either. And no one was as tall as Thianna.

Karn grabbed the chair and dragged it to the middle of the floor. He stepped up onto it and stood slowly, bending at the knees and being careful not to bang his head again on the ceiling. Then he turned a slow circle.

He needed to look at the room from Thianna's vantage point. There. One of the ceiling beams had a crack running for most of its length. The gap, only visible when standing on the chair, or standing in a frost giant's daughter's shoes, was easy to spot.

Karn poked a finger in and felt something. He couldn't

get a grip, though, so he took out his knife and carefully slid the blade into the gap. He pressed down and scraped an object out of the small aperture. It fell, and he caught it in his hand. It was small and made of iron.

"A key," said Karn, so thrilled that he spoke out loud. There weren't any markings on the metal. Nothing to indicate where he was supposed to take it. " 'First to a Castle in the Briars, where ends all of life's desires . . .' "

"What's that?" said Fosco. The innkeeper had returned bearing needle and thread.

Karn instinctively closed his fist around the key, hiding it.

Fosco indicated the chair.

"Not tall enough already, kid?"

"Oh, no," said Karn. "I, ah, just missed my friend."

Fosco eyed him strangely, then he went over to the mattress and began to sew it up.

"Life's a struggle, kid. Ups and downs. Nobody's free of problems. Rich, poor, wee folk, big folk. We all get our share of troubles. There. There's your mattress stitched up good as new." Fosco dusted off his hands and stood. He paused in the doorway and turned around. "Still, it's like my mother used to say, 'Better to be alive with worries than dead with no complaints.' "

Karn grunted agreement. His mind was still racing with excitement at his discovery of the key. Where was the lock that it fit? How did it work with the end of all of life's desires?

Then Fosco's parting words slowly penetrated his mind.

Better to be alive with worries than dead with no complaints.

"I know," whispered Karn. "I know where ends all of life's desires!"

Grave Hill was a knoll to the west of the city. Karn studied the rows upon rows of tombstones. It wasn't how his own people marked the resting places of their dead. But it was easy to see what it was for.

"It's like a stone forest," said Nesstra.

"What are you doing here?" said Karn, startled by the sudden appearance of the wood elf. He has spent an uneasy night with the bathtub shoved up against his door, waiting for intruders to return. In the morning, he had slipped out of Fosco's before the sun came up, leaving from a back exit. He'd walked a zigzag path around the city, slipping in and out of various shops and doubling back several times, trying to throw off any unseen pursuers.

He'd even left by the east gate and then walked all the way around to the western side of Castlebriar. Only when he was sure no one was tailing him had he finally come to the graveyard.

"Followed you," said Nesstra. "We've gotten quite a bit of exercise, don't you think?"

"I wanted to come alone." Karn scowled.

"I told you I'd help."

"Why would you do that?"

"You helped me."

Karn considered that. "I didn't really."

"You tried to help me then," Nesstra said. "A stranger. You were being brave even if you weren't effective."

"It was two against one," Karn said, defending himself. "I *did* hold them off until you freed your darts."

"Exactly," replied the elf. "We made a . . . a good team."

There it was again, that hesitation. Maybe this wood elf really needed a friend, so much so that she'd attach herself to a stranger's mad quest. He did understand that. Karn missed having Thianna at his side. It would be nice to have someone he could rely on. And Nesstra was certainly a good fighter. And a fellow gamer too. Maybe they could get in a few more sessions of Charioteers when this was over.

"I met with Greenroot last night," he confessed. "I've already got dark elves to watch out for. He thinks there are others who want hidden things to stay hidden."

Nesstra was silent for a moment as Karn's information sank in, then her words came out in an explosion.

"I can't believe you went to Greenroot without me!" she yelled, her gold skin reddening in anger. "Why are you cutting me out?"

"I don't—uh . . ."

"Don't want help? Don't think I'm capable?"

"It isn't that."

"Don't want to share your treasure?" she demanded, poking him hard in the sternum.

"Don't want you getting hurt!"

Nesstra blinked. *"What?"*

"I don't want you getting hurt, all right?" Karn said. "I think things are about to get dangerous."

Nesstra was quiet for a moment. Karn wondered what she could be thinking. Then she tapped the slender darts strapped to her thigh.

"Let me worry about who gets hurt." She walked to a tombstone and rested a hand on it. "Tell me why we're here."

"Because this is the end of life's desires," Karn explained, resigning himself to her company but also glad of it. "Once you're dead, you don't want anything anymore. I didn't see it at first, because Norrønir bury our own dead in mounds, and, well, some of the dead in them are still pretty greedy."

"The dead are *greedy?*"

"Long story. Tell you another time. But I wonder why the dark elves haven't figured this out yet."

"They live underground. They don't bury their dead in the earth like humans do. The Svartálfar float the deceased out on boats on a big subterranean river and then set the boats on fire."

"You know a lot about it."

"They're still elves, right? Even if they don't like the

sun." She turned around and leaned on the tombstone. "So what's our next move?"

"We're looking for something that is 'over Oak and under Corn.'"

"'There to seek the soundless Horn,'" Nesstra finished. "Let's get started. After your morning stroll, we don't have that much daylight left."

There were a couple of tall oak trees scattered about Grave Hill, though nothing that resembled corn. Nesstra scrambled up both of them, all the way to the top—she was so nimble!—but she reported finding no clues among their branches.

"The riddle didn't make sense," the elf complained. "Oak trees are taller than cornstalks, aren't they? How can something be over an oak but under corn? Shouldn't it be 'under oak and over corn'? Maybe we have it wrong."

"I don't think so. Anyway, it's all we've got to go on."

"But it doesn't make any sense."

"If it were easy, everybody would be doing it! The horn would have been found years ago."

Karn studied the tombstones. They ranged from simple slabs with a name and date carved into their surface to elaborately wrought headstones with statues and ornamentation. Not surprisingly, the higher on the hill they climbed, the fancier the grave sites became. But the tombs also got older as they climbed higher. Nothing seemed to fit the riddle, however.

"We're going about this wrong," said Karn. "We'd spend a month combing over every single tomb."

"What are you thinking?"

"Greenroot said the horn came to Castlebriar when it was still a Gordion outpost called Castrusentis. That means we can eliminate any tomb with a date after Three AG, when the Gordion Empire fell. We only search the oldest, and the oldest are the highest."

"To the top of the hill."

"To the top of the hill."

The oldest grave markers at the crest of the knoll were extremely weathered. After all, they were nearly a thousand years old and older. Their designs also made the most use of ancient Gordion deities. Karn saw several likenesses of the horn-shouldered figure and the god on horseback that he'd first glimpsed on public buildings in the ruined city of Sardeth. He also saw quite a few images of Cybelle, the mountain mother, goddess of town and city walls, fertility, and . . .

"Corn."

"What?"

"Look for images of the mountain mother. Cybelle. She's the goddess of corn. Thianna had her statue in her room. Look for her on tombs that also have images of oak trees."

Nesstra and Karn ran among the tombstones. They were both buzzing with excitement. It didn't take long.

"Found it," the wood elf said.

Karn came to where she stood, looking where she pointed.

A simple slab, though a large one. It had a carving of an oak leaf in a circle. Under this was a carving of the goddess Cybelle. And between them, a keyhole.

"'Under oak and over corn,'" observed Karn.

"I don't know what we do next, though," said Nesstra. "Maybe I can try picking that lock."

"You don't have to."

"Then what do we do?"

"We use this," Karn said.

Nesstra gaped at the key in Karn's palm.

"What else are you holding out on me?"

"What? Don't you have any secrets?" said Karn.

Nesstra didn't answer.

The key slid easily into the keyhole. Karn twisted it in the lock. There was a soft click, followed by a louder one, and then the slab sank slowly into the ground with a grinding noise. In the hole now revealed, they saw a staircase leading down into the earth.

They started down the stairs, Nesstra leading the way. The sunlight only penetrated a few feet into the passage, but she didn't seem bothered by the dark.

"Wait up," Karn said. He slipped Thianna's phosphorescent stone out of his shirt, where it hung on the cord about his neck. Giving it a shake, he activated its wan light.

"Oh, right," said Nesstra. "Thanks."

The steps ended at the start of a narrow corridor. The walls on either side were decorated with patterns that looked like the rings of tree stumps. At the end of the passage, a great slab of stone was held up by a large shield propped under it. The shield was rectangular, around three feet in height and two feet wide, and slightly curved, and had an elaborate design painted on its face. It had obviously been placed deliberately to prevent the slab from sealing off whatever lay beyond.

"That's a scutum," said Karn. "The troops of the Gordion Empire carried them a thousand years ago."

Nesstra didn't pause for the history lesson. She ducked under the slab. Not wanting to be left behind, Karn dropped to the ground and crawled under as well. But he eyed the ancient shield warily as he scooted through, taking care not to bump it. If it were to give out, they'd be trapped when the heavy stone slid down.

He found himself in a much larger space, circular with a domed ceiling. The floor had the same tree stump pattern as the walls outside. The center of the chamber was dominated by a huge stone sarcophagus, the lid of which was carved to look like a body, lying horizontal across the top.

"Obviously, this is meant to represent whoever is inside," said Karn. He brought the light close. The figure was robed and bearded.

"He looks like a scholar," Nesstra said.

Karn nodded, but he was concerned. The figure held two hands up in front of his face, as though he had been clasping something, and his lips were puckered.

"It's not here," said Karn.

"What do you mean?"

"Look at the carving's hands. He was holding a horn. It's made to look like he was blowing it. They buried his body and put the horn in the hands of his statue. Then sealed this whole place up. Someone's been here since and taken it out."

"Maybe it was just a carved horn—part of this statue."

"They didn't break it off. They slid it out."

"Maybe it's in the sarcophagus. With the body."

Karn studied the slab. It looked as if it weighed a ton. It also looked undisturbed, mold and the dirt of ages smeared evenly across its seal.

"I don't think anybody's opened this in a millennium."

"It has to be here!" said Nesstra. "It has to be."

"Well, it isn't," he said, feeling defeated.

"Who could have taken it?" She looked around the room frantically, as if searching for a thief.

"I'm guessing whoever left that scutum shield."

"No, that would mean—"

"That the horn was taken over a thousand years ago,"

Karn finished, "by a soldier in an army that doesn't even exist anymore."

"I can't believe this. I can't."

"I don't know why you are so upset," said Karn. "After all, I'm the one searching for Thianna. It's not like—"

He stopped speaking. Something peculiar had caught his attention.

"What's with your ears?" he asked.

"They're long," replied Nesstra irritatedly. "Don't tell me you're just noticing."

"No. I mean, why are they twitching?"

"What?" asked the elf.

"Your ears; they're twitching."

Nesstra stilled, her ears lifting as she listened intently. Then her expression turned to alarm.

"We're not alone," she said.

They both faced the passageway. There was a faint light at its far end, and the soft sound of footsteps coming down the stairs. Many footsteps. Karn slid White-storm from its sheath at the same time that Nesstra drew two of her slender darts.

Karn bent to look under the stone slab. Wood elves, both men and women. They wore scarves to hide their faces. Each carried a small round shield of a type known as a buckler. The faces of the shields were painted with the now familiar tree stump pattern.

"This can't be good," whispered Karn. Then one of their number spotted him.

The strangers all drew swords.

Beside him, Nesstra hurled one of her slim darts. It caught an elf in the leg. He hollered and went down.

The rest of the group reacted, bringing their small shields to the front. Nesstra's next dart was batted aside.

"We're pinned," whispered Karn. "Nowhere to go."

"Sure there is," hissed Nesstra. "We can go through them." She tossed another dart. This one struck home in a woman's arm. Karn saw the woman drop. But they still faced too many opponents.

Then a man stepped forward and raised a small bow.

Karn jumped aside quickly as an arrow sped past him. He took cover behind the scutum—the first time in a thousand years the ancient Gordion shield had been utilized for its intended purpose.

Without any sort of projectile weapon, he was useless unless Nesstra could take out the archer. But he stood ready to chop with Whitestorm if anyone came ducking under the slab.

Then Nesstra yelped and fell backward. An arrow clattered on the wall behind her. She clutched her side, something wet on her fingers. She'd been grazed.

Nesstra tried to stand. Her legs wobbled.

"Oh no," she said. "Poisoned."

Then she fell over.

"Nesstra!" Karn called. He tried to reach her, but a second arrow drove him behind the shield.

The strangers cheered and broke into a run. They'd be

on him in seconds. More than he could take on his own. Nesstra was dying, and he'd be joining her in moments unless he could think of something.

Karn looked at the heavy stone slab. Not the best solution. Just the only one. He grabbed the scutum tightly on either side. He hauled with all his strength.

The shield came away with a horrendous scraping noise. Karn fell to the ground, the large shield across his chest. With a loud thud, the enormous stone slid down, closing off the passageway. Then things were silent apart from his and Nesstra's labored breathing. The strangers were on the other side of solid rock. They couldn't reach him anytime soon. But neither could he reach the passageway to the stairs.

They were safe for the moment, but they were also trapped. Possibly forever.

 CHAPTER NINE

The Order of the Oak

"It's bad, isn't it?"

Karn knelt beside Nesstra.

The wood elf winced in pain as the poison worked its way through her system.

"I can't feel my legs," she said. "I'm paralyzed."

"I'm so sorry," said Karn.

"No," she replied. "Paralysis is good. If it was— poison—might not know how to treat it." She tugged on her satchel with an arm that was rapidly losing its coordination. "Here. Take."

Karn undid the flap and dug through the contents— glass vials, leather pouches, wrapped paper packets, a single round stone, small clay jars, as well as additional darts.

"Don't prick—finger," she warned.

"What do you need?" he asked. "Tell me what to do."

"The red powder," Nesstra said. "Mixture of sage, primrose, watercress, other herbs—will cure paralysis."

Karn dug frantically through her gear.

"Found it," he said, holding up a small vial of the medicine.

"Rub in wound," Nesstra directed.

Karn lifted her shirt carefully.

"Oh goodness," he said, voice heavy with fear.

"What—wrong?" she asked.

"Your skin. Around the wound. It's so pale."

Nesstra turned her face away. "Ignore it," she said. "Rub it in."

Karn did as instructed, applying the entire dosage of the medicine to her injury. The cut itself was slight—the arrow had done little more than graze her side. But he was worried about the gray-white flesh, which looked sickly. He hoped it wasn't necrotic. When he finished, he slid her shirt back down to hide the sight of the pale skin.

"Hang in there," he said, patting her awkwardly. "I dragged you into this. For Neth's sake, this wasn't even your quest! I promise you, I won't let you die!"

Nesstra hid her face in the crook of her arm. Karn wanted to tell her she didn't need to be ashamed to show pain and fear, but he didn't quite know how. So he just held her, sitting quietly and waiting for the antidote to take effect.

"Let's see you get out of this."

Yelor was gloating. Or gloating as much as was possible with two badly swollen ears.

"Stick around and you will," Thianna replied. "Though you're looking pretty banged up. Maybe you shouldn't."

Yelor scowled.

The frost giantess was bound to an even bigger tree trunk than the last one, with bigger chains than before. Two more dark elves were standing a good fifteen feet away from her, both with loaded crossbows pointed at her belly. They had orders to fire the minute she muttered anything that sounded even remotely like a spell. They were in the main workroom of the lumber mill now, where the huge circular blade hung above the saw pit, but the pit had been covered up with boards.

"There have been some interesting developments in the city," Yelor said. "We may not need you much longer. You should have cooperated when you had the chance."

"Right. Like you'd just let me go," sneered Thianna.

"True, you were never leaving here," replied the elf. "But there are ways to dispose of you that are more or less—entertaining." He touched one of his ears. "I think you owe me some entertainment now, don't you?"

Thianna heard noises from the far end of the room,

like something heavy being lifted on a winch through the doorway. And something else. Something bestial.

"Hear that?" asked Yelor, smiling darkly. "My agents found it wandering out of the woods last night. It maimed two of them before they caught it. They're putting it in the saw pit now."

Whatever it was made a strange hissing noise, unhappy with being snared. An elf swore. Clearly the mystery creature wasn't cooperating.

"My conversation is too clever for you. Is that it?" Thianna laughed. "You needed someone to talk to more on your own level."

"Charming. But this little pet is for you, not me. Consider it my going-away present."

"You shouldn't have."

"It's no bother. But you must be wondering what it is. Well, I'm not going to tell you. That's a surprise for later. But I will tell what it's not."

Yelor came as close to Thianna as he dared. It wasn't very close. He whispered like a child with a naughty secret.

"It's not a vegetarian."

"Do you think they'll try to lift the slab?"

"Maybe," replied Nesstra. She was on her feet again. Karn was amazed by how fast the wood elf's strength was returning now that her medicine had chased away the paralysis. "But then again, they looked like they were trying to kill us. Wouldn't it be easier for them to just leave us in here forever?"

"Or wait a week and come back when we'd long since died from lack of food and air," said Karn. "I hate to agree, but I think you're right."

"That's what I'd do," said Nesstra. "I mean," she added hastily when she saw his expression, "that's what I'd do if I were, you know, a member of a group of cold-blooded killers or something. Who are they, anyway?"

"Masked faces. Shields with the same symbol that's marked on the wall here. I'm guessing they're some sort of ancient secret society that doesn't want the horn found. Greenroot warned me someone like this might try to stop us."

"They've done more than try."

"It's my fault. I didn't know what else to do."

Karn bent and wedged his fingers under the slab. He heaved, but the heavy rock didn't budge. He tried again, but he was just acting out his frustration. The slab wasn't going anywhere. He doubted even Thianna could have lifted it.

"I knew what I was getting into," said Nesstra.

"I don't see how you could. But thank you."

Karn still knelt, feeling along the crack where it met the chamber floor. Nesstra went to him and took his chin in her hand, commanding his full attention.

"Don't thank me," she said with a startling intensity. "And don't feel regret on my account either, okay?"

She crouched beside him and undid her satchel.

"You saved me back there," she said. "How about we call it even if I get us out of here?"

Nesstra unwrapped a small packet. Karn saw that it contained a greenish claylike substance.

"Help me pack this under the crack," she said. "But be careful."

"What is it?"

"Let's just say it goes boom."

"Explosives? What are you doing with explosives?"

"Getting us out of here."

"Yeah, but you have to tell me what you're doing with explosives!"

"If we live through this, you'll know. But it's going to take all I've got, and—" She gazed at the chamber. "Rounded walls. The blast will circle around. We won't be safe, even hiding behind the sarcophagus. I think there's only one place where we'll be properly shielded. But it's going to be a little gross."

It took the two of them to lift the stone lid of the sarcophagus. They looked down at the occupant. Neither was in a hurry to join him.

"He's really well preserved," said Karn.

"Some kind of charm in the room, I bet."

"It would explain why the wood of the shield hasn't

rotted." He gritted his teeth. "I guess there is no sense putting this off."

"After you."

"Why do I go first?"

"I have to light the fuse."

Karn couldn't argue with her logic. He steeled himself and set a foot in the sarcophagus, then climbed in. He did his best not to bump anything, but it was hard not to in the cramped space.

"Wait a minute," he said, climbing back out and retrieving the ancient Gordion scutum.

"What do you want that for?" asked Nesstra.

"It's our only clue."

Karn climbed in again, then moved as far from the opening as he could. He wanted to give her space, as she'd have to move fast once the fuse was set.

"Ready?" she called.

"Ready."

Nesstra lit the flame, then dove into the sarcophagus. No time to worry about where she landed. Karn hoped the body didn't mind. Once the wood elf was inside, the two of them lifted the heavy stone lid as rapidly as its weight permitted and slid it back across the stone coffin. Then they were sealed in, alone with a soldier from a thousand years ago.

"So, this is a grave," said Nesstra.

"Yeah," said Karn. "For some reason, I tend to find

myself in them startlingly often. Can't say I'd recommend the experience."

She smiled at his attempts at humor. Karn was grateful for her help and companionship, but she presented almost as big a mystery as his quest. He studied the wood elf in the light of his phosphorescent rock. Her normally golden skin looked wan in the dim illumination. It was almost as if—

The explosion was loud despite the thick stone. The lid of the sarcophagus even jumped a little bit, then settled back down. Putting their backs to work, they shoved it aside.

Karn looked at the slab. It had shattered in several places. Chunks of rock still hung in the doorway, but there was enough space to crawl through.

"You carry that explosive stuff around with you?" he said in amazement. "Aren't you afraid you'll blow up?"

Nesstra didn't answer.

They picked their way across the rubble. Karn drew Whitestorm from its sheath. He held the scutum in his other hand.

"I bet they left a guard," he said. "Just in case we didn't die like we were supposed to."

"Shame on us," said Nesstra. She plucked a small, egg-like object from her supplies. Karn wondered what in the world it could be. At this point, nothing would surprise him.

Cautiously, they tiptoed to the staircase. The tombstone above had been reset, but a small lever on the wall was clearly intended to activate it from this side.

"Get ready to fight," Karn said as he threw the switch.

Sure enough, a wood elf cried in surprise as they emerged into the open air of Grave Hill. He swung a sword at Karn, who surprised himself with the ease with which he blocked the blow with his newly claimed shield. Then Nesstra broke the egg-thing on the man's back. A foam substance erupted from it, swelling to engulf him. In seconds, the wood elf was stuck in a large, sticky blob.

"Sorry," said Karn apologetically to the elf. "But you started it."

"Put it back," the stranger replied. "What you have found should not be found."

"We haven't found anything," said Karn. The elf's eyes widened. "It wasn't there." He saw the man's disbelief and added, "I'm telling the truth. It looks like it was moved centuries ago."

"Then let us hope it is still lost to the world," said the elf.

"Why? Why do you care? And who are you, anyway?"

"We are the Order of the Oak," said the wood elf. "We exist to keep dangerous artifacts hidden from the world. You will find nothing here but death. Go home to your cold wasteland while you can."

"I came to find my friend Thianna," said Karn angrily. "I'm not leaving until I do."

They left quickly, in case any more members of the

mysterious Order of the Oak were nearby. Karn sheathed Whitestorm, but he had no strap on which to sling the shield. He hefted it in his left hand, impressed by its weight and feel. Then he stopped walking.

"What is it?" said Nesstra.

"Words," he said. "Words that I'm sure weren't here before."

He turned the shield around so that she could see the underside. Above and below the handgrip, characters painted in Common now appeared. Karn suspected there were two more verses of the riddle Orm had given him. Karn and Nesstra read them together.

> *A little finger holds the fate,*
> *Where a crescent commands a straight.*
> *Upon the arc where shatters wheel,*
> *Alter course and come to heel.*
>
> *In Sunken Palace waters reign,*
> *King and Dragon find their bane.*
> *When snake and cockerel sundering,*
> *Seek ye then the Marble King.*

"What does it mean?" said Nesstra.

"I don't know what it points to," said Karn. "But I'll tell you what it means. It means we're back in the game."

CHAPTER TEN

Finger-Pointing

"The horn is missing."

Leflin Greenroot was clearly surprised to have visitors this evening. He turned his attention from Karn to Nesstra to Karn again and finally to the ancient Gordion scutum that Karn held before him.

"We found the secret location of the Horn of Osius," Karn explained. "Only it wasn't there. Someone took it."

"Quiet," said Greenroot, snapping out of his stupor. "Don't talk of such things in the street. You had better both come inside and tell me everything."

Greenroot made them tell their story three times. He grilled them about every tiny detail. They were in his main living area. The ancient shield was laid facedown on his large table so that the mysterious second and third verse of the riddle could be read.

"So the horn is really missing," the dark-skinned wood elf mused.

"That's what we've been telling you," said Karn. "But what I don't understand is why the Order of the Oak didn't know. Aren't they the ones who hid it in the first place?"

"But they weren't the ones who took it," said Nesstra.

"No, but they clearly wrote the poem," Karn explained. "Which means someone from the Order of the Oak entered the chamber after the horn was taken and penned the second and third verse on the back of the shield. But the Oak elf we met didn't know."

"They've forgotten—that is, I *imagine* they must have forgotten a bit of their own history," said Greenroot. "An occupational hazard when all your teachings are secret and tied up in riddles."

Karn tapped the shield.

"It's Gordion, right?"

"Yes," said Greenroot. "Remarkably well preserved." He turned it faceup. "But the markings should be able to tell us some more about it."

Greenroot went to a bookcase and pulled out a scroll. He unrolled it on the table beside the shield. Karn saw it was an illustrated guide to the various shields used by different Gordion military divisions.

"This one," said Greenroot, tapping an image on the

scroll. It matched the shield on the table in color and design. "It's the shield of a Thican auxiliary soldier. The auxiliaries were people from conquered territories who were conscripted into the Gordion army. They would fight together as their own legion, separate from the native-born Gordion soldiers."

Nesstra snorted. "Come join our empire," she said. "Just don't stand too close."

Karn wasn't listening. Puzzle pieces were slotting together in his mind.

"So a horn from Thica is buried in Castlebriar. Long ago, when it was the Gordion outpost called Castrusentis. And later, a soldier from Thica forced to fight in the Gordion army is stationed there."

"And the soldier finds the horn," Nesstra added excitedly. "And takes it. But why?"

"Thianna could use the horn," Karn replied. "If the soldier was from Thica, then it's possible he could too."

"I think we can assume that he could," said Greenroot.

"So the soldier could compel reptiles," said Karn. "If you could command a wyvern—or a dragon—what would you do?" He turned to Greenroot. "Tell me about Thica's history with the Gordions."

"It's not a pleasant one. Thica used to be a mighty empire in its own right. Then they lost all their colonies in Katernia to the empire in 739 EE. The Thican island-continent fell to the empire a hundred and twenty-three years later. Our mystery soldier was probably stationed in Castrusentis a few centuries after that."

"Maybe not too happy about being a conscript, or seeing his own country conquered by another," said Nesstra.

"So where does he go?" asked Greenroot.

Karn tapped the scutum.

"He goes where the riddle says he goes. 'Where a crescent commands a straight.'" Karn walked to the bookshelves. "Leflin, can I see all your maps of the Gordion Empire? Particularly the ones after 616 EE."

"What are we looking for?" asked Nesstra.

"We're looking for crescents and straight lines. And I think we'll know when we see it."

Several hours later and they were still no closer. There weren't many naturally occurring straight lines, even fewer inside all the various territories held by the Gordion Empire over the centuries. They combed over map after map, working by candlelight now that the sun had set and peering at every little detail until their eyes were blurry. Greenroot called for a break and served them a strong plant root—infused beverage that he recommended drinking through a straw to avoid sediment.

Karn sat in a high-backed chair and sipped his drink. Just as the first sentence of the riddle had indicated the city of Castlebriar and Grave Hill, he was sure the first sentence of the second stanza would reveal their next destination. He felt as if the answer was staring him in the face, hidden in plain sight.

He was so preoccupied in thought that he didn't notice he'd finished his root tea until he reached the bottom of the glass with a loud slurp.

Greenroot flashed him a look of irritation. Karn realized he was probably being very uncouth by elf standards.

"Sorry," he said. "We don't use straws. We just drink out of . . . cattle horns." When the elf's mouth curled in distaste, Karn added, "Um, it's not as bad as it sounds."

Feeling somewhat embarrassed, Karn took the rye grass straw out of his cup and studied it. It was a hollow plant stem, slender and straight as an arrow. Straight. Narrow. With liquid passing through.

"We're going about this all wrong," he exclaimed, leaping from his chair and rushing to the table. The others joined him in surprise at his outburst.

"We're not looking for a straight line," Karn explained. "It's a play on words. We're looking for a *strait*. You know, a narrow passage between two larger bodies of water."

"Of course," said Greenroot, shoving some books off a large continental map. The three of them pored over the map with renewed energy. Karn saw it first.

"Look," he said. He indicated a thin channel of water between Thica and their own continent of Katernia. The strait separated the northern Somber Sea from

Uskirian Empire

Zoldak

Mosh

Tarbul

Muspilli Mountains

Sacred Gordion
Supremacy

Caladium

Mittosha

Fortress of
Atros

Syrium

Gordasha

The Sparkle Sea

Ithonea

THICA, SACRED GORDION SUPREMACY,
AND USKIRIAN EMPIRE

0   45   175   350

miles

the Sparkle Sea to the south. A long peninsula extending from Thica's western side even looked like a hand, thumb, and forefinger together with a pinkie extended.

"And here's the finger," said Karn, "pointing to this crescent-shaped bay. But how does it hold the fate?"

"That I can explain," said Greenroot. "The city of Gordasha sits here on the western side of the strait. An enormous chain stretches across the water to the finger here, where the Thicans have a fortress. By ancient treaty, the Gordashans control the raising and lowering of the chain, and they only permit those ships that they approve to pass through the channel."

"'A little finger holds the fate, where a crescent commands a straight,'" quoted Karn. "It's obvious."

"Right, obvious," said Nesstra. "Could it be any more obvious? Maybe if the riddle were printed in black ink on black paper."

"That's where the horn is," said Karn, ignoring her. "I imagine the rest of the riddle won't make sense until you get there."

"So you mean to pursue this?" asked Greenroot.

"I don't know," said Karn. "I'm here to find Thianna. If she's still in Castlebriar, I can't leave. But I don't know how far on this quest she got. Only that if the dark elves find the horn first, they won't have any more need of her."

"You really don't care about the horn?" Greenroot

studied Karn. "You aren't motivated by greed or power or the lure of magic?"

"I told you, I want to find my friend. I won't let her down."

"Perhaps I need to reassess my opinions," said Greenroot. Then he noticed Nesstra. She had left the table sometime during the conversation and now stood at a window, holding one of the room's candles up in front of the glass. She seemed to be absently waving it back and forth. "What are you doing? Come away from the window."

Nesstra started, and she stepped away sheepishly.

"I'm sorry," she said. "I was just—just looking at my own reflection."

"Vanity I understand," said Greenroot. "But have some sense too. These are confidential matters we discuss."

"Tell me about Gordasha," said Karn, to pull Greenroot away from chiding Nesstra. "It was the capital of the Gordion Empire, right?"

"Not exactly," scoffed the elf. "It's the current capital—and really pretty much all that remains—of the Sacred Gordion Supremacy, the self-proclaimed inheritors of the legacy of the fallen Gordion Empire. They control the strait, which is one of the main fortifications preventing the Uskirian Empire from expanding south. The Uskirians have laid siege to it several times over the centuries, but it's never fallen. Gordasha is a huge city."

"Bigger than Castlebriar?"

Greenroot snorted.

"Try half a million people. Much bigger than anything you Norrønir can imagine."

"It doesn't matter," said Karn. "If that's where my path takes me, that's where I go." He looked at Nesstra. "I don't expect you to leave home. But I want to thank you for everything you've done."

Nesstra looked at Karn sadly. "I told you," she said. "I didn't want you to thank me. We're even, and you don't owe me anything."

It was then that the dark elves attacked.

The window Nesstra had been standing in front of suddenly shattered. A rocklike object came crashing through. It landed on the table in the center of the map, belching a choking, noxious smoke. The parchment turned brown and singed around the projectile.

Greenroot's front door shuddered as someone outside pounded it with something heavy.

"Upstairs," Greenroot ordered, tearing a curtain from the wall and hurling it over the table.

Karn snatched the shield and started for the staircase, but Nesstra was hesitating.

"Come on," he yelled.

The gold-skinned wood elf seemed confused, then she followed him.

Greenroot ushered them into his bedroom, shutting the door and locking it behind him.

From a cabinet, he took out a sword and a shield. Karn saw with surprise that it was a buckler. One adorned with a familiar pattern. He stared at the tree stump design in disbelief.

"You're one of them," he said accusingly. "You're a member of the Order of the Oak."

Nesstra's darts were out. Karn pulled Whitestorm from its sheath.

"Save your weapons for the enemy downstairs," said Greenroot.

"But—" said Karn. "Your society tried to kill us."

"And I'm trying to save you now," said Greenroot. "Get to the window and onto the roof. You can cross to the house next door."

"Why should we trust you?"

"Don't trust me, then. But only a fool fights in a flaming forest."

The doorknob to Greenroot's bedroom began to hiss and smolder, the metal melting like candle wax. Some alchemical concoction at work. The intruders would be through in moments.

"Why not just destroy the horn? You could have done it centuries ago." Karn guessed when the elf didn't answer. "Because you might need it yourself one day. You don't want anyone else to have it, but you don't want to get rid of it either!"

Greenroot scowled. "Perhaps our motives are not as pure as yours, Karn Korlundsson. Perhaps that's why I am buying you this chance. Now, go!"

Nesstra was strangely silent in all this.

Then the door burst open, and several dark elves rushed in. Leflin met them with his sword and shield. Two against one wasn't fair odds, but their small knives didn't have the reach of his longer blade.

"Go," Greenroot snarled.

Karn didn't listen. Instead, he raised the ancient scutum and charged. He barreled into an elf and sent the assailant crashing down the staircase.

"Evening your odds," said Karn to a surprised Greenroot, who now faced only one opponent. Then Karn opened the window.

"Nesstra," he called, "we have to go now."

The she-elf was still hesitating, but Karn pulled her along. Together, they climbed out of the bedroom and onto the sloped roof of the house. They were able to jump across the gap to the next rooftop relatively easily.

"Leaving the party before it's over, are you?" said Tanthal. Karn saw the dark elf looming above him, along with another. "We can't have that, now, can we?"

The elf with Tanthal drew daggers and advanced. Karn raised the scutum and readied his grip on Whitestorm. But he was on the roof's edge, facing an opponent on higher ground, with his back to a drop.

The dark elf came at him fast. Karn caught a dagger on his shield, turned another with a flick of his sword hand. Once again, Whitestorm moved easily in his grasp. Orm's blessing had made the sword lighter and easier to wield.

Karn's opponent tried again. Karn worked his way sideways across the roof, trying to put distance between his back and the drop. Why wasn't Nesstra helping with her darts?

Karn saw an opportunity and bashed his opponent with his shield. As the elf staggered from the blow, Karn noticed a strange powderlike cloud come off his armor. Sawdust!

"This is taking too long," said Tanthal impatiently. He shoved his own underling forward into Karn. They toppled together, tumbling over the roof's edge.

Surprisingly, Karn's fall was cut short. The scutum was lodged between this roof and a neighboring house. He dangled from it. Beside him, the dark elf fell with a scream, followed by a thud.

"Oh, now, this is delightful," sneered Tanthal, bending to peer at Karn hanging one-armed from the shield. "I told you the bigger victories would elude you."

"You talk pretty bold for a guy who's just betrayed his friend."

Tanthal raised a boot, about to send Karn crashing to the ground.

A jet of white flame suddenly arced over Karn's head. Tanthal fell back, surprised and cursing, shielding his face with an arm. The flame spat again, driving the elf farther away. Karn saw his armor was smoldering but unburnt. It must be resistant to fire.

Tanthal fled at a third burst. But where had the attack come from?

"Don't just stand there," said a new voice. "Help him up."

Then Nesstra appeared, reaching down uncertainly to grip Karn's sword arm. Awkwardly, she took White-storm, then guided him to a grip on the roof. He was able to release his hold on the shield and climb to safety.

A strange cloaked figure wielding a staff stood on the neighboring roof. Was the staff the source of the flame? Was it some sort of magical totem, like the wizards in the old stories?

"Who are you?" he said.

"One who would see you succeed in your quest," said the stranger. "Go quickly before the dark ones regroup."

Karn didn't hesitate. He grabbed Nesstra's sleeve and dragged her across the rooftops and away.

 CHAPTER ELEVEN

Together Again

"I know where Thianna is."

Karn and Nesstra were at street level. He was rapidly leading them toward the city's east gate. Nesstra kept looking back. Karn thought she was afraid of pursuit or worried for her fellow wood elf.

"Don't worry," he said. "I think Leflin knows how to take care of himself. Now we have to rescue Thianna."

"But—how can you know where she is?" asked Nesstra.

"The elf I fought—he had sawdust on his clothing. I remember spotting a lumber mill just across the West-water River. That's where the elves are hiding. That's where they are keeping Thianna."

"A lumber mill?"

"Well, it's not exactly a place that tree-loving wood elves would just drop by, is it? It's perfect for hiding out from the Order of the Oak."

"We only just got away," argued Nesstra. "Now you want to go knock on your enemy's front door?"

"Not when you put it like that—of course not," snapped Karn. "But I came here to rescue Thianna, and that's what I'm going to do."

"Leave here, Karn," said Nesstra with sudden urgency. "Go back to Norrøngard and live your life."

"You can help me or you can desert me. But I'm going."

Nesstra reached out hesitantly to touch Karn's arm. The gesture made him stop walking.

"Tell me the truth—would you still try to save Thianna even if you knew it was impossible? If doing so might mean your doom as well?"

"I told you before, I'd do anything for her."

The familiar sadness overcame the golden elf's face.

"I've never seen friendship like that. I never even believed it existed."

Karn dropped his gaze, embarrassed at Nesstra's display of emotion. He wondered what sort of lonely life the little elf came from.

"This is the best time for a rescue," Karn said, returning to practical matters. "While the dark elves are searching for us all over the city. Will you help?"

Nesstra pondered this a moment.

"I'll come with you," she said.

"You'll help?"

"I'll come."

Having exited Castlebriar and crossed the Westwater, Karn and Nesstra clung to the thinning woods until the mill was in sight. Crouching behind a stack of felled trees, Karn watched the small cluster of buildings. Nesstra started forward. Karn stopped her with a hand on her arm.

"Wait," he said.

Sure enough, a dark elf stepped out of the central building.

"They left a guard behind," said Karn. "I wonder if he's alone."

"How do we get past him?" asked Nesstra. "And which building do we search first?"

"Let me think," said Karn. He studied the area, his mind breaking up the terrain like squares on a board game, running moves and strategies.

"She's in the main building," he said.

"How do you know?"

"I don't, but I'd bet on it. No lights anywhere else. Most of the elves are in the city looking for us. They've left a minimal guard, maybe only the one, so she'll be in the same building the guard is in."

"Okay, so that still leaves the question of how we get to it without being seen."

"That's easy. We swim."

"Swim?"

"They won't be watching the water. We can come up right alongside the mill's dock." Karn gave Nesstra an apologetic look. "I'm afraid it may be cold for you, though."

"For me? Won't you be cold too?"

"I'm a Norrønur," Karn snorted. "You Nelenians don't know what cold is."

Despite Karn's bravado, when it came to it, he was impressed to see that Nesstra entered the water without complaint. She slipped right into the chilly waters without so much as a goose bump showing. For his part, Karn found it awkward to swim with both Whitestorm and the Gordion shield. The river was rapid near its center, but by staying close to its banks they could make their way upstream and toward the mill without too much effort. Twenty minutes later, the pair climbed out onto the shore, dripping wet but unnoticed, in the shadow of the main building. A ramp designed for sliding timber down into the water made for a convenient ascent to the second floor.

As Karn was about to enter the mill by a second-story doorway, Nesstra touched his arm.

"Whatever happens," she said, "believe me when I say I think Thianna is lucky to have a friend like you."

Karn smiled, unsure how to react to this. Then they entered the mill.

Karn and Nesstra found themselves in a large, open space. A circular blade hung over a saw pit dominating the room. But that wasn't what commanded Karn's attention. All his focus was for the large girl bound to a great tree trunk.

"Thianna!" Karn called, racing forward.

"Karn?" said the frost giant's daughter. "Karn, is that you? What are you doing here?"

"I'm here to rescue you," he replied.

"Sweet Ymir!" exclaimed Thianna, beaming. "Did Orm send you? How did you find me?"

"Let's get you out of here first," said Karn. "Then I'll tell you."

He set about examining her chains. Her captors had wrapped them in fur, though why they'd want to keep chains warm he couldn't imagine. While he studied them, Thianna's eyes shifted over his shoulder to his companion. The giantess's enormous smile faltered as Nesstra stepped forward.

"What are you doing with *her*?" the giantess said.

"She's been helping me," said Karn, confused.

"No, she hasn't," said Thianna.

"Yes, she has," said Karn.

"No, she hasn't."

"Yes, she has," insisted Karn. He couldn't understand

Thianna's reaction. Did Thianna have something against elves?

"I don't know what you are doing with that person," said Thianna, "but she hasn't been helping you."

"We met at the Windy Willows," said Karn. "I saved her from a mugging, and she's been helping me search for you ever since. Nesstra, tell Thianna that you've been helping me."

"I'd like to, Karn," said the elf. "But that's not what I've been doing."

Nesstra struck Karn between the shoulder blades. He felt something crumple softly against his back. Then a sticky yellow foam was pouring over his arms and oozing rapidly down his legs. He tried to run, but he was stuck fast. Unable to move his limbs, he twisted his head to bring the elf into view.

"Nesstra—what are you doing?" he said. She shook her head sadly, regret plainly visible in her dark eyes.

"I told you not to thank me."

"He saved my life."

Desstra had shed her wet disguise as Nesstra for the black-and-orange leathers that marked her as both Underhand and not. Though she had wiped off the golden makeup from her forearms, face, and neck, there were still streaks of it remaining in the folds of her long ears. No matter. She had more serious concerns than cosmetics.

"He thought you were a wood elf," said Tanthal. "A fellow surface dweller." They stood on the bank of the same watercourse Desstra had only recently used to sneak into the lumber mill. They had come outside to be out of earshot of the other elves. Tanthal exercised a few practice swings with Whitestorm. Yelor had taken the key and shield for examination, but Tanthal had claimed the sword for his own.

"I was poisoned. Paralyzed. He gave me the antidote."

"Doesn't mean he wouldn't hesitate to kill you now. You're a dark elf. A pale, sickly thing that lurks in caves and crawls in the dirt with the worms. That's how they see us."

Desstra wasn't so sure. The Norrønur boy had felt so guilty at bringing a stranger into harm's way. *I promise you, I won't let you die!* he had said.

"You weren't there," she told Tanthal. "You didn't see the concern in his eyes."

Tanthal spat in disgust.

"Then it shows what a good actress you are! Desstra, remember the stone I gave you to carry."

"It's hard to forget such a valuable gift. A rock." Yes, she thought. Keep right on rolling your eyes. Maybe you'll find your brain back there.

"Be like that stone," admonished Tanthal, "strong as the rock of our home. You've done very well these last few days. Don't taint my good opinion of you by letting your weak heart spoil it all now."

Desstra gazed down into the flowing waters. With the nocturnal vision of all dark elves, she could see her reflection in the river. Her skin looked silver in the light of the moons. Not sickly pale like it appeared in the sunshine. Perhaps Tanthal was right. The dark was her home. She was back with her kind, where she belonged. But Karn wasn't home. And he wasn't with his kind. He'd come all this way for Thianna, and he'd told Desstra how different Thianna was from him. She recalled how willing he was to do anything for her, despite their differences. Even die.

Would Tanthal die for her? She didn't think so. She remembered the way he'd shoved a fellow elf down the roof in an effort to get Karn. Tanthal wouldn't die for her, but she was pretty sure he'd kill her if it served his purposes. Was that what it meant to be strong as the rock of your home?

"What happens now?" she asked.

"'A little finger holds the fate, where a crescent commands a straight. Upon the arc where shatters wheel, alter course and come to heel.'"

"Yes, yes. I'm the one who found the riddle, remember? 'In Sunken Palace waters reign, King and Dragon find their bane. When snake and cockerel sundering, seek ye then the Marble King.' But what do we do?"

"We follow the next verse of the riddle to Gordasha. We find the horn. We take it back to the Svartálfaheim Mountains. I'm hailed as a hero, and you get to graduate and shed that gross orange lizard skin for proper armor.

Then, when the Underhand masters the use of the horn, you can laugh with me as our people force that old worm Orm to burn Norrøngard down. Thousands die. Everybody wins."

"Sure," she said. "Everybody."

"I am so dumb."

"No argument here," replied the giantess. She was still bound to the tree trunk, only now Karn was tied up as well. He was lashed to a chair positioned a few feet away from her. At least they were facing each other.

"I really should have seen it. I mean, when we went into the grave, Nesstra—I mean Desstra—she didn't really need a light to see."

"Dark elves wouldn't."

"And the skin under her shirt was all pale. When I saw her belly—"

"You saw her belly?"

"She was injured. I treated the wound. The skin was all white."

"And that didn't clue you in?"

"I thought it was the poison."

"Sure. Okay. Poison often turns people into dark elves."

"I'm ignoring you," Karn said, frowning. "But the cold didn't bother her, either. That really should have tipped me off that she wasn't from Nelenia."

"I'll give you that one," said Thianna. "None of you take to cold like an Ymirian."

Karn stamped his feet in frustration.

"Stupid, stupid, stupid," he said.

"Sure was," Thianna replied.

"You don't have to keep agreeing with me!"

"Then say something I disagree with!"

Karn scowled. Then he grinned. "It's good to see you, Thianna."

"You too, Short Stuff," she replied, teasing him with her first nickname for him. "I wish it were under better circumstances. But I'll take what I can get. How'd you find me?"

"I just looked for a wave of destruction and knew you'd be at the center," he laughed. "No, really, it was a bit more complicated than that."

Karn gave Thianna a quick rundown of everything that had happened since the wyvern snatched him away from trading in the markets of Bense.

"But what about you?" he asked. "How did you get here?"

"After I left Norrøngard last winter," she said, "I found a ship in Bense that would take me across to Araland. I worked in Pil Meck for a while, loading cargo. Seems I'm good at lifting things."

"You think?"

"Yeah, well, I got bored, so I went farther south. I spent a few days in Tidge. It's a little town on the Shyburn River. I had just gotten into some interesting trouble there when the wyvern showed up."

"You could talk to it, though? It didn't just snatch you out of the sky like it did to me?"

"Yeah, but I didn't really know what it was after. I thought maybe Orm just wanted his sword back. Anyway, you know what happened next. The dragon sent me to Castlebriar to search for the horn."

"He didn't have any trouble convincing you?"

"I was heading in that general direction already. Flying is a lot faster than walking. And he promised me more answers about my past if I found the horn. Anyway, I found the dark elf team headquartered here in the mill. They had stolen the Grave Hill key from the Order of the Oak, so I stole it from them. I hid it in my room at the Windy Willows, where you found it. I was just on my way to see Greenroot about it when the dark elves grabbed me."

"It must have taken quite a few of them."

"I did make them work for it."

"I imagine. Anyway, what do we do now?"

"Oh, that's the fun part," said Yelor, striding into the room, along with just about every elf in the mill. "Now you get to die."

"What's fun about that?" said Karn.

"We get to watch," replied the elf.

❖

Several elves carried Thianna's tree trunk to the edge of the saw pit. Karn's chair was hauled over as well. The boards covering the pit had been lifted up in one corner. An elf with a long pole jabbed savagely at something below. A hissing came from the dark. Karn wondered what kind of creature was down there. He'd never heard anything like it. The noise sounded like a snake's hiss, but it was punctuated with shrill howling sounds—almost a caterwaul.

"Oh, someone's not in a good mood," said Yelor. "Don't worry. It'll have a happy tummy soon."

"Planning to jump in, are you?" said Thianna.

"I think its appetite calls for something bigger," replied the elf. "If only there was something large and useless lying around that we could feed it. Oh wait, there is."

Karn looked away from the gloating Yelor. Suddenly, he recognized Desstra among the elves. He studied her now that she had transformed from wood elf to dark elf. Her pale white skin was almost skeletal against the black-and-orange leathers of her Underhand armor.

"I guess you liked me better when I was Nesstra the wood elf," she said scornfully.

"Wouldn't you?" he replied. "Nesstra was my friend."

"That was an act," she said.

"It didn't have to be. If you can pretend something so well, you can be it."

"This is who I am—the *real* me," she said. "Do I disgust you now?"

"You don't disgust me at all," said Karn. "You disappoint me. I just thought you were someone better than you are."

"We're all better than you," Tanthal sneered. "Even the least of us. Even Desstra. Too bad you won't live to see us overrun Norrøngard with dragon fire."

"I saved your life," said Karn, ignoring Tanthal and keeping his gaze on Desstra.

The little dark elf approached, bending and putting her hand on Karn's chest. She gripped the collar of his woolen long coat for a moment.

"Thank you for that," she said, stepping away. "Goodbye, Karn. At least you found what you came for." Then Desstra turned and walked away.

Tanthal shook his head.

"Just like Desstra to leave when the fun starts," he said.

"Enough," said Yelor. "We need to be off. Let's get this going-away party started." He motioned to the elves holding Thianna. They upended her tree trunk with a heave and tipped it over the edge of the saw pit. The frost giantess slid right off the log, disappearing into the darkness of the pit with a cry of "Troll dung!"

Before Karn could shout his anger, he was lifted and tossed, chair and all, into the hole after her.

CHAPTER TWELVE

Here, Kitty, Kitty

Karn lay in a pile of splintered wood. The chair had smashed to bits when it struck the hard-packed dirt floor of the pit. It had mostly broken Karn's fall. Mostly.

"Are you okay?" cried Thianna, rushing to him. Free of the tree trunk, the slack in her chains made them easy to slip off. Karn climbed unsteadily to his feet. They stood in a small circle of light cast by the hole in the pit above.

"I think so," he said. He pulled the phosphorescent stone from his pocket and shook it until it glowed. "Out of the stew pot . . ."

"And into the fire," Thianna finished. "Never been too crazy about fire."

In the shadows outside their pool of light, something hissed loudly. The saw pit was long and rectangular, to accommodate cutting tall trees. Whatever it was sounded as if it was at the far end. Karn wrinkled his nose at a musky smell in the air.

"What is it?" he asked.

"Guess we're about to find out," Thianna replied.

Karn looked around the pit. Aside from piles of sawdust, there was a bucket of water nearby that had obviously been placed for the mystery creature to drink. But he didn't see anything of use.

"If only we had some sort of weapon."

"I might be able to do something about that." Thianna selected one of the chair legs. Sticking it in the water bucket, she stirred the wood in the water and chanted, "Skapa kaldr skapa kaldr skapa kaldr skapa kaldr."

Smiling, Thianna raised the chair leg, now with a sizable chunk of solid ice on one end.

"Instant club," she said. Then, to Karn's look of incredulity, she added, "I've been practicing."

"I can see."

"Let me make you one too."

Unfortunately for them both, whatever the something was, it chose that moment to spring out of the darkness at them. Amazingly, it seemed to leap nearly the whole length of the pit.

Thianna had an impression of a fuzzy face and paws with wicked claws, but also of a long, scaled tail. Then it was on her, and it was time to act.

The frost giantess brought her club of ice around in a

vicious swing. She struck the creature hard on the head, knocking it aside. It sprang away again, vanishing into the dark.

"Ymir's rotten toes! What in the world was that?"

"Surprised? I'm told it's called a tatzelwurm," called Yelor from above. "It's apparently native to the hills of these parts. Also called a springwurm."

"I can see why," said Thianna.

"Well, you are the clever one," said Yelor. "But do carry on. Don't let me interrupt you again. It's quite entertaining watching."

"It's even more fun down here," called Karn. "Why don't you join us and see?"

Yelor made to answer but was interrupted by the sound of shouting from elsewhere in the mill. "Go and see what that is," he said irritably to an underling.

Thianna kept her eyes on the darkness, holding her makeshift club at the ready.

The shouting noises turned to sounds of a struggle. Karn and Thianna heard Yelor swearing, then the noise of running as the dark elves were pulled away.

"What's going on?" Thianna asked.

"Trouble for them can only be good for us," Karn replied.

"Yeah, well, I don't see how it helps our immediate circumstances," she said.

Then the tatzelwurm sprang again.

This time it came at Karn. Suddenly, a feline face was

barreling right at him, vicious claws extended. Without a weapon to defend himself, he thought he was doomed. But the tatzelwurm's attack fell inches short of its mark.

Thianna, nearly as fast as the creature, had gripped it by the tail and yanked it back before the claws found their target. It spun around to face her, and Karn got a good look at it.

The tatzelwurm was like a cross between a wildcat and a snake. It had the head and forelimbs of a cat but a long, legless body like a serpent. The hissing and caterwauling suddenly made sense.

Unfortunately, Thianna now had a tatzelwurm by the tail. It coiled on itself, swiping at her. Karn ran forward and kicked it savagely in the side. It hissed and spun back and forth, not sure whom to attack.

"Let go of it," Karn yelled.

"Let go?"

"Yes, pick up your club and let go. I can't drive it off if you're holding its tail."

Thianna understood, releasing the tatzelwurm and grabbing her club. She struck the creature in the flank, and when it spun to face her again, Karn gave it another kick.

Under assault from both sides, it leapt back into the darkness of the far side of the pit.

"That thing can really make an impressive jump!" said Thianna.

"Admire it later, kill it now," Karn said. Then he looked

down at his long coat. The tatzelwurm's attack had been a nearer miss than he realized. The fabric of his coat was torn. He saw a small pouch tucked under his collar. It didn't belong to him. Karn pulled it out, realizing instantly that Desstra must have slipped it into his clothing when she had said goodbye.

He had no reason to trust Desstra, but the pouch hadn't immediately exploded or caught fire. It was bound with a small string. He pulled it open—a strong but not unpleasant smell wafted out. Karn saw that it contained what looked like crushed leaves.

While Karn puzzled over the herb, Thianna was advancing slowly toward the other side of the pit. She reasoned that the tatzelwurm's big advantage lay in its ability to jump great distances. If she could close the distance, she'd remove that advantage. She swung her club back and forth to discourage attacks.

What that smell? Sniff sniff sniff.

Thianna stopped her advance. She had heard a voice, distinctly, from the darkness.

Something smell good! Sniff sniff. Something smell very good! Big girl with stick have smell?

"I don't have any smell," she called.

"Who are you talking to?" asked Karn from behind her.

"The tatzelwurm, I think."

"What? How is that even possible?"

"I don't know," said Thianna, though she thought she

might have an idea. The Horn of Osius gave its user the ability to talk to reptiles. The Thicans she had encountered could all communicate mentally with their wyverns. Had her experiences awoken this ability in her—a gift from her human heritage? The tatzelwurm was clearly part reptile.

"Tatzelwurm," she called, "is that you?"

The creature sprang out of the darkness again. But this time it stopped just out of Thianna's reach. Its paws were on the ground, claws retracted, but its nose was twitching fiercely. It stuck its face in Thianna's own.

Sniff sniff sniff. Big girl not smell nice. Bad bad bad.

"Speak for yourself, buster. I've been tied up for days without a bath."

Must find good smell. Sniff sniff.

The tatzelwurm sprang past Thianna, bounding toward Karn. She raced after it.

When she reached the Norrønur, he was pinned against the far wall, clearly uncomfortable but unharmed. The tatzelwurm was running his nose up and down Karn's body, looking for the source of the scent.

Smell smell smell, sniff sniff sniff. Me want that smell.

"What's it doing?" said Karn. Thianna realized he couldn't hear the creature in his mind the way she could.

"Something's driving it wild. Some scent. Are you carrying anything smelly? What do you have on you?"

Karn held out the pouch.

"Is it this?" he asked.

Yes! Sniff sniff! Good good!

The tatzelwurm sprang at the pouch, knocking it with its nose. A little of the herb fell to the ground. The creature dropped and rubbed its whiskers in the crushed leaves.

Yes! Yes! Yes! Sniff sniff sniff! More! More! More!

It writhed on the ground, flipping onto its back and making a strange noise.

"Is it purring?" Thianna asked. The sound was more of a *purr-hiss-purr-hiss.*

"I think so," said Karn, smiling. He tossed some more of the substance over to the animal, which practically tied itself in knots, it was squirming so much in ecstasy.

Sniff sniff sniff!

"What is that stuff?" said Thianna.

"It's catswort," he explained. "Also called catnip. It drives cats crazy. Apparently, our friend here likes it better than eating us."

Much better. Girl smell bad. Sniff sniff! More more more!

"Apparently so," said Thianna. "Um, good kitty. Snake. Kitty snake."

Good kitty snake! Yes! Sniff sniff sniff!

"Karn, save some of that."

Karn clutched the pouch back to his chest.

"You want more?" Thianna asked.

Yes! More! Kitty snake want more!

"We can do that. But we have a problem of our own. Maybe you can help us with it."

What problem bad smell big girl have? Me help, give more sniff sniff?

"Yes."

"We're stuck in a pit." Thianna gestured around.

Bad elves put us all here.

"Yes. But can you get us out?"

For an answer, the tatzelwurm sprang again, right up and out of the pit. Then its long tail flopped over the edge. It hung all the way to the ground.

Climb! instructed the tatzelwurm. *Climb. Give more sniff sniff!*

Karn and Thianna burst out of the lumber mill, with the tatzelwurm cavorting merrily around them. The scene outside was chaos. Wood elves clashed with dark elves in a fierce battle. The wood elves' faces were masked, but they carried the distinctive buckler shield of the Order of the Oak. They fought with swords and bows. The Underhand agents of the dark elves fought with maces, daggers, darts, and short swords.

Karn saw Leflin Greenroot dueling fiercely with Yelor. Then they were spotted and several dark elves broke off from their melees to engage with him and Thianna.

Unfortunately for the elves, Thianna had a much longer reach. She knocked them around savagely with her ice club. They hung back after that, moving apart to try to split her focus. Karn wished again that he had a weapon.

"Now, this I'm going to enjoy," said Tanthal, stepping out from the shadow of a building and approaching Karn. He held a sword, grinning. It was Karn's father's sword.

"That's mine," the Norrønur boy said.

"All the more perfect when I cut you down with it," the Svartálfar boy replied. "It's quite a prize." Tanthal pretended to admire the blade. "Even if the red-gold tint is a bit garish for my taste. I think I'll call it Norrønbane. And use it specially for killing Norrønir."

Karn spoke through gritted teeth.

"The sword already has a name."

"I'm sure it's had several. Now it's Norrønbane."

"The sword's name is"—Karn's voice rose to a shout—"Whitestorm!"

Suddenly, the blade jumped of its own volition. It shot from Tanthal's grasp, almost pulling the elf over as it flew from him. Whitestorm crossed the distance between them, reversing its point as it did so. Karn gaped as the hilt settled comfortably into his hand.

"You c-c-can call your sword?" Tanthal stammered in shock.

"I guess so," said Karn. "It looks like a dragon's gifts keep on giving." Reunited with his weapon, he adjusted his stance for a fight. "Now, you were saying?"

Tanthal spat and drew both a mace and a dagger. He came at Karn swiftly.

Karn raised Whitestorm to block the first strike, but Tanthal's dagger was right behind it. Karn kicked the elf hard in the side, knocking him back and throwing off his strike.

Tanthal recovered and came at Karn again and again. The third time, Karn caught the blade of the dagger and, with a twist of his wrist, sent it clattering to the ground.

"Nice," said Thianna, suddenly beside him. "I took care of my two and came to see if you need help. But you don't seem to."

"I've been practicing," Karn replied. "Hey, I'm no fool. Every day for an hour since the battle at Dragon's Dance."

Faced with two attackers and short one weapon, Tanthal chose to flee. Karn let him go. Now that he had found Thianna, his concern was getting her to safety. Then he had a thought.

"Hey, where's the tatzelwurm?" he asked.

Thianna pointed.

The kitty snake was having the time of its life. Clearly still giddy under the influence of the catswort, it was pouncing on one dark elf after another. With an exultant caterwaul, it would come leaping out of the sky to knock a hapless elf into the dirt. Then it would bound again, soaring into the air and returning to earth to crush another unfortunate elf beneath it.

Fun fun fun! Pounce pounce pounce! Sniff sniff sniff! it said in Thianna's mind. Several dark elves decided to make a run for it. The tatzelwurm noticed them and set off in joyous pursuit.

"I'm not certain it's coming back," Thianna said, laughing.

"That's probably just as well," Karn replied. "I wasn't sure what to do when the catswort ran out."

Between the springing kitty snake and the Order of the Oak, the battle was quickly winding down, though it looked as if the dark elves had given nearly as good as they got. Several of the wood elves were injured, and a few of them were down.

"Can't say it hasn't been fun," said Thianna.

"True," replied Karn. "But I'll be glad when we're home."

"Home?"

"Well, yes. We can go home now."

"Whoa!" said the giantess. "I'm not going 'home.'"

"Why not? The horn is gone. The dark elves have been stopped. We can go tell Orm he has nothing to worry about."

"You go tell him. I'm headed to Thica."

"I didn't come here for Orm. I came here for you."

"I didn't ask you to," said Thianna, a touch of resentment in her voice. "I'm here to see the world. You want to see it with me, great."

"You tried the world," Karn argued. "It was dangerous. I had to rescue you from the world. Now it's time to go."

"Technically, neither of you are going anywhere," said Greenroot. The wood elf had approached while they were quarreling. Karn saw that he had a vicious cut across one eye and into his cheek, but he didn't seem to feel it.

"What are you talking about?" said Karn. "The horn is gone. The dark elves have been stopped. You have the shield and the key. You can follow the trail if you want or bury it forever. You don't need us, and you don't need to worry about us."

"And you owe us," said Thianna. "Seems like we've done all your work for you."

"True, you've alerted us to our own forgotten history. And led us to our enemies."

"But?" said Karn.

"But you and your friend are loose ends who know too much. I told you that the Order plays a long game. Weighing the good of the whole world on a timeline of centuries."

Several wood elves had appeared to surround them now.

"So we're what? Your prisoners?"

"Let's call you our guests for now."

"Guests who can't leave," complained Thianna. "How are you better than they are?" She gestured to where the surviving dark elves had been rounded up and disarmed. Karn saw that both Tanthal and Desstra were among the captives. Despite himself, he was glad that Desstra was still alive. He still had a hard time separating the wood elf who had been his friend from the dark elf who had betrayed him.

"We're better because the Underhand would use the horn to lay waste to the surface world, whereas the Order of the Oak exists to prevent such things from happening."

"So if you have to disappear a few kids, that's all right," said Thianna.

Greenroot had the decency to look away.

Karn glowered. None of this had anything to do with him. He had come to save his friend, and now he had to convince a secret society that he didn't care a flip about that he didn't care a flip about its secrets, either. Neth take both the Order and the Underhand! He glared at the wood elves and the dark elves.

"Hey," said Karn, suddenly alert. "What's Tanthal doing?"

The dark elf had something in his lips. Karn saw that he was blowing on a small, thin whistle. It didn't make any sound that he could hear, but then Karn had experience with instruments meant for other ears than human.

With a screeching noise, a swarm of enormous creatures suddenly dropped out of the sky. Karn thought they were wyverns at first. Then he saw that they were giant bats.

The hind claws of the bats raked at the wood elves, driving them back. The Order of the Oak raised their bows. Several of the creatures were brought down. But Tanthal and Desstra managed to climb onto the backs of two of them. In seconds, they were far overhead.

Greenroot swore. He grabbed a bow and fired a clearly useless arrow after them.

"They're gone," he said.

"You can't go after them?" asked Karn. "You don't have any way to fly?"

"No, we don't," Greenroot replied.

Karn looked at Thianna. He had come all this way for her. He thought his journey was nearly over. Now the dark elves were heading to Gordasha, armed with the second and third stanza of the riddle. Flying, they'd be there in days or sooner. Whereas on foot or horseback, it would be weeks before the Order of the Oak could follow. The Horn of Osius would fall into the dark elves' hands. He hated what he was going to say, but he had no choice. It was the right thing.

"We do," said Karn. "And now it looks like we're your only hope."

CHAPTER THIRTEEN

Fly by Night

"You just left them behind."

Desstra clung to Flittermouse. The cold night air blowing through her hair did nothing to cool her temper. The star-filled sky was wasted on her as well. She was grateful the bat had rescued her, but furious that Tanthal had abandoned the rest of their team.

"The bats can only carry one person each," Tanthal explained. He rode beside her on his own wing, close enough that they could talk. He was smug and completely unapologetic. Desstra felt he was treating their quest for the horn like a game of capture the banner. He didn't care who got hurt. His only concern was that he was winning.

"But you didn't even try to help them," she protested. "We fled and left them to their fate."

"You're welcome to turn around," the dark elf replied. "I'm sure it will make their defeat so much more bearable if you go down with them."

Desstra scowled at him, but she made no move to alter Flittermouse's course. What could she do on her own?

"We have a mission," Tanthal went on. "That mission is more important than any one person. Their sacrifice will mean our success."

"Your success."

"Of course. And your graduation. Remember that."

"How could I forget?" she said. You never let me, she thought. In need of a distraction, she checked the supplies in Flittermouse's saddlebags. She had extra gear, including another set of her darts. In the east, the horizon was beginning to glow in anticipation of the rising of the sun. Dark elves hated sunlight. But she hadn't minded it so much when she was pretending to be Nesstra the wood elf.

"Oh, don't worry," said Tanthal, misinterpreting her expression. "I suspect we haven't seen the last of that Norrønur boy you like so much."

"I don't like him," she said, too quickly.

"Good. Because I have a thought."

"Whatever it is, I'm sure it can wait until you're more intelligent."

"My thought is this," continued Tanthal, unruffled. "The next time we encounter Karn Korlundsson, we should kill him."

"Kill him?" Nesstra said.

"Of course. And you should be the one to do it."

"Me?" She had already betrayed Karn. But after he had saved her life, could she really kill him?

"A great idea, don't you think?" Tanthal asked. "What better way to prove that you can be strong as the rock of our home? Think of it as your final exam."

Oh wonderful. More humans.

The wyvern was perched in the lower branch of a beech tree. Its tail was coiled around the limb for balance while it tore greedily into a rabbit with its teeth.

"Actually, these are elves," said Thianna. Karn had led her, Greenroot, and several other wood elves across the bridge and to the location in the Blackfire Forest where the wyvern had remained hidden.

Do you think I care about the difference? it thought in Thianna's mind. *If it weren't for you and your kind, I'd be far from here. Nesting on a mountain peak so high none of you could ever climb it. Well, maybe you could. But you take my point.*

"It's good to see you, too," Thianna said.

If I were glad to find you still alive, the wyvern thought, *it would be a tiny emotion buried beneath my irritation at encountering all these strangers.*

"This is the creature you came on?" Greenroot said, incredulous.

"Yes," said Karn. "Thianna first, and then it brought me."

"With such a large wingspread, it can overtake the bats. And they can only travel by night. The sun will be up soon. We can get to Gordasha ahead of them."

"We?" said Karn.

"Neither you nor Thianna are experienced warriors. It only makes sense for two of us to go in your place."

I did not sign on for this, thought the wyvern.

"You want to ride it," said Thianna, "you're welcome to try."

The reptile snarled and bared its fangs.

Over quite a few of their dead bodies.

"Relax," the giantess said to the wyvern. "I don't think that's going to happen."

"You're talking to it? You understand it?" asked Greenroot, who like everyone else present was only getting one half of the conversation.

"Yup," said Thianna. "And it's not real happy to see you."

That's putting it mildly. Although only Thianna could hear it, the wyvern hissed again to demonstrate its displeasure.

"See?" said Karn. "Only we can ride it. Only she can talk to it."

"You're going to let us go now," said Thianna. "And you're going to trust us to fix your mess for you."

"But we won't be bringing the horn back to you," said Karn. "We'll be taking it to Orm so he can destroy it."

"Destroy it?" There were shouts of objections from the other wood elves.

"It's that or the dark elves get it," said Thianna. "Take it or leave it."

Greenroot frowned, then he nodded.

"Very well. We will trust you to see this through. Such trust does not come easy for us. But it seems the circumstances demand that we learn."

The wood elves gave Karn and Thianna what supplies they had, as well as some coins. They offered them each a bow and a quiver of arrows, but neither Karn nor Thianna knew how to use them. Thianna settled for a sword, having lost the one given her by Orm. It was a type known as an arming sword, a one-handed weapon with a straight, double-edged blade and a simple cross-guard. The elves kept the scutum shield and key.

As they were preparing to depart, Karn swatted at several insects that were buzzing around the phosphorescent stone on the cord around his neck. They were attracted by its light, and more and more of them were coming as the morning approached.

"Does anyone have a small cloth bag?" he asked. "Something soft. I've got an idea."

After Karn had put his notion into effect, it was time for goodbyes.

"You've more than proved yourself," Greenroot said.

He reached into a pocket and handed something to Karn. "It's time we honored that."

"What is this?" asked Karn. He held a small silver ring in his hand. The face of the ring was cast in the same tree stump design of the bucklers.

"It marks you as a friend to those who know," the wood elf said. "You may find it will open doors for you that are otherwise closed. At the very least, it may spare you a knife in the back."

"Um, thanks," said Karn, slipping the ring onto a finger. "Though the friend I trust more than anyone is standing right next to me."

Are all humans as talkative as these? thought the wyvern as it carried them into the sky.

"Elves," said Thianna. "Those were elves."

"So what is Gordasha, anyway?" asked Thianna.

"According to Greenroot," replied Karn, "it's the capital of the Sacred Gordion Supremacy. Though apparently there isn't much left of the Supremacy but the capital."

Karn was seated in front of Thianna as they rode the wyvern, feeling a bit like a little kid pressed against the much larger girl. They had tried the reverse, but he couldn't see anything around her wide shoulders, and her long hair whipping in the wind was always in his face.

"I thought the Gordion Empire fell a thousand years ago," she said.

"It did," Karn explained. "Or rather nine hundred eighty-three years ago. It broke in half then. The Supremacy is sort of the last gasp of one of those halves."

"Okay. But do you even know where it is?"

"Hey, I spent hours last night poring over maps at Greenroot's house. I probably know this whole continent better than anyone who isn't a professional mapmaker by now."

"New career for you? Cartographer?" Thianna teased. "If farm boy or tavern owner doesn't work out."

"Right. I'd have to learn how to draw first. Though come to think of it, maybe I could make a game of it. Some sort of war game, moving armies around on a map. What do you think?"

"Maybe. What do you use for the playing pieces?"

"Bats," said Karn with sudden urgency.

"You use bats for the pieces?"

"No! Bats!" Thianna looked where Karn was pointing. Directly ahead of them, she saw their enemy.

"How are they even flying in the daytime?" she asked. "The sun's been up for hours. Aren't bats nocturnal?"

"How should I know?" said Karn. "But there is no way we'll pass them without being spotted."

Sure enough, the dark elves caught sight of the wyvern. The bats flew apart, circling in a wide arc in an obvious attempt to flank them.

"I'm wishing now we'd taken one of those bows," said

Thianna, though she knew that she could never fire it effectively in the rushing air.

Karn drew Whitestorm while Thianna readied the sword gifted her by the wood elves.

"Maybe I should call this Elfbane," she laughed, remembering Karn's fight with Tanthal.

"I'm not sure the wood elves would appreciate that," said Karn.

"Tanthal's Tears, then," suggested Thianna.

"You'd need a pair of them. *Tears* is plural."

"Don't be such a stickler."

The enemy closed in on them, and the time for banter was over. By unspoken agreement, right-handed Karn would defend on that side. While Thianna, who was proving adept with either hand, would defend their left flank.

Karn saw with relief that Desstra was coming at them from the left, so he wouldn't have to face her. He was afraid if it came to it, he might hesitate to swing a blade at his onetime friend. Against Tanthal, he had no such reluctance.

The dark elf came in fast. Karn raised Whitestorm in anticipation, but at the last minute, Tanthal pulled up. The bat flew across them, its back claws raking savagely at Karn's head and arms. Karn threw himself aside, narrowly avoiding a serious laceration. He almost tumbled off the wyvern, but Thianna caught him with her right arm and hauled him back in place.

At the same time, Desstra drove her bat under them, stabbing upward with one of her darts. In desperation, Thianna kicked the elf girl's wrist, throwing off her aim.

Then the bats were out of range. They began their curve in preparation for a second pass.

"If they try that again, aim for the patagium," instructed Karn.

"The what?" said Thianna.

"The patagium. The leather bit between the wing bones."

"Why didn't you just say that?"

"Because it's called the patagium. You should know the proper name."

"I don't have to know what it is to hit it!"

Having crossed sides, Thianna would now face Tanthal. Unfortunately, this matched Karn with Desstra.

"Can't this thing go any faster?" said Karn. He was unhappy at the prospect of facing the she-elf.

Tell the idiot boy that he should try flying all night without a rest, replied the wyvern.

"He says this is the best he can do," Thianna relayed.

The way you paraphrase my words leaves something to be desired.

Then the elves were upon them.

This time, Tanthal attacked with his own weapon. He had traded his mace in for a long gray sword more suited for opposing someone of Thianna's reach. Their blades clashed loudly as they swung at each other.

Karn and Desstra were less enthusiastic in their combat. He swung at her halfheartedly, and she jabbed weakly at him with her darts. In combat, it was important to look your opponent in the eye. Instead, they both kept their gaze on each other's hands.

Karn heard a shout from the left. Thianna had scored a hit.

Tanthal broke off, flying wide. Seeing this, Desstra steered her bat away as well.

Karn noticed that the dark elf had tied blindfolds over her mount's eyes. That explained how they had gotten the bats to fly in the daylight. It also meant they were flying by hearing alone.

"It's time," he whispered in Thianna's ear.

"Get ready," she said, speaking to her mount.

The dark elves came around, readying for another pass. Karn sheathed Whitestorm and withdrew the small cloth bag with the contents he had gathered from the Blackfire Forest.

"On my mark," said Thianna.

The elves approached.

"Dive!"

The wyvern folded its wings to its side. Pulling in its limbs and ducking its head, they dropped like a stone.

The bats both dove after them, but the wyvern had pulled ahead with the benefit of surprise.

Karn waited until the bats were squarely in their wake. Then he opened the bag.

The insects swarmed out. Moths, fireflies, other

buzzing things. Everything he could gather with the glow of the phosphorescent stone.

The bats—starving from their long flight—broke off their pursuit to snatch at the insects as Tanthal and Desstra fought to stay in their saddles.

The wyvern extended its wings, bringing them out of their dive. Its larger wingspan and greater speed meant that the smaller, weaker bats could never hope to catch up.

Tell the boy I've revised my opinion of him, thought the wyvern. *He's only a half-wit, not a complete idiot.*

"The wyvern says you are pretty smart," said Thianna.

I begin to think I am in need of a new translator. My current one is severely underqualified.

"Relax," said Thianna, patting the reptile's neck. "This is a day where everybody wins."

Having left their pursuers behind, they passed the time with Karn pointing out the countries and landmarks as they flew east. They crossed the green rolling homeland of the gnomes, then the enormous landlocked Sea of Catara. Next they crossed the beautiful, mountainous realm of the high elves. Karn told the giantess how the elves had once ruled most of the continent, long ago before even the Gordion Empire.

"Dark elves, wood elves. What's a high elf?" she asked.

"I think it's like other elves, only snootier," he replied.

"Wonderful. Can't wait to meet one someday."

By late afternoon, they were admiring lush green landscapes vastly different from anything in their lives in the far north. They knew they were heading somewhere warmer and more densely populated than their own remote corner of the world. Finally, they came to the territory of the Sacred Gordion Supremacy. The Muspilli Mountains, home to several active volcanoes, provided an impressive land barrier to the north, explaining why the control of the strait was so crucial.

Gordasha, when they saw it, proved to be an enormous city, bigger than Bense, vaster than Castlebriar, greater even than the ruins of Sardeth. A formidable double wall surrounded the city on all sides, protecting it from land on one side and sea on every other. Towers were set at intervals along its length, and soldiers could be seen marching along its ramparts. Inside this barrier, buildings were packed together as tightly as cobblestones in a Gordion road. Greenroot had said it was home to half a million souls. Finding the Horn of Osius would be like searching for a single pebble on a rocky coast. But that wasn't the worst of their troubles.

A fleet of warships choked the waters to the north of the city, while to the west of the land wall, an enormous army was camped. Karn and Thianna saw a multitude of tents, troops, huge siege engines, and great, ferocious beasts that looked like nothing so much as giant warthogs, armored and saddled for riding.

"What in the world are those?" said Thianna. "War pigs? Who rides war pigs?"

"The Uskirian Empire," said Karn. "Gordasha is under siege."

"There must be thousands of troops. Hundreds of thousands."

Karn studied the battlefield. His mind took it all in, studying the defenses. He saw cannons, bowmen, spearmen. But not in numbers equal to the invaders.

"Thianna, the city may not be able to stand up to all this. Gordasha may be about to fall."

And this is where you two want to go? thought the wyvern. *My estimation of your intelligence has taken another dip.*

"We'll just have to find the horn before it falls," said the frost giantess. "Because when those walls come down, Gordasha is the last place we want to be."

CHAPTER FOURTEEN

Breaking the Line

"Imagine trying to get through that army on foot," said Karn. "It's hard to believe there are so many soldiers in the world."

They were soaring above the Uskirian forces, gazing down in wonder at the thousands of troops camped outside the walls of Gordasha. Neither Karn nor Thianna had ever seen anything on this scale.

"And this is just one army," said Thianna.

"Our biggest battles only had a few hundred people in them, maybe a thousand," Karn said. "Look how disciplined they are. They move with such ... such mathematical precision. We just bang on our shields with our axes and yell until the enemy pees themselves."

"That's better than us giants," Thianna replied. "All we do is lob rocks at each other's heads."

Karn couldn't see what two young people could be expected to do in the face of such an army.

"What are we doing here?" he said.

Finally, a sensible question, thought the wyvern. *Shall I turn around?*

"You know you love it," whispered Thianna to the reptile, patting its neck. "But you've got the easy part. Once you get us inside, that's when the real fun starts."

They saw huge siege engines being erected. A giant cannon, cast to look like the head of a boar, was being wheeled to the front lines. It was just like the war pigs that made up the Uskirian cavalry. Soldiers moved to and fro like ants. In the sea to the north side of the peninsula, the fleet of Uskirian warships was keeping its distance. The ships stayed moored just outside the range of the defenders' cannons.

"The battle hasn't started yet," Karn observed. "The Uskirians are still moving their forces into position."

"Lucky us," said Thianna. "I hate being late to a party."

Inside the city, Gordashan troops marched back and forth across the ramparts and towers. Archers, spearmen, and cannon. The double walls were each fifteen feet thick. The terrace between the two walls was wide enough for two wagons to move abreast and crowded with troops. Two enormous city gates were shut by massive iron doors. Another gate was shut against any water traffic on a small river that flowed through the fortification.

"What's that?" said Thianna, pointing to a structure that looked like a high, straight stone bridge. It stood on multiple arches and ran across the land and through the wall.

"An aqueduct," Karn explained.

"What kind of duck?"

"No, aqueduct. A watercourse. It carries fresh water from the mountains all the way to the city. Probably built a thousand years ago by the Gordion Empire. Nobody can build them like that anymore."

Thianna whistled.

"So where do we put down?"

Karn scanned the city interior.

"There's a patch of parkland inside the walls," he said, indicating the area.

The wyvern was just adjusting its course when their flight path was suddenly, abruptly, and quite rudely interrupted.

Then Karn, Thianna, and the wyvern were all screaming, yelling, and hissing as they tumbled through the air. Their limbs and wings were entangled in a heavy rope net. Weighed down with rocks, it had been cast by a catapult to pluck them from the sky.

"We're going to crash," Thianna hollered. "Brace yourself!"

I just want you to know, thought the wyvern, *I'm holding you responsible for all of this!*

The ground rushed at them. They were plummeting too far, too fast. Karn knew their time was up.

The tent deflated like a bladder.

It broke their fall, collapsing under them as it carried them to the ground. The wyvern shook them from its back, flapping its wings to toss off the tent and netting.

"We're not dead?" Thianna wondered aloud.

Don't think this gets you off the hook, the reptile shot back.

Karn stood up.

"We're not dead," he answered. Then he took in their surroundings. They stood in a circle of spears, all aimed at them by fierce soldiers riding atop savage war pigs. And the soldiers themselves were like nothing Karn had ever seen. Gray-skinned, white-haired creatures with pointed ears on their heads and large tusks protruding from their wide mouths. Their bestial appearance was in stark contrast to their finely embroidered clothing. These were Uskirians, Karn realized, and they didn't look at all happy to have visitors.

"We're not dead ...," Karn repeated, taking in the angry faces. "Yet."

Thianna drew her arming sword. In response, the Uskirians prodded her with their spears.

"Cut that out," she snapped, batting a spear away like it was just a buzzing insect.

"Thianna," said Karn, "we're in the middle of an army. Not even you can fight your way out of this."

Thianna considered whether this was true. She shrugged and put her weapon away.

"For now," she said, glaring at the soldiers.

With a great deal of hissing and snapping of teeth, the wyvern had a rope tied around its neck. *Your fault! Your fault!* it screamed in Thianna's mind. Karn and Thianna were left unbound. They weren't even disarmed. Escape was impossible. It was obvious that it was obvious.

The three of them were marched through the encampment at spear point, where Karn got a close-up look at the attackers' capabilities. He had to admit he was impressed. There was a refinement to the troops' armor and gear that spoke of wealth and sophistication, as well as an appreciation for design. Karn and Thianna marveled at row upon row of richly embroidered tents erected to house the encamped forces. An enormous pavilion, positioned in the shadows of the aqueduct, was obviously the command center of the entire army. It was made of multiple tents of varying sizes, some with peaked roofs, others with domed roofs. Hundreds of flags crowned their peaks. The flags showed the face of a boar glaring from the center of a flower-petal design.

"It's like a mobile palace," Karn observed.

"It's like a big pile of rugs," Thianna retorted.

The wyvern was dragged to a hitching post. It saw what was intended and immediately reared up in protest. For an instant, the spearmen turned all their attention to the reptile. Thianna chose the moment to throw herself into them. They went over like bowling pins.

Fly, she thought to the wyvern.

It burst into the air while the Uskirians were still trying to extricate themselves from under a frost giant.

A few spears were hurled in its wake, but they fell short. The wyvern flew across and behind the ancient aqueduct, disappearing from sight.

Call me if you live through this, Thianna heard it say in her mind. She was hauled to her feet by angry soldiers, their weapon points pressing into her back.

Karn and Thianna were walked past guards who wore helmets that covered their whole heads. The metal of the helmets had been cast to look like the tusked faces that lay underneath. It was beautiful and frightening at the same time. The soldiers' armor was made of interlocking rings of flattened metal, reinforced with rectangular metal plates at the front and back. The craftsmanship was more sophisticated than any armor Karn had ever seen. Again, he felt like a bumpkin from the edge of a far more complicated world.

Once they were through the tent flap, the heavy green canvas of the exterior gave way to rich red tapestries of finer materials. They saw that the tent was subdivided by curtains into numerous hallways and rooms. All the walls were embroidered, largely with beautiful flower patterns. The flowers seemed an odd design for an army engaged in a war.

Karn and Thianna were led down passages where numerous underlings ran back and forth, carrying messages or bearing supplies. No one paid them the slightest attention. Finally, they came to a room where an impeccably dressed Uskirian with a braided white beard and an enormous turban sat upon a throne on a dais and presided over a room full of officers and court officials who stood chatting in groups or sat on pillows and cushions.

An Uskirian wearing a fancy cloak and a large turban approached them. He bowed slightly.

"Welcome to the court of Shambok Who Borders on Spectacular," he said in perfect Common. "I am Dargan Urgul, Speaker to Barbarians."

"We aren't barbarians," Karn replied, somewhat miffed. Dargan's white eyebrows rose.

"You speak Uskirian?" he asked.

"Is that what I'm speaking? I guess I do."

Dargan studied them.

"You are strange spies, I'll give you that," he mumbled to himself.

"We aren't spies!" Thianna protested.

"No?" said Dargan. "I think that is highly unlikely."

"I don't care what you think," she roared.

"My dear, I spoke that last sentence in Herzerian. And yet you understood it immediately. Common, Uskirian, Herzerian. Such a command of language can only mean you are spies, scholars, or diplomats." Dargan glanced at their clothing disdainfully. "And, your pardon, but judging by the rough manner of your dress and your muddy appearance, you clearly aren't scholars or diplomats. So I say spies."

Karn looked down at his own clothes, with his torn pant leg and muddy boots. Norrønir weren't exactly the best when it came to personal hygiene, but he knew that he seriously needed to bathe and change.

"We don't actually speak all those languages," Karn explained. He brushed self-consciously at the mud on his shirt. "In fact, I'm not sure which language I'm speaking now. It's kind of hard to explain."

"Try me," said Dargan.

"I'm not sure we should say," said Karn.

"We were sent by a dragon to find a lost magic item that we think is hidden in Gordasha," blurted Thianna.

"Thianna!" Karn gasped in shock.

"Look," she explained, "it's not like he's going to believe us anyway. Or it matters if he does." She turned to the Uskirian. "We don't really care about your war. We aren't planning on staying for it. We just need to get in and out of Gordasha quickly. And you've sort of cost us our ride."

"You don't care about the war?" he said.

"Well, yeah. Like I said, we're not here for it," replied the giantess. "I mean, not that war isn't bad, right?"

Dargan rubbed his brow. "I admit I will be sorry to see these uncivilized realms tamed," he said. "They always lose some of their uniqueness and vitality when they are brought to heel."

"Listen to you! 'Uncivilized'! 'Brought to heel'! You're really big on your own superiority, aren't you?" said Thianna.

"I mean no offense," said Dargan. "I've often thought it would be pleasant to travel the world before our empire brings enlightenment to the far corners of the earth. I'm intrigued by other customs, especially primitive ones. But Shambok Who Borders on Spectacular requires that we fight this war. So fight we must."

"He likes war, does he?" asked Thianna.

"Oh no. He chafes under its yoke, but he has a duty."

"I'm sorry," interrupted Karn. "Did you say he 'borders on spectacular'? Why isn't he just 'Shambok the Spectacular'?

"A very good question." Shambok spoke from his throne. Karn and Thianna realized that the room had grown silent.

The Uskirian leader stepped down from the dais and made his way to where they stood. As elaborate as all Uskirian dress appeared to be, his clothing was the most lavish yet.

"I am only on the verge of being spectacular," Shambok

said. "I cannot be fully spectacular until I fulfill my destiny."

"What is your destiny?" asked Karn.

"So pleased you asked." The Uskirian leader beamed. Then Shambok clapped his hands. Musicians approached from the corner of the room, bearing a variety of lutes and flutes. They began to pluck and blow delicate notes. Then, to Karn and Thianna's surprise, the Uskirian leader began to dance and to sing.

> *"When I was young,*
> *Just a wee lad,*
> *My father said, 'Shambok,*
> *All your siblings are bad.*
> *Kill them all*
> *Or they'll get you.*
> *There's room for only one at the top.*
> *There's no place for number two.'"*

"What's that instrument?" said Thianna, pointing at one of the long-necked lutes.

"Shhh," said Dargan. "It's called a tanbur. Now, listen."

Suddenly, Shambok was joined by a line of backup dancers.

> *"When you're an Uskirian,*
> *There's more to life than fun.*

You have to take the whole wide world
With saber, scimitar, and cannon gun.
The civilization that we bring
Is such a fine and worthwhile thing. . . ."

Shambok twirled around the room now, cajoling various courtiers to join in the dance, while his backup dancers broke off into pairs and whirled around him.

"When you're Uskiri,
You have to travel every sea.
You have to conquer every land
For the empire's glory."

The lights in the tent dimmed. Servants used candles and small mirrors to cast a spotlight on Shambok, who twirled rapidly in a tight circle as he sang.

"You've got to break the strait
To fulfill your legacy.
So you hammer at the walls
Of the Sacred Gordion Supremacy."

"Ouch," said Karn. "Shambok really forced the rhyme a bit there."

"Quiet," Dargan said. "Music critics are often fed to the war pig."

"'Conquer Gordasha.
Open up the Sparkle Sea.
You will be great.'
And here Dad got a bit oracular.
'When you do this thing,
They'll call you Shambok the Spectacular!'"

Shambok ended in a dramatic leap to his knees, arms flung wide. Colorful ribbons burst from the corners of the room and crisscrossed in the air, and all the courtiers clapped.

Awkwardly, because it seemed expected, Karn and Thianna clapped too.

"That was . . . ," Thianna began.

"Impressive," Karn finished for her, before the frost giantess could say something rude. "That was truly impressive. You should be a dancer."

Shambok sighed.

"Frankly, I'd rather dance than wage war, but how else is culture to be spread?"

"I can think of several ways."

"Not available to us, I'm afraid. We Uskirians are charged with enlightening the world. Ti-Emur is an impatient god, for only when all peoples are brought together under the banner of the Uskiri can the god of war rest. He must lead, and the gods of wisdom and benevolence follow only in his wake. We were doing all right with it too, but then we got blocked at the Gordashan Strait. Dargan, why don't you enlighten the barbarians?"

Dargan bowed and spoke. "It was one hundred and fifty-four years ago that Yarak Uskir the Bone Breaker founded the Uskirian Empire. That was when he declared himself Uskir the Stupendous. He decreed that no Uskirian after him could hold so exalted a title unless they succeeded at opening up the Gordashan Strait so that the glories of the Uskiri could move into the Sparkle Sea and beyond. But none since have broken the double walls of Gordasha. However, Shambok Who Borders on Spectacular will triumph where all others failed."

Shambok nodded in acknowledgment of Dargan's faith. "And so it's my turn to hurl Uskirian bodies against the wall. It is a heavy burden, but one I must bear. Do you understand?"

"Not really," said Karn.

"Maybe if I sang the song again," Shambok said hopefully.

"Not necessary," Thianna said quickly.

"Oh, very well," Shambok replied, disappointed. "But by the Seven Sons of the Moon, dancing has made me hungry! Take the spies away, and we'll figure out what to do about them later. Something gruesome, I imagine."

"What do you mean, 'gruesome'?" asked Karn.

"Torture, interrogation, that sort of thing," said Shambok. "So unpleasant, but what choice do I have?"

"Are we friends?"

Desstra had to shout to be heard above the noise of the wind and the sound of the waves crashing on the rocks.

"What?" Tanthal shouted back.

They were swooping low over the waters of the Sparkle Sea. The walls on the south side of the city, below the Great Chain that closed off the strait to Uskirian warships, were undermanned compared to the land walls and northern seawalls.

"I said, are we friends?" Desstra yelled again. She ran her fingers over Flittermouse's fur. She felt closer to the bat than she did to Tanthal. The two dark elves had seen the Uskirian army looming ahead and diverted east, out of range of any catapults, cannons, or ballistae.

"Don't be absurd," said Tanthal. "Of course we're not friends." His lip curled in derision. "Now focus, Desstra. We have work to do."

She wanted to say that she was well aware of their work. She wanted to remind him that approaching the city by sea had been her idea. But Desstra said nothing. She checked that all her gear was firmly secured and watertight. Then she rose up in the saddle.

"Now," Tanthal commanded. In unison, the two dark elves leapt from their bats. Their movements were perfectly synchronized as they dove through the air and splashed into the cold waters of the Sparkle Sea. Then Desstra and Tanthal were swimming hard to reach the rocky shoreline.

Ten minutes later, panting with the exertion, they climbed out onto the thin strip of rocks at the base of the city walls. A large pipe, protected with an iron grate, spilled rushing water out into the ocean. It was the egress for the River Lux, which ran through two-thirds of the city before disappearing underground.

"Anytime now," said Tanthal impatiently.

"I'm on it," snapped Desstra, reaching in her satchel and bringing out a small vial of a very strong acid. She applied it to two of the bars of the grate, then stood back as they sputtered and hissed.

"Oh, cheer up, stupid girl," Tanthal says. "You don't really want friends."

"I don't?" she asked.

"No, you don't." Once the bubbling acid subsided, Tanthal grasped the iron and pried it apart. "You think that the world is divided into friends and enemies? Well, you are wrong. It's divided into winners and losers. And there's always more of the second category than the first. 'Friends' is just what the losers call each other to take the sting out of defeat. I'm better than a friend to you. I'm a winner! And following me is the only way you'll be a winner, too. You want to graduate? Don't worry about being my friend. Worry about finding the Horn of Osius and carrying out my orders."

Tanthal ripped the bars from the grate. He pushed into the tunnel, struggling against the force of the water.

"Stupid of the Gordashans to leave this way unguarded," he mocked.

"Give them a break," said Desstra as she crawled in after him. "There's no reason for them to expect an invader to carry the sort of gear we have."

She passed him one of two nets of finely woven silk. It was the web of a large species of diving bell spider that lived in the caves of their home.

"You're right about that," Tanthal said, pulling the material over his head so it would trap oxygen and allow them to breathe in the waters of the subterranean river. "No one else in the world is the equal of the Underhand. Now, let's go prove it."

CHAPTER FIFTEEN

City Under Siege

Karn and Thianna were disarmed and tied to a tall, wooden tent pole in the center of a room.

"I apologize for the necessity of this," Dargan Urgul said. "I almost wish I could free you both and travel with you to your rustic land."

"Rustic!" Thianna objected, but Karn cut her off.

"Why don't you?" he said.

"Because I remember what happened to Shambok's last Speaker to Barbarians when he displeased our ruler."

"What was that?" asked Thianna.

"He invited him to dance," the Uskirian answered.

"That doesn't sound so bad," she said.

"On hot coals."

"Oh."

"Exactly. Now I will bid you goodbye and take my leave of you."

Dargan bowed, very formally, and left the room.

Karn and Thianna were alone.

"Well," said Karn. "Here we are, tied up again."

"So what do we do now?" she asked. "If we were chained, I could try a freezing cantrip, but this rope fiber won't get brittle like metal would."

"Leave this one to me," said Karn. "Whitestorm," he whispered. "Whitestorm," he said again, louder. Then he yelled as quietly as possible. "Whitestorm!"

The sword came flying into the room, flipping end over end to land in his hand. It was an awkward grip, given that his arms were tied at his side by ropes wound around a pole.

"Watch the point of that thing," said Thianna.

"Sorry," he said. "It's a little hard to maneuver."

It took some effort, but with Thianna's help, they were able to eventually clasp the blade between them and slowly saw its edge against the ropes. At last, the ropes slipped to the ground and they stood free.

"Now where?" Karn asked. "We're still in the middle of an army camp."

"I got this one," said Thianna. "Up."

Thianna grabbed the tent pole and, wrapping limbs around it, shimmied to the ceiling. Once there, she tore at the canvas at its top.

"I wish I had a blade," she muttered.

"You do tend to go through swords rather fast, I've noticed," said Karn.

"Yeah, well, mine don't come when I call."

"Mine didn't used to. You kind of have to stick it in a dragon's mouth for that."

"Sticking my head in once was enough," said Thianna. "Would you get up here?"

Karn wasn't as skilled a climber as a girl raised in the Ymirian Mountains, but he managed to join her with a little effort. Night had fallen while they were being treated to Uskirian hospitality, the darkness providing cover. The surface of the pavilion sank under their feet and offered very little in the way of handholds, but they eventually made it to where a section of the tent abutted the ancient stone of the aqueduct.

"You want to climb that now?" Karn asked.

"I've got an idea," Thianna said cryptically.

Compared with climbing the tent, scaling the weathered stone blocks was relatively easy for the northerners. Soon they stood on the top of the aqueduct. It had a flat surface like a long, narrow bridge.

"You going to call the wyvern now?" asked Karn.

"No," said Thianna. "Being shot out of the sky once is enough. I've got another plan."

"What's that?"

Thianna knelt and pried at a stone slab. After a few

moments of grunting and heaving, she levered the stone up. Inside, the moonslight shown on rushing water coursing through a large, brick-lined tunnel.

"Okay," said Karn, "but unless you have a way to turn that off, I don't see what good it does. Not that we both couldn't use a bath."

"Speak for yourself, Norrønboy," she said. "I always smell wonderful." She raised an arm and took an exaggerated sniff of her armpit. Then she knelt and placed a hand just above the rushing water. "Skapa kaldr skapa kaldr skapa kaldr," she chanted. Thianna stood back so that Karn could survey her handiwork. She'd frozen the water upstream so that the tunnel leading to the city was rapidly emptying out.

She leapt down the now vacant hole.

"That's not going to hold for long, I imagine," Karn said.

"Doesn't have to," Thianna answered. She placed her hands against the frozen block she'd made and muttered some incantations. As Karn watched, Thianna fashioned a rough chair of ice that grew from the front of the block.

"One ride coming up," she said.

"You have got to be kidding," said Karn.

"Hey, you wanted to get to Gordasha ahead of the dark elves. I'd like to see them try this."

"I'd like to see anybody try this," said Karn. "Anybody but us."

"Come on, Short Stuff. It'll be fun." There was an

ominous creaking from the frozen water. "But, um, you better hurry and make up your mind. This is about to blow."

"Can't believe I'm doing this," said Karn, jumping down to join her.

They sat on the seat, pulling their hands and feet in from the sides of the tunnel.

The creaking intensified. Karn could feel the tremendous force building up behind them. He had a tense moment during which he hardly dared breathe. Then the ice broke loose, and his head snapped back as they shot through the tunnel faster than an arrow fired from a bow.

"Sweet Ymir's feet!" hollered Thianna. "This is incredible!"

Karn and Thianna zoomed through the tunnel. They had never traveled so fast in their life, even by wyvern. The roar of the waters behind echoed through the tunnel, and it sounded as if they were riding the advance of a thundercloud. Karn remembered being caught in an avalanche last winter, being carried along by an enormous force. This was similar, only this time he'd chosen the wild ride.

By the dim light of the phosphorescent stone, they began to see small side tunnels leading off to the right and left.

"We're inside the city now," Karn said, yelling above the sound of the water. "How do we stop?"

"Good question," Thianna replied. She held her hands palm outward to either side and began to chant.

"Uh-oh," she said.

"Uh-oh?" asked Karn. "What do you mean, 'uh-oh'? 'Uh-oh' is *not* encouraging."

"I mean, 'Uh-oh, we're not slowing down.' Too much friction."

"What do we do?" Karn asked.

"You could try screaming and see if that helps."

They whizzed along in the darkness. Thianna chanted her incantation. If their ice chair slowed at all, they couldn't tell.

"We must be halfway through the city by now," said Karn, though he had no real way to judge their speed.

"I think I see a light up ahead," she said.

"Where?"

Before Thianna could answer, they soared into the open air, landing with a splash in a large body of hot, steamy water.

They were in a man-made pool, surrounded by bathers in various stages of undress lounging in the warm water. The walls of the room were tiled in elaborate mosaics. A waterfall behind them issued from the large mouth of a statue of a strange animal that had the front quarters of a rooster but the hindquarters of a reptile.

"So much for a low-key entrance," he said.

"You—you came out of the fountain!" exclaimed an elderly woman.

"What?" said Karn, still catching his breath.

"The waters shut off a few moments ago," a man said. "We just complained to the proprietors when you came flying out of it."

"We're with the public works department," said Thianna, climbing from the pool and helping herself to a towel that belonged to a man too shocked to object. "All fixed now."

"Um—thanks," said the stunned woman, her gaze looking uncertainly at the ring of muddy water surrounding Karn where he stood in the pool.

"Don't mention it," he said as he took Thianna's hand and she hoisted him up. "Just, um, doing our job, is all."

Karn and Thianna left the room quickly. They passed smaller rooms with other pools.

"This is some sort of wealthy bathing house," Karn explained.

"Bathing *house?*" Thianna repeated. "If you're into bathing, what's wrong with just jumping in a river?"

"It's a Gordashan thing."

They were beginning to draw looks as they walked through the corridors, still dripping wet.

"You've bathed in your clothes?" a young man asked incredulously.

"Saves on time doing laundry," Karn replied.

Thianna spied a locker room and led Karn inside.

"We're trying to save the world, right?" she asked.

"That's the idea."

"Then I guess that's a good-enough excuse." She quickly helped herself to several sets of clothing, riffling through the cubbies in search of something large enough to fit her. Capes were clearly in fashion. As were long tunics. She found one that suited, though it didn't come much past her waist.

Karn hated to steal. The Norrønir had a dim view of theft. But he admitted the need was great. He took a strange, conical cap that draped forward in the front. Silly, but clearly a standard Gordashan accessory. He handed one to Thianna.

"This looks ridiculous," she said.

"Doesn't matter," he replied. "Put it on. It's obviously all the rage in these parts. And you stand out enough as it is."

Thianna grumbled but donned the cap.

"Perfect," said Karn, although secretly he thought she looked absurd. "We're just two fellow Gordashans returning from a bath. Nothing suspicious about us," he said, laughing at the way the Gordashan cap on Thianna's head kept scraping the ceiling. "Now, let's go save the world."

It was late at night when they emerged onto the street. The aqueduct had carried them all the way through the city to this upscale bathing establishment between a palace and a large racetrack called the Hippodrome. Karn admired the real-life inspiration for the Charioteers board game.

"Like the coliseum in Sardeth," he said. "Only it's horseshoe-shaped, not oval."

"Also, it's not in ruins," said Thianna. "But let's put some distance between our clothing and its previous owners."

Together, they rushed into the still-busy streets ahead without a clear sense of direction. Karn worried that Thianna's extreme height would make them conspicuous, even in Gordashan clothing. As it turned out, Karn was the one who stood out more. There were people in all shapes and sizes and species—humans, elves, dwarves, and rodent folk—but most of those who weren't covered in fur had the same dark hair and olive skin as Thianna. Karn's pale northern skin and blond hair was the exception here, not the rule.

They decided to sleep on the rooftop of a large public forum. It was a circular, grand colonnaded plaza, and its many statues and carvings of gods and heroes made for easy climbing. "It can't be any worse than the Ymirian winter," Karn joked. But the warm air of this southern, seaside climate turned out to be pleasant.

"Do you hear that?" he said as they settled in for the night.

Thianna listened for a moment. "Music? Chanting?"

"I think it's coming from outside the city," Karn said.

"It sounds like 'Over the walls! Over the walls!'"

"The Uskirians."

"Yeah, well, we know Shambok loves his music."

"There is that," agreed Karn. "But this isn't for him. This is to demoralize the people inside. Wear them down before the battle even starts."

"Isn't that cheating?" asked Thianna. "Where's the glory in fighting your enemy if they aren't at their full strength?"

"I guess so," said Karn.

"The dark elves will cheat too," the giantess observed.

"We've beaten them so far."

"I think actually it's been pretty even."

Karn winced at her choice of words, remembering that Desstra had said he and she were even.

"How can someone pretend to care when they don't?" he asked. "Tanthal hates anyone who isn't Svartálfar. You can see it in his face. But Desstra . . . I thought . . ."

"The best liars make themselves believe what they are saying," said Thianna. "At least until they don't need to."

"I wonder."

"Well, don't."

Karn didn't say any more after that, but he lay awake for a long time before sleep came.

206

The sunrise woke them up early. They stood, stiff and sore, but they could see the entire city laid out before them.

"I thought Castlebriar was big," said Thianna in amazement.

"Castlebriar made Bense look tiny," Karn agreed. "But Gordasha makes Castlebriar look like some backwater village."

"You got that right, Norrønboy," said Thianna. "If the world has a center, this must be it."

Gordasha wasn't just enormous in scope and scale. It dripped with history and culture. Statues and obelisks, pillars and columns were dotted throughout the city. The gleaming white of its buildings—brick, stone, and plaster—and the beautiful red tiled roofs were such a sharp contrast to the wood and mud of Norrønir construction. To say nothing of Ymirian ice caves. Cypress trees were planted in orderly rows along many streets and in front of many houses. This impressed Karn as much as anything. The idea of deliberately planting a tree was completely foreign to someone who grew up on the edges of the great Norrønir forests.

"Trees are something you chop down to make boats and houses," he said. "Not something you use for decoration."

"Look there." Thianna pointed.

They could also see the Uskirian fleet amassing in the

Somber Sea to the north of the city, and a view of the nearly mile-long Great Chain, which ran from the tip of Gordasha to the Fortress of Atros on the Thican coast. Thianna took her first glimpse of that not-so-distant land. She felt a longing, a desire to forget about quests and responsibilities and just run away. . . .

"That's it, you know. Mother's home. All my answers. I didn't know we would be so close."

"You'll get there," said Karn, laying a hand on her arm.

"If I could just walk across that chain . . . ," Thianna said softly.

"I don't think that's what the chain is for," Karn replied.

"Why don't the Uskiri attack the Thican fortress? It's a lot smaller than a whole city. If the chain is all that's stopping them, why not drop it from the other end?"

"I don't know," said Karn.

"I thought you knew a lot about history."

"I know a lot about history for a barbarian living on the edge of the world," he said. "Not so much for someone here in the middle."

As it was, however, an answer wasn't long in coming. An Uskirian ship, perhaps thinking along the same lines as Thianna, strayed too close to the Thican coastline. In response, a tower amid the fortress unveiled what looked like a huge parabolic mirror set on a swiveling base. The mirror was rotated and positioned so that its surface could catch the sun's rays. This was then reflected into a tight beam of focused light.

The Uskirian ship realized what was happening and tried to pull away. Unfortunately, it wasn't fast enough. Fires broke out on its deck. As the beam swept back and forth, the vessel was quickly engulfed in flame. Karn and Thianna saw tiny figures leaping into the water as the warship, the integrity of its hull destroyed, sank into the dark waters of the Somber Sea.

"For Neth's sake," Karn exclaimed. "They have a death ray."

"Sweet Ymir," said Thianna, impressed despite herself. "That's one way to discourage visitors."

CHAPTER SIXTEEN

Fishing for Clues

"First order of business," said Thianna.

"Figuring out what the arc that shatters wheel is?" suggested Karn. "Or finding a Sunken Palace where the waters reign?"

"Food," said Thianna. "I've been a prisoner a lot more than you lately. And neither elves nor Uskiri seem to appreciate how much we frost giants eat."

"Food it is," said Karn.

They climbed down from the forum rooftop and made their way to the streets. They didn't see a market, but suddenly Thianna stopped walking and sniffed the air.

"Fish!" she exclaimed. Karn smelled it too.

"That way." He pointed.

They followed the scent to an alley, where a strange sight awaited them. A small person, a dwarf by the look of it, though his skin was of an olive complexion and his nose was more aquiline than bulbous. His beard was also curly and, unusual for the dwarves of Karn's homeland, trimmed short. Doubtless, this was a concession to the heat, though Karn had never known a dwarf not to have a long, braided beard.

The dwarf was cooking on a small portable grill. And he was doing something else.

"Are you *fishing*?" Thianna asked.

The dwarf looked at them. "Shh," he said. "Not so loud."

"You're fishing in the street?" the giantess said again. Sure enough, the dwarf was holding a pole with a line that disappeared through a small hole in the ground. She grabbed the line and lifted it, testing its length.

"Cut that out," the dwarf snapped, swatting her hand. "You'll scare them off."

"But you're fishing. In the street."

"That's what a street fisher does," he replied irritably. "Now, buzz off."

"Forgive my friend," said Karn. "Her stomach is steering her manners. We were hoping you could sell us some breakfast."

"Ah," said the dwarf. "Coin goes a long way to cover ill behavior."

They bought two grilled fish from the street fisher, which he wrapped in an oval-shaped flat bread he called a pita.

"Aralish money?" the dwarf said when they paid, holding up a coin to stare at it. "Don't see that very often."

"Is that a problem?" Karn asked.

"Problem, no. Not really. Money is money. And I like money."

"But where do the fish come from?" Thianna asked around a mouthful.

"How should I know?" said the dwarf.

"You don't know?" asked Karn. "Then how did you know they were there?"

"My father taught me. And his father before him. It's a local secret." The dwarf eyed them with suspicion. "You're not with the Fisherman's Guild, are you?"

"No," they both said.

"Good. And good day." He waved them on with a hand. "Enjoy the Mensis Imperativae."

"The what-what?" asked Thianna.

"You haven't heard? The imperator has called a celebration for today, to petition Mensis to return and save us all from the dreaded Uskiri. For all the good that will do."

"Mensis?" asked Karn.

"Mensis. The god. The one that lives in that big, domed basilica that dominates our skyline. Say, you aren't

212

from around here, are you? Aralish coin. And you don't know Mensis, the horn-shouldered one."

"I've seen him," said Karn, remembering the altar they had found in Sardeth. "What do you mean, 'return'?"

"Well, two nights ago, strange, glowing lights were seen over the dome. They rose into the air and drifted off to sea. People took it as a sign that Mensis had abandoned the city."

"Not exactly a vote of confidence in your chances against the invaders," said Thianna.

"No, it isn't," agreed the dwarf. "Though if you're here, then they're your chances too."

"What can you tell us about the Marble King?" Karn asked.

The dwarf frowned.

"Not a thing. You ask too many questions. Enjoy the fish and the festival. Good day and all that. Now, move along."

"Please," said Thianna, shocking Karn with her politeness. "It's important that we know. We have to find the Marble King."

The dwarf's frown deepened.

"You're not guild. Are you working for the city guard?" he asked.

"No," said Karn. "We aren't with anyone."

"I'm sorry, but I'm selling fish, not information. That's my final word. Move along."

Karn and Thianna left the dwarf reluctantly, stepping away from the alley.

"Well, look here," said an ominous voice behind them.

Karn's hand was instantly on his sword hilt, while Thianna had balled her hands into fists. After living under constant threat for so long, they were surprised to find the danger wasn't directed at them.

Three large men had entered from the alley's opposite end. They surrounded the dwarf, who did not look at all pleased to see them.

"The Fisherman's Guild said we get to make an example of you," said one of the men, smacking a fist into a meaty palm. "I like making examples."

The men had weapons, but so far they hadn't drawn them. The dwarf, however, was clearly in for a beating.

Karn looked at Thianna.

"Shall we?" he asked. "It's not our problem, but . . ."

"I don't like bullies," Thianna said. "Besides, I need a new sword."

"What are we waiting for, then?" said Karn.

Sliding Whitestorm from his sheath, he rushed back into the alley, bellowing a Norrønir war cry. Karn struck one man with the flat of his sword. Thianna pummeled another with her large fists. As her opponent retreated, she caught his own weapon and yanked it from his belt.

"Thanks," she said, holding up another arming sword with a wide cross-guard. "Needed one of these."

When his own opponent drew a blade, Karn was relieved. "Now I don't need to hold back," he said.

Karn held Whitestorm high, inviting the man to step in. When his opponent took advantage of the opening, he brought the sword down hard. The man parried as expected. Karn twirled Whitestorm in his wrist, snaring the other man's sword and sending it spinning from his grasp.

Thianna thrust her new blade right through her opponent's cap, ripping it off. The man clutched his bald scalp.

Then the dwarf boxed the third man on either ear with two wet, slimy fish. The three men yelped and ran.

"How do you learn to move so fast?" the street fisher said, eyeing Thianna with new appreciation.

"It's easy," she replied. "Just spend twelve years dodging frost giants."

The dwarf nodded.

"Don't believe I'll take that up," he said. "The name's Idas, by the way. And I'm obliged for your help."

"My name is Karn Korlundsson," Karn replied. "And this is Thianna Frostborn."

"Strange names, but I will take help when I can get it."

"Who were those men attacking you?" asked Thianna.

"Fisherman's Guild. They don't like when we get our fish from the street," Idas explained. "Then we don't have to buy at the docks. It's nothing new, but I'm in your debt, nonetheless. So, how can I repay you?"

"You can tell us about the Marble King," said Karn.

"You sure you wouldn't rather have another fish sandwich?" Idas asked hopefully.

"The Marble King," Karn repeated.

"Though if you want to throw a second sandwich in on top of that, I won't object," added Thianna.

Idas sighed.

"All right." He glanced around before continuing. "The Marble King is a legend. One our current ruler would rather forget."

"Why is that?" Karn asked.

"Well, he was a revolutionary. You know, a trouble-maker."

"He was a soldier, wasn't he?" Karn remembered the story that Greenroot had told him. He suspected it was connected.

"Yes," said Idas. "Also, he was a dactyl named Acmon. A seafaring dwarf. Like me. He came from Thica originally, but he was a conscript, conquered and drafted to fight in the Gordion army. They conquered people and then drafted them to fight their next war. The Gordions sent him to Castlebriar, where something happened to him. Some say he found a magic horn. He came back to Gordasha—it was called Ambracia then—and launched a rebellion."

"This rebellion—he had some help, didn't he?" said Karn, putting pieces together. "Some really big, scaly, fire-breathing help."

"Sure did," said Idas. "Legend says he had a dragon.

Together, they drove out the Gordion Empire. He ruled for several years then. It was a good time to be a dactyl, let me tell you."

"Then what happened?" Thianna asked.

"Oh, what always happens. The Gordion Empire retook the city. He was overthrown. The king and the dragon both vanished."

"Vanished?" asked Karn.

"Folks said they died fighting the empire, but no one ever found either body—king or dragon. And that's how the legend got started."

"The legend?"

"Of course. Every vanished king has a legend. You know, that he'll return one day, in the hour of our greatest need, et cetera . . . et cetera . . . to save his city."

"You don't believe it?" asked Thianna.

"Don't know. I tell you what I do believe. Gordasha has been under siege before, and he's never come back. But we've never faced an army like this. I think the Uskirians will come over the walls this time. Or through them. So I hope the Marble King returns. Because it's going to take a miracle to save the city."

"Hey, what are you doing there?" called the city guard. "That area is restricted."

Desstra and Tanthal were crawling out of the ingress of the River Lux. The water ran aboveground for most of its journey through the city, until it poured into subterranean caverns that fed into the sea. An iron grill was meant to discourage trespassers, but the bars were spaced widely enough for the elves to slip through.

They had spent the night in the tunnels. Cave dwellers themselves, they had been more comfortable there than anywhere they had stayed since leaving Deep Shadow. The bright blue sky and oppressive heat of this southern land was hard to bear, even for Desstra, who was less dismissive than Tanthal of other places and cultures.

"The bars are for a reason," said the guardsman as the elves came blinking into the sun. "It's dangerous down there."

"I apologize." Tanthal smiled with fake congeniality. "You see, we were out walking our pet rat when we took a wrong turn."

The man was confused by Tanthal's words and friendly attitude. He smiled uncertainly. Desstra reached in her satchel, fumbling for a sleeping draught in case an opportunity presented itself.

The guardsman's smile dissolved into a look of alarm when he saw the knife protruding from his belly. He opened his mouth to cry, but Tanthal clapped a hand on it and steered the dying man over to the ingress. He shoved the guardsman through the gate. The man disappeared into the cascading waters.

"You were right about one thing, human," Tanthal said. "It is dangerous, all right."

"It wasn't necessary to kill him," Desstra protested.

"It wasn't necessary not to either," replied Tanthal, rinsing his blade in the water.

"But—but he was nobody. He had no connection to our mission. Nothing to do with us at all."

"Exactly. Nothing to do with us at all. Just a nobody." Tanthal wrinkled his lip in irritation. "You're beginning to bore me, Desstra. Why don't you remind me of your value by stealing us some breakfast?"

"Steal it yourself," she snapped, not ready to dismiss his ruthlessness. Killing enemies under orders was one thing. But killing a random individual, when it could be easily avoided, was another.

"If you insist," said Tanthal, holding up his knife for her to see. "Though I imagine your methods will be a little easier on the locals."

Desstra glanced at the shining blade.

"Put that away," she said. "Breakfast is on me."

"Will you look at that?"

Karn pointed over the heads of people crowding the streets to the procession beyond. At a time like this, he wished he were as tall as Thianna. Still, most of what there was to see was raised high above the crowd.

A line of pageant wagons was being slowly pulled down the street. These were two-story structures mounted on six-wheeled wooden carts. The lower room was a dressing area for the performers, while the upper floor served as a small stage. The whole thing was pulled by people or, in some cases, horses. Karn thought it was a wonder they didn't tip over.

He noticed a wagon featuring a model of a creature that seemed to be half rooster, half reptile. The animal had the head and legs of a bird, but the wings and tail of a dragon. He recalled seeing the creature emblazoned on banners about the city.

"What is that?" Karn asked another street fisher.

"Cockatrice," the dwarf explained. "Nasty animal. But it's sort of a Gordashan mascot." Then he got a tug on his line and turned his attention to his work.

"And there's the horn-shouldered guy again," said Thianna.

Sure enough, they saw an actor dressed as Mensis doing battle with fierce creatures with enormous tusks in their mouths. The monstrous figures were dressed in animal skins and had rusty armor and weapons.

"Those aren't supposed to be the Uskiri, are they?" Karn asked.

"I think they are," said Thianna, whose head was almost as high as the foot of the stage. "Not a very good likeness, is it?"

"Not at all," agreed Karn. "I guess they don't want to go making your enemy look too impressive, but still."

"Speaking of enemy," said Thianna, "look out."

Karn followed Thianna's gaze to the other side of the

street. There, he saw the dark elves, Desstra and Tanthal. The elves' attention was directed on the pageant wagons. So far, they hadn't noticed the two friends.

"Well," said Karn. "Now we know they made it into the city."

"Do we try to take them?" Thianna asked.

Karn looked at the cruel elf boy.

"It would feel good to wipe the sneer off Tanthal's face," he said.

Then he looked at the pale-skinned slender girl he thought had been helping him. It was still painful to think of her as the enemy. Then his attention was caught by the sudden twitching of Desstra's ears. He'd seen that before. He knew what it meant.

"Duck," he whispered, pulling on Thianna's arm in an effort to get his tall friend to bend. Unfortunately, they weren't fast enough. Desstra's eyes went wide as she saw them. He saw a glimpse of resignation pass across her face, then the elf's hand dropped to her satchel.

"Forget ducking," Karn exclaimed. "Run!"

Desstra rolled an egg sac across the street. She timed it perfectly with the gaps between cart wheels and pedestrian feet. The projectile came to a stop, and a choking, debilitating gas billowed out.

Several Gordashans began to cough, eyes watering fiercely, but Karn and Thianna weren't among them. The Norrønur pulled his friend through the crowd as, behind them, the dark elves ran across the street.

When they had gone a little distance, Karn turned. The elves had vanished amid the throngs of people. In a fair fight, Karn thought, he and Thianna stood a decent chance. But the crowd added to their danger. It was the knife in the back he feared, or the gas bomb arcing out of nowhere.

"We need to get away," he said. "Somewhere open where we can see them coming."

"Somewhere open," said Thianna. "Okay."

She reached and gripped the stage of a passing pageant cart, hauling herself up. Then she turned and held a hand for Karn.

Another costumed Mensis and a man with lion and bull sock puppets on his hands stood gaping at them.

"You aren't supposed to be up here," the puppeteer said, moving the mouth of the lion sock puppet as he spoke.

"Sorry," said Karn, scanning the crowd for signs of the dark elves. "Won't be here long."

"You need to get down," the man said, now speaking with the bull puppet.

"There they are," said Thianna, pointing.

"There who are?" asked the lion and bull together. Karn gave the man points for staying in character even if it was pretty ridiculous.

There was Desstra, arm poised to throw another egg sac.

"Don't try batting at those," Thianna warned. "Trust

222

me, it doesn't work. If only we had something soft to catch them in." She glanced around the stage.

Desstra lobbed the egg.

Thianna ripped the lion puppet off the shocked performer's hand. "Hey," the man protested. She inverted the sock, catching the egg sac inside the leg cuff. Then she twisted it closed, trapping whatever gas might come bursting out, and swung the sock puppet around her head. She let go, sending it coursing to a rooftop, where it could do no harm. A purple cloud erupted where it struck.

"What was that for?" the man said, speaking with the bull.

"She's, uh, not a fan of puppet theater," Karn replied with an apologetic shrug.

"True." Thianna nodded. She gestured at Karn. "Come on."

Thianna ran and leapt from the stage. She landed on the pageant wagon next in line. It was a longer jump for Karn, but he managed it.

He turned and saw a second projectile heading their way. On impulse he hurled Whitestorm into the air. The sword struck the sac, which exploded harmlessly high over the heads of the crowd. This drew appreciable oohs and aahs from the onlookers. They thought it was just part of the festival.

"Whitestorm!" Karn called as the sword began to drop. It swooped back into his hand.

"Neat," said Thianna. "But how many more of those explodey things does she have?"

"Don't know," said Karn. "She never seems to run out of them."

The jump to the next cart was too far to make, even for Thianna. Then help came from an unexpected source.

A new cart emerged from a side alley. It was slightly longer and lower than the others. And possibly not as well made. Its stage featured a dwarf in a crown confronting a dragon prop. This new entry drew cheers from the crowd, but frowns from the guardsman among them. The cart forced its way into the procession, right ahead of them.

"They're not supposed to be here," called the bull puppet from the previous wagon.

Karn nodded.

"The Marble King."

"Go away!" shouted the bull. "You're ruining the festival!"

But as the longer, lower wagon turned to join the line, Karn and Thianna jumped together, landing on the new stage.

"Well, hello," said the dwarf dressed as the Marble King. "Where'd you two come from?"

Karn gestured at the previous wagon. Then he peered at the dwarf.

"Idas?" he said.

The street fisher smiled.

"Guess I'm more of a believer in the Marble King legend than I let on," the dwarf said.

"Hey there." Thianna greeted Idas. Then she pointed. "We've got company."

Desstra and Tanthal had climbed onto the back of the stage.

"Friends of yours?" Idas asked.

"Not really," Karn replied. "You might want to stand back."

"I'll just nip downstairs," said the dwarf. He lifted a hatch in the stage floor and ducked through.

"I'll take this one," said Thianna, moving to face off against Desstra.

"Thanks," said Karn, relieved not to be fighting the girl.

"Don't thank me," said Thianna. "I'm eager for a rematch." She drew her arming sword and flashed her characteristic grin.

Not taking her eyes off the giantess, Desstra nodded and drew out her slender darts. She welcomed the fight as well.

Karn turned to face Tanthal.

"Let's finish this," said the Norrønur, glaring at the dark elf.

"My sentiments exactly," replied Tanthal. He held aloft his mace and dagger. Then the time for talking was over and weapons clashed.

CHAPTER SEVENTEEN

Getting into the Act

Fighting an opponent who had two weapons was a challenge. Karn wished he still had the Gordion shield. Tanthal was on the offensive with his mace, using his dagger for parrying and for quick counterattacks. The longer reach of Karn's blade, not to mention the dragon's touch, kept things even, but only just. The Norrønur was being driven slowly backward. Despite Karn's months of practice, Tanthal was the better fighter. Karn's trick with Whitestorm had surprised and unbalanced him when they battled at the lumber mill. The Norrønur wouldn't catch the dark elf off guard again, and Thianna wasn't able to lend any help.

The giantess had her own problems. Furious, she was

pursuing the little elf around the stage, but Desstra leapt and dove like a skilled acrobat. Thianna grew angrier and angrier as her strikes failed to connect. Meanwhile, her own clothes were being rent from near-misses of the slender darts.

"Stand still, why don't you?" the larger girl growled.

"I'll stand on your head if you'll just fall over, you big oaf," the elf replied.

Thianna dove at her and came up empty.

"Troll dung! Where'd you go?" she exclaimed, looking around.

Just in time she saw Desstra atop the dragon. Thianna kicked it hard with her boot, sending it toppling sideways. Desstra slipped, catching a wing with one hand. She dangled perilously over the street.

Cheers erupted from the crowd.

"This isn't a performance!" the little elf cried as she swung back onto the platform.

"Then stop dancing!" Thianna roared.

"A little help here!" Karn was fending off all of Tanthal's blows, but he was out of room with nowhere to go.

"Kind of busy myself," Thianna answered, whose sword missed Desstra but clipped a chunk off the dragon's wing.

The procession reached the gates for the grounds of the enormous basilica, the great dome of which dominated the Gordashan skyline. The road led through the gates and up the hill to the doors of the church. The strategist in Karn wasn't crazy about entering an area with only one way out, but he had more immediate worries.

Tanthal increased the speed of his blows. Karn's guard was weakening as he tired. Then the trapdoor flew open. Idas climbed out, bearing a wooden sword. Behind him, a half-dozen other dactyls emerged, similarly armed.

"Time to return the favor!" Idas yelled. The dwarves charged the dark elves. They whacked Tanthal mercilessly with their pretend weapons. With relief, Karn joined them in their assault.

Desstra was surrounded on all sides, unable to leap and jump.

"Show's over," Thianna said. "Time to take your bows."

Suddenly, the pageant wagon rocked. City guards were clashing with the dwarves towing the cart. The stage swayed precariously.

"Can't you see we're fighting here?" Thianna yelled.

Then the pageant wagon tumbled over and Thianna, Karn, dark elves, and dactyls crashed to the ground.

Karn leapt clear as the cart collapsed, landing on the soft grass of the parkland. He saw Tanthal under a pile of dwarves, Desstra atop the remains of the dragon, Thianna picking her way out of the wooden wreckage. More guardsmen came running up. He counted at least twenty of them, all armed with spears and shields. No one was going anywhere.

"I'm sorry, Idas," he said to the street fisher. "We've wrecked your parade."

"That wasn't your doing, kid," said the dwarf. "I told you the authorities weren't big on the Marble King's legend. I'm surprised we got as far as we did."

"Well," said Thianna, joining them, "fun's over now."

"Those dreadful cannons have my teeth on edge."

The man on the golden throne looked like he was having a bad day. Karn thought that the enormous jeweled crown on his head looked too heavy to be comfortably worn, while his expensive clothes and fur-lined cape must have made him incredibly hot in this southern climate. He was speaking in Common, though with an accent not that different from that of the dwarves Karn had met in the city.

The sound of a cannon erupted. It was followed seconds later by the noise of a projectile striking stone. The Uskirians had begun their bombardment at the close of the festival, firing at both the land walls and the northern seawalls.

"It's hard to think straight with all the cacophony," the Gordashan imperator said.

Karn and Thianna were in a large, marble-floored and marble-columned room, the most exquisite chamber either of them had ever been in. They, along with the dwarves and elves, had been brought to the palace, an ancient structure dating from the time of the original Gordion Empire, now the seat of power for the current ruler.

"Can't we close the windows?" the imperator asked. When no one rushed to obey, he scowled and ordered, "Close the windows or throw yourselves out of them!" This got the attendants scurrying.

Not nice, Karn thought.

The imperator plucked a date from a tray, bit into it, made a sour face, and discarded it to the floor. A servant immediately appeared to pick up the chewed fruit.

"Well," the imperator said, "I suppose you had better bring forward the rabble-rousers who ruined my festival."

The guardsman prodded Karn and Thianna in the backs, as well as the elves, and thwacked the shorter dwarves about the head to drive them forward.

"Kneel," the captain of the guard said.

Karn saw the dactyls drop immediately, and he started to do likewise. Then he noticed Thianna hadn't budged. Neither had the dark elves.

"Kneel before the imperator," the guard captain repeated.

"He's not my imperator," said Thianna. "Didn't even know what an imperator was this morning."

Karn groaned. Antagonizing their captors probably wasn't wise.

"I said, kneel," ordered the man. He was growing red in the face.

"Make me," growled the frost giant's daughter.

Guards kicked them from behind, causing their legs to buckle. Rough hands on their shoulders forced Karn, Desstra, and Tanthal to their knees. Karn fought it, but he was held down and couldn't rise.

Thianna, however, was still standing. Despite his reservations about the wisdom of her actions, he felt a surge of pride for his friend.

"Kneel!" The guard captain was shouting now. Thianna stared him down, unflinching. The man gestured and two more guards joined the ones already trying to bend Thianna's knees.

It was comical, four grown men tugging and shoving at the giant girl. She glanced at them hanging off her limbs, then raised her chin.

"I prefer to stand."

The guard captain drew his sword, preparing to run her through.

"Thianna," Karn warned.

"Oh, enough of this," said the imperator, rising from his throne. "Let the barbarian stand. We can cut her down easily enough later." He strode forward. "So this is the group who wrecked the Mensis Imperativae?"

"Yes, Your Eminence," the guardsman replied.

"Two barbarians. And aren't you a nasty lot?" he said, turning his attention to Desstra and Tanthal. "Elves, but not a type I've ever seen before. You four are a bit of a curiosity."

The Gordashan imperator stopped before the dactyls and sighed.

"You people need to give up this 'cult of the Marble King' nonsense. Really, it's not doing you any good. Look where it's gotten you now."

"Well, I've never been invited to the palace before," said Idas.

The imperator gave a tight-lipped smile.

"Take them away and cut their heads off," he said, indicating the dactyls.

"They weren't with us," Karn spoke up. "They had nothing to do with us. We just jumped on their stage."

The imperator raised his eyebrow at the captain of the guard.

"True?"

"Yes, Your Eminence," the man replied. "While the dactyls joined the procession without proper authorization, we don't think they were involved with the foreigners."

"They weren't," the boy said suddenly. "Whatever you think we were doing, the dwarves had nothing to do with it."

"Curious," said the imperator.

"Your Majesty," an older advisor interjected. The ruler motioned him forward.

"The cult of the Marble King has a lot of followers in

the city," the advisor said. "Perhaps now is not the time to make a public spectacle of them."

"But the festival has been ruined," the imperator complained. "We needed a morale boost, and now we have a disaster."

"If we can separate the dwarves from these four, we can deal more harshly with them without risking the disfavor of the population."

The imperator brightened at this.

"So you say your squabble has nothing to do with the dactyls?" the ruler asked Karn.

"Nothing at all," Karn continued. "We just leapt onto their wagon when we were fleeing those two." He indicated the two strange elves.

"Very well," the imperator sighed. "Give the dwarves a whipping and send them home."

Several of the guardsmen moved to carry out this order.

"Good luck, kid," said one of the dactyls as he was led away.

"Now," said the imperator. "Suppose you tell me what you four are doing in our fair city."

"It's very easily explained," said Tanthal. "I'm sure we can come to an understanding. If only I might approach your throne . . ."

"You might not," said the imperator. "Not without a sword in the gut, that is."

Thianna snickered at this.

"Please, sir," said Karn. "We don't have anything to do with your war. We're very sorry for your situation—"

"Our situation?"

"Being under siege."

"My boy, Gordasha has been under siege many, many times in its illustrious history. The Uskiri will give up and go home after a few weeks. We will weather this siege as we have all others." As if to disprove his point, a particularly loud cannon shot boomed outside. The imperator winced.

"It's so hot in here," he said. "Someone, open a window at once!"

"But, Your Eminence," replied a servant. "You just ordered the windows closed."

The imperator batted the servant away.

"Well, open the windows again," he shouted, then he glared at Karn. "I suppose we had better just kill you all. Starting with the human boy."

Four men strode forward from a curtained antechamber. Karn stiffened at the sight of them. They were blond-haired, blue-eyed, and big-shouldered men, dressed in fashion he recognized.

"You're—you're Norrønir?" Karn said.

"What of it?" asked the imperator. "The Norrønir make marvelous palace guardsmen. I've never encountered fiercer fighters. They call themselves 'the Sworn,' which I suppose means they'll swear their loyalty to you . . . as long as you pay them enough."

"Sorry, son," said a man Karn assumed was the leader of the Sworn. He drew his ax. "Nothing personal."

"Wait," Karn said. "I don't even have my weapon. There's no honor in this. Cutting down an unarmed opponent."

"Honor doesn't apply to foreigners," the guardsman replied.

"I'm Norrønur too," Karn protested, wishing he hadn't traded in his clothing for the ones in the bathhouse.

"So you've got blond hair—" the man said, readying his ax.

"I'm Karn Korlundsson," said Karn, putting as much authority into his voice as he had used outside the gates of Castlebriar. "My father is a hauld. Korlundr hauld Kolason. Of Korlundr's Farm."

"Korlundr's Farm?" the man said. "I know that farm." He stared at the boy. The hardness in his eyes shifted. Then he slid his ax into his belt. He stepped from Karn and his three men stepped away as well.

"What are you waiting for?" said the imperator angrily. "Kill him."

"Kill him yourself," the man replied. Karn couldn't help but feel a swell of pride at the lack of fear in the man's voice. "He is a Norrønur. And deserving of an honorable death."

"I pay you very well," the imperator insisted. "You've always killed on my command before."

"What you Sacred Gordion So-and-Sos want to do to

each other is one thing," the man replied. "But no gold is worth my honor. The Sworn will raise no weapon against him."

The imperator fumed. His guardsmen had clearly never hesitated to carry out his orders before. But then this was the first time they'd ever encountered a fellow Norrønur.

"Please, sir," Karn said again. "We aren't a part of your war. If you'll just let us go, we'll leave without any more trouble."

"But you wrecked my festival," he said. "That was as much to entertain the people as it was to honor Mensis. To give them something to focus on other than these blasted cannons."

As if to underscore the point, another explosion sounded.

"Close the windows. Why aren't the windows closed?"

Confused servants rushed to obey. Or at least to try to.

"I can tell this guy is a really fair and balanced employer," said Thianna. This got the imperator's attention. He looked at her again, standing so tall above everyone else in the room.

"Hmmm," the ruler said. "Here is the situation. I'm sure the walls will hold. But there is growing unrest in my city. At times like these, a ruler needs to remember that it is important to prevent panic among the citizens. Keeping them entertained is the thing. The festival hasn't worked. We need another diversion."

He surveyed the prisoners.

"Your foreign squabbles aren't our concern," he said. "But we will allow you to resolve them nonetheless."

"What do you mean?" Desstra said.

"You four will race in the Hippodrome," said the imperator. "Tomorrow, you can work out your differences on the track. The winners can go free, and the losers, well, the losers can pay for raining on my parade with their lives."

CHAPTER EIGHTEEN

A Day at the Races

"No way those are the horses."

They stood in the stables of the Hippodrome, their boots crunching on the sand floor. The sun had only just risen. The four prisoners had been roused from their cells early in preparation for the day's event.

First order of business was to pick their chariots. The guards had laughed when Karn asked about the steeds. Neither he nor Thianna had understood what was so amusing until now.

"I admit," continued the giantess, "I don't have much experience with horses, but I'm pretty sure they don't look anything like those things."

"Watch who you are calling a thing!" the thing that

wasn't a horse growled. "I could always do with a second breakfast."

The creature before them had a body like a lion, but its tail was thick and plated like an insect's carapace. It curved up over its back and ended in a wicked barb like the stinger of a giant scorpion. The animal's head was framed by a thick mane, out of which curved horns protruded, but the face amid all this hair was humanlike. Or almost. It was oversize, and the wide mouth showed multiple rows of razor-sharp teeth.

"You talk?" said Karn. He had never seen anything like this beast in his entire life.

"When there's someone worth talking to," replied another.

"Mind your manners," said a well-dressed man walking up to join them. "These young people are your charioteers for today."

"You have got to be kidding," the creature replied.

"I never kid about such things," the man said. "They race by order of the imperator himself."

"Do they know how to drive? Have they even been on a chariot before?"

"I haven't," admitted Karn. "Though I, um, played a board game recently that was similar."

"That's just perfect," the first creature said with an edge of sarcasm. "We call numskulls like you meals on wheels."

All the creatures guffawed.

"Don't mind him," said the man. "This is as pleasant as they get, I'm afraid. But let me introduce myself. I am Lymos, and I am the master of the games here at the Hippodrome."

"What are they?" Karn asked, pointing to the creatures.

"They are called manticores," Lymos replied. "As to what they are: they are rude, deadly, and, regrettably, fond of bad jokes. But they are quite fast. Also, they frequently devour our charioteers."

"Devour?" asked Tanthal.

"Yes," said Lymos. "They eat them whole. The risk adds an interesting dimension to the race."

"I bet," said Thianna.

"You don't know the half of it," said one of the manticores.

"Our name means 'man-eater,'" another explained.

"But we'll eat girls too! We don't discriminate!"

The manticores all laughed uproariously.

"How does the race work?" asked Karn. Recalling Charioteers, his gamer's mind was eager to understand the rules of the real thing.

Lymos nodded his approval at the question.

"You race in teams of two," he said. "You and your companion—"

"Thianna," the giantess answered.

"Thianna," the master of the games continued, "will race in one chariot. While your two pale friends—"

"We aren't their friends," Tanthal interjected. "Quite the opposite."

"Merely a figure of speech," said Lymos.

"Our names are Desstra and Tanthal. We're dark elves from the Svartálfaheim Mountains in Norrøngard," Desstra explained.

"Wonderful," said Lymos. "Foreigners make for such interesting contestants. And are you proficient at working as a team?"

Desstra looked sidelong at Tanthal.

"Yes," she said. "Regrettably."

"Good, good. Desstra and Tanthal will race in another. One member of each team will drive. The other will fight. You will race with two other teams. One of them is the imperator's favored team. They rarely lose. The fourth team will be backed by one of the city's many political factions."

"What do you mean?" asked Karn.

"Chariot teams are sponsored by various elements inside the city. You will find that racing in Gordasha can be very political."

Lymos led the four of them to where a row of chariots were parked. The chariots were simple, two-wheeled vehicles. There wasn't much to them apart from a floor and a semicircular, waist-high guard. Well, waist-high for anybody but Thianna, Karn observed. Each was painted a different bright color—red, green, black, and gold.

"What's with the weapons on the wheels?" asked Thianna. Sure enough, each of the chariots had thin scythe blades extending outward from the wheels' axis on both sides.

"Ah, those." Lymos smiled. "For shredding your enemy's chariot. Or lacerating a manticore's legs."

"Let me guess," said Karn. "It adds another 'interesting dimension' to the games?"

"Exactly!" said Lymos. "My, you're picking this up quickly."

"It's obvious enough," said Tanthal. "Which one is mine?"

"The imperator's team rides in the gold chariot," Lymos explained. "The other team has already spoken for the green. That leaves the black and red chariots for you to choose from."

"I prefer the black chariot," said Tanthal.

"No surprise there," Karn said. "But what makes you get the first pick?"

"Because I claimed it," the dark elf replied.

"Black, it is," said Lymos. "Karn and Thianna will command the red one. Now you must select a manticore to pull."

Lymos walked the four of them over to where a pride of manticores waited. The creatures were lounging around. One was rolled onto his back, paws batting at dust mites in the air like a giant cat. They smiled evilly as their new drivers approached, exposing three rows of razor-sharp teeth.

Tanthal walked up to one.

"Are you fast?" he asked.

"Fast enough to swallow you whole when you wipe out, skinny boy," answered the manticore.

"I have no intention of wiping out," said Tanthal. "Unless that's your way of admitting that you're a poor racer."

"What?" roared the beast, gnashing his teeth in Tanthal's face. "How dare you?"

"He's brave, I'll give him that," said Thianna.

"That or an idiot," said Karn.

"So you are fast?" Tanthal asked.

"I'm the fastest there is," the manticore boasted. "I'll show you fast."

"Good," said the elf. "Then I'll let you pull my chariot." He turned to Lymos. "I'll take this one."

"Psst, kid," another manticore said to Karn. "Come here."

Karn wasn't sure he wanted to approach a man-eater, but he summoned his courage and stepped forward.

"That's not how you pick 'em, you know," the manticore said.

"Really? He seemed pretty fierce," said Karn.

"Fierce has nothing to do with it," said the creature.

"So how do you tell if a manticore is fast?" Karn asked.

All the manticores snickered.

"You look for the lightest."

"You all look about the same size," Karn said.

"Not the smallest," the animal said, rolling its human-like eyes. "The lightest. The one who isn't carrying a load in his stomach, if you take my meaning."

"I'm not sure I do."

"We eat people," said the manticore. "Or whole cows and boars when we can't get fresh humans. Do you know how much a cow weighs? That's a lot to carry around in the stomach. You need to look for the manticore that's most recently lightened his load."

"Oh troll dung," Thianna swore. "I know what he's talking about."

"Well, you got half of it right." The manticore laughed. "But it's got nothing to do with trolls. Unless we ate one."

"You mean—?" began Karn.

"Yup," said the creature. "You should pick the one of us who pooped the biggest and the most recently. How are you going to run five times around the track if you're clenching your haunches because you have to go? We usually poop about half an hour before the race."

"That's disgusting," said Tanthal, catching wind of their conversation.

"Think so?" The manticore grinned. "Wait until you hear the catch."

"There's a catch?" asked Desstra. Karn was surprised to hear her speak up. So far, she'd kept silent in his presence.

"Oh yeah." The manticore laughed again. "If we're too hungry, we might just decide to stop the race and eat our drivers."

"So you have to figure," volunteered another, "have we pooped enough to be fast, but not so much as to be starving?"

"I've got no interest in evaluating manticore wastes," sneered Tanthal.

"Told you that one was a fool," said another. "All the smartest bettors and bookies are down here every morning. Some of them even bring their own scales."

"Bettors and bookies?" said Thianna.

"Oh yeah," a manticore said. "Wagering on the races is big business. They usually ask us what we've eaten, how we feel, did we make a bowel movement yet. Was it big? How big was it?"

"Yuck." Desstra couldn't help herself. All the manticores laughed.

"Of course, every now and then, one of them gets too close and we eat a bookie!" said one. "Which messes up the odds."

"I caught a little gnome yesterday who was poking through my poop with a stick," replied another.

"Hardly a mouthful, gnomes," said another.

"I did not need to know that," said Desstra. "Seriously."

"Seriously you do," said a manticore. "You've got a lot

more riding on today's race than money. You four are all betting your lives."

"Okay, we get it," said Karn. "So, who wants to tell me what they had for breakfast?"

"That is one big stadium," said Thianna. "It makes Orm's coliseum in Sardeth look tiny."

"Better not let him hear you say that," said Karn.

"Aw." The giantess grinned. "He's a pussycat."

Karn noticed Desstra looking aghast at how casually they discussed the mightiest of linnorms. Good. She should realize who she had betrayed.

The Gordashan Hippodrome was a race course laid out in an elongated horseshoe shape. Lymos told them the stands could hold a hundred thousand spectators. The course was divided by a low wall called a spina. It was crowded with statues, columns, and obelisks. These were treasures pillaged from all over Katernia in the days of the Gordion Empire.

The chariots were hitched and driven into four starting gates. Two hard-looking men made up the imperator's gold team, but Karn and Thianna were surprised to see that the green team, dactyl dwarves, represented the cult of the Marble King.

The charioteers busily adjusted their light armor and checked their weapons. Karn's and Thianna's own swords were returned to them, as was the dark elves' gear. "To add another interesting dimension to the race," Lymos had explained. Tanthal was admiring the scythes on his chariot's wheels. He obviously approved of the deadly accoutrements.

"Obviously, I'll drive and you'll fight," Karn told Thianna.

"Why is that obvious?" she replied, making Karn feel good. But she stepped up into the chariot and drew her arming sword, making some experimental thrusts and lunges from the car.

"Be healthy," said a voice beside Karn. He turned and saw one of the four Norrønir from the imperator's personal guard, a scruffy man in rough clothing.

"What are you doing here?" he asked the man.

"My name is Ynarr Ulfrsson," the man replied.

"Do I know you?" The name didn't mean anything to Karn.

"I was at the Battle of Dragon's Dance," Ynarr said, eyes downcast. "In the employ of your uncle."

Karn drew back, alarmed. When Uncle Ori had seized control of Korlundr's Farm, he had hired four thugs to help him enforce discipline.

"It was a stain on my honor," Ynarr continued, holding up a placating hand. "I should not have hired myself to such a man. I was hungry and he had coin. I did not realize the things he would ask of me. Then I was knocked unconscious and left for dead. When I awoke, I fled south."

Karn sized the man up. A thug and a coward too, running from Norrønir justice.

"So why are you here?" he asked.

"I thought to leave my shame behind in Norrøngard, but I come all the way to the other edge of the continent, and I see you again."

The man handed Karn his own shield. It was wooden, round, about thirty-two inches in diameter, and rimmed with leather, and had an iron boss in the center to protect the hand grip. The wood had been painted green.

"Please take this," Ynarr said. "Let it defend you as you race."

Karn was suspicious of gifts from former enemies.

"Why would you give this to me?"

"I know now I fought for the wrong side," Ynarr replied. "Perhaps the gods will see me helping you, and they will help me to regain my honor."

Karn took the shield. It was heavy, but he had missed carrying one since losing the scutum.

"It's not magical," Ynarr said, glancing at Karn's sword Whitestorm.

"That's okay," said Karn. "It's a strong Norrønir shield. That's good enough."

Ynarr seemed pleased with the compliment.

"Live through this challenge, Karn Korlundsson," he said.

"Thanks," said Karn. "If you survive the siege, I hope you live to find your honor."

The manticores were snapping at each other as they lined up at the start. A few brave bettors and bookies made final assessments of their "recent business" too. One got too close and almost got bitten by the manticore from the gold team.

Karn and Thianna surveyed row upon row of seats filled to capacity.

"I'm not sure there are this many people in the whole of Norrøngard," Karn said.

"Numbers don't matter," said Tanthal. "Only the will to win and the ability to fight."

"I hope for your sake you play this better than you played Charioteers in Nelenia," Karn replied.

Tanthal scowled and busied himself adjusting his armor.

Karn turned his attention to the master of the games. Lymos had taken a position in a raised box and was addressing the crowd.

"By special order of the imperator, His Highness Adrius the Fourth, Ruler of the Sacred Gordion Supremacy, Monarch of the City of Gordasha, First Among Equals, we dedicate this race to Mensis and the rest of the Gordion gods. Let the procession begin."

The manticores all started forward. They were to make one circuit around the course for the crowd to see and evaluate them. Karn gathered that this was to allow for last-minute bets.

The gold team stood unsmiling and haughty beneath the cheers of the spectators. Judging by the number of green banners, Karn thought that the dactyls too had quite a few supporters in the stands. Tanthal glared a challenge to everyone who made eye contact as he passed, but Desstra seemed as overwhelmed by the size of the crowd as Karn was.

As they approached the halfway mark, Karn considered the way the features of the track were duplicated in Charioteers. Despite the tension of that evening in the Windy Willows, he had enjoyed a good game. He had believed Desstra to be an ally then, when she had pretended to be Nesstra Sunbottom. Karn caught the dark elf glancing his way and scowled. Then he noticed two statues set at the far end of the spina.

"Look at that," he said, nudging Thianna. The frost giantess was flexing her arms for the crowd and waving. Her enormous size seemed to have impressed quite a few of them, who were waving back and even throwing flowers.

"I could get used to this," she said. "Look at what?"

"Those two statues," said Karn.

One depicted a dactyl dwarf wearing the armor of a Gordion auxiliary. The dwarf was crowned with a laurel leaf. The other statue was of an enormous dragon. Long and sinuous, it stretched down the spina without taking up too much room on either side.

"Like the pageant wagon," said Thianna.

"A statue of the Marble King and his dragon," said

Karn. As they came around the curve, they could see that the dwarf was holding up a horn. They recognized it immediately. There was no doubt that it was a depiction of a Horn of Osius. "That's him, all right. Or at least what he looked like."

"Why place it here?" she asked.

"Because the empire conquered him," said Karn. "He must have commissioned the statues during his rule, for his palace or a market square or someplace. When he was overthrown, the empire transferred the statues here like any other spoils of war."

"That's a pretty realistic statue," said Thianna, looking at the dragon. "It's almost a smaller version of Old Grumpy Worm."

Karn studied the carving. Thianna was right. There was a certain resemblance to Orm Hinn Langi, although this dragon was considerably smaller than the greatest of linnorms. Of course, there wasn't a big-enough chunk of marble in the world to render Orm full-scale, but the similarities were there. With certain differences. It was hard to tell with dragons, but Karn thought this one looked female. Its head wasn't as broad as Orm's, and the dragon had a sleekness to it that the Doom of Sardeth didn't possess.

The chariots completed their circuit around the track. The imperator announced the names of the racers—he called Tanthal and Desstra "Tantrum and Dessie" to the dark elves' great annoyance and Thianna's amusement.

Flags were raised.

"On your marks, get set . . . ," said the imperator. "GO!"

The flags came down.

The race began.

Karn felt the reins jerk in his hands, then the rush as the chariot surged forward. The wooden wheels rumbled over the ground. The jolts were bad enough that even Thianna seemed unsteady on her feet.

Karn wore the heavy Norrønir shield on his back to keep his hands free. Also, for protection if they were in the lead. He didn't want a spear or dart taking him from behind. As Karn watched the imperator's team pulling ahead of the rest of the chariots, he thought that might have been optimistic. Driving the chariot wasn't easy.

"Faster," he yelled to the manticore pulling them.

"Faster means hungrier," the creature said, but Karn felt their speed increase.

The track narrowed quickly after the starting gate, forcing the four vehicles closer together. Thianna was faced with a javelin being jabbed at her by a dwarf. She chopped at the short spear with her sword.

Tanthal flung a dagger at the giantess's unprotected flank. Karn pivoted, placing the heavy shield between them. The dagger sank into the thick wood, sticking with a loud *thwack*.

Tanthal glared and drew his mace. Karn steered away

to the right. The scythe on the wheel tore at the side of the dactyls' chariot, rending a gash in the painted wood. Angry, the dwarf jabbed again at Thianna with the javelin. The giantess knocked the spear aside, then grabbed the shaft and hauled it free of the dwarf's grasp. Without missing a beat, she swung it left, crashing into Tanthal's mace and batting it down just as the elf attempted another blow.

Then the chariots approached the curve—the most dangerous part of the course. Tanthal flung a projectile at the gold team as they slowed to take the bend. The imperator's favored charioteers choked from the noxious gas. Then their speed carried them out of the cloud.

The dactyls saw their opportunity and clashed with the weakened gold team. Thianna, her reach made even longer with a javelin, kept the dark elves at bay. Karn heard jeers from the audience. Rocks pelted Tanthal in the back, encouraging him to be more daring. He got the point. Ripping one of Desstra's darts from her leg pouch, Tanthal hurled it not at Thianna but at their manticore. The animal yelped as the dart sunk into his haunch, but the poison didn't work on the man-eater. The angry manticore shouldered the dark elf's own animal. It stumbled on its legs and veered sideways as the two elves fought to stay aboard. Karn and Thianna pulled ahead.

As the chariots completed their first lap, a golden marker on a pole was tipped over to count off their progress. The gleaming metal was cast in the image of the same half bird, half reptile Karn had seen on public buildings all over the city. A cockatrice. *Snake and cockerel,* he thought. But he didn't have time to consider it.

The dactyls had taken the lead in their second lap but took the curve too fast. Their chariot swung too far left, crashing into the wall below the stands. A dactyl was thrown from the chariot.

The reins jerked in Karn's hands. His own manticore veered off course, twisting into a path that brought him directly in line with the frightened dwarf. Karn tugged on the reins, but the creature fought him.

"Thianna," he called. She understood instantly. Holding both weapons with one hand, Thianna grabbed the reins with her other and gave a savage jerk. The manticore was pulled back on course. It roared in anger.

Karn glanced behind him. The black chariot's manticore opened its jaws wide. Without pausing in its stride, it scooped the unfortunate dwarf up and swallowed him whole. The audience broke into enthusiastic cheers.

"That dwarf was mine!" roared their own manticore.

Thianna whacked it hard on the head with her javelin.

"Ouch," it hollered.

"You shouldn't eat things that talk," she yelled back.

The gold team pulled ahead as a second golden cockatrice was tipped over to mark the passage of another lap. Karn saw Desstra remove several small spider egg sacs from her satchel.

"Watch out," he said, expecting incoming projectiles.

Instead, Desstra turned and tossed the egg sacs behind her into the sands of the race course.

The terrified dactyl took the curve too fast again. His beast tripped on its own paws. The chariot tipped, crashed, and burst apart. The dwarf was on his feet instantly, racing for the stands as his own manticore shook free of its broken yoke and set off after him.

Karn's manticore leapt right over the broken wood, dragging the chariot straight through it. Both wheels came off the ground for an instant. Karn tugged hard on the reins to brace himself. Thianna, too tall for the low waistguard, tumbled over the front of the chariot. She landed on the startled manticore's back.

"Get off!" it screamed at her. "Heavy, heavy, heavy!"

"Quit complaining," Thianna replied. "This isn't the way I prefer things either."

"Two more laps to go," Karn yelled to Thianna. The giantess still clung to the manticore. She had no easy way to get back into the chariot, and they both knew the terrible fate of anyone who stood unprotected on the race course in front of the fearsome creatures.

Ahead of them, a wheel of the gold chariot crushed one of the egg sacs Desstra had tossed onto the track. It exploded in sticky goo. The substance foamed and swelled, engulfing the wheel, then the chariot car itself. Wheel and car tore themselves apart. The driver was pulled free, dragged behind the manticore, while the other team member went down in a mass of splintered wood.

"No you don't," said Thianna. Guessing their own manticore's intentions, she jerked savagely on its mane.

"I swear I will eat you, girl," it growled at her. She rapped it hard on the head for this. "Stop that! I'm a man-eater. It's what I do!" It yelped again as she clocked it a second time.

Karn turned his eyes away from the black team as they reached the wreckage. He tried to block out the enthusiastic shouts from the crowd.

Now there were only two teams.

They had a clear lead on the dark elves. And their opponents had to be running short of darts, egg bombs, and daggers.

Clinging tightly to the creature, Thianna studied the marble statues of the dwarf and dragon. She saw the shattered wheel of the dactyl chariot.

"'Upon the arc where shatters wheel, alter course and come to heel,'" she said. Suddenly she understood. The curve of the Hippodrome was the arc where chariots were most likely to crash.

"Stop!" she ordered.

"What?" Karn and the manticore both said at once.

"Stop!" she called again.

"But if we stop—" Karn began.

"I will so totally eat you both," the manticore finished.

"I said, stop!"

The frost giant wrapped her arm around the manticore's neck and hauled back on its head with all her might. It twisted back and forth, roaring, forepaws claw-ing at the air.

It stopped.

Karn saw the dark elves racing past them. Tanthal was embracing his certain victory, but Desstra had a look of confusion. Karn knew how she felt.

"What did we stop for?"

"Karn," Thianna explained, "this is the arc that shat-ters wheel."

"Gonna eat you both," the manticore said, its jaws stretching impossibly wide. Three rows of gleaming teeth made it clear that the beast wasn't joking.

"I said no eating things that talk," said Thianna. She punched it hard right on the end of its nose. The manti-core squealed and clamped its paws to its face. Karn saw tears welling in its eyes. And fear.

"Now be a good kitty and stay quiet," the giantess commanded.

"I've said it before," said Karn. "There's strong, and there's Thianna strong."

But the frost giantess wasn't listening to him. She had approached the statue of the Marble King and was look-ing at its base. Then she began to stomp the ground.

In the stands, the audience was divided between boo-ing and cheering. Half of them were upset that the red team had forfeited the race, but the other half were im-pressed to see a manticore punched.

"What are you doing?" Karn asked. The giantess was

picking her leg up high and bringing it down heavy right behind the statue.

"Whoever wrote the riddle likes to play on words. It said 'straight' when it meant 'strait.' I am thinking it's done the same thing again with 'heel.'"

"I get it," said Karn with dawning comprehension. "It's another play on words. 'Come to heel' means stop, but it also means to come to the King's heel. But why all the stomping?"

For an answer, Thianna brought her foot down hard one more time. With a great, cracking sound, a huge slab of rock collapsed. It fell into a hole revealed in the ground. Karn heard a splash.

A sound alerted him to the approach of guardsmen. Looking toward the finish line, he saw Desstra struggling to get Tanthal's attention. The vain elf appeared to be enjoying his victory, but his companion realized something more important was going on.

"I don't think we can stick around here any longer," he said.

"My thoughts exactly," his friend replied. Then she jumped into the hole, disappearing into the darkness below.

CHAPTER NINETEEN

The Sunken Palace

Karn dropped into darkness. He didn't fall for long. He landed with a splash in cold water. Sputtering, he broke the surface, spitting out a mouthful as his eyes adjusted. The only illumination came through the hole in the ceiling above. Sunlight spilled down in a tight circle.

"Glad you could drop in," said Thianna next to him.

"Can you touch the bottom?" Karn asked, treading water. She didn't seem to be paddling and kicking, though she was lifting her chin to keep her mouth in the air.

"Barely," she said. "Tippy-toes."

Karn nodded. He pulled the phosphorescent stone on its cord out of his shirt and shook it awake. Shouts were echoing from the race course above. Thianna noticed too.

"We shouldn't linger," she said. She waded into the darkness. He swam after her. They were in a long tunnel. Not a natural cavern, Karn saw, as the walls were built of brick. He guessed that it was leading them north. But after a stretch, they came to a low stone pier. Thianna hauled herself out of the water, then held a hand back for him.

They followed the tunnel to an archway and into another chamber beyond, where the pier stopped. The walls of the room disappeared in the darkness of a cavernous space. Elaborate stone columns were set in ordered rows throughout the chamber. They could only see the first few, but they could guess there were more.

"No two of these columns are alike," said Karn.

"They're all pretty fancy," said Thianna, studying the architecture. It was almost like a cathedral, or . . . "Welcome to the Sunken Palace," she pronounced.

Karn saw movement disturbing their reflections in the water. "Fish," he said, pointing.

"Blind, I think," said Thianna, unsurprised. "From living in the dark."

"You guessed this was down here?" he asked.

"Yeah," she admitted. "I kept thinking about the street fishers. All that water coming in the aqueduct had to be going to more places than just a few public baths and fountains."

"This is some sort of cistern," Karn said.

"Whose sister?" asked Thianna.

"Cistern," he said. "Underground chamber for holding water. Idas said he learned how to street fish from his father. His grandfather taught him, on and on going back generations. This place was probably constructed by the empire a thousand years ago, then built on top of and forgotten. The locals know there's fish down here, but they don't remember why."

"Makes sense," said the giantess. "Shall we?" She hopped into the water again. Her head went right under. She came up sputtering.

"Okay, this one's deeper. You might want to be careful going in."

"Or you could hold your breath, and I could stand on your shoulders."

"Ha, ha, very funny," she said. Then she grabbed Karn's ankle and yanked him in. He fell, splashing into the water. He came up sputtering and grinning. It was good to laugh again. To laugh with her. A small splash fight ensued. But only for a moment. They had work to do.

Together they explored the Sunken Palace.

"Look at that," said Thianna. Some of the columns weren't as tall as the rest. The shorter ones stood upon the broken-off heads of old statues. Some of the heads were upside down or on their sides. Karn didn't know if it was deliberately disrespectful, or if the ancient Gordions were just using what worked best, fitting the pieces in any way they'd go.

"I bet the Gordions looted these columns from all over Katernia," he said. "That's why none of them match."

"They sure like to nab things," said Thianna. She remembered the statuary on the spina.

"Do you hear something?" Karn asked.

"Water, lots of it."

The sound grew louder as they approached. By the time they reached its source, it was a roar. A column of water fell from out of the darkness above, splashing down on a raised stone block, like a dais for a throne.

"'In Sunken Palace waters reign,'" they said together.

"Another play on words," Karn pointed out. "Reign and rain."

They dog-paddled over and set about examining the dais, but it was plain and unadorned. Whatever decorations it might once have had, the stone had been worn smooth by centuries of erosion.

"There's got to be something more here," said Thianna.

"'King and Dragon find their bane,'" Karn quoted. "We're looking for a king and a dragon."

"Over there," said Thianna.

Two columns were placed in line with the waterfall. They were in a row by themselves. Each was short, and their plinths stood upon broken statuary to make up for their lack of height. One twisted column rested upon what was clearly meant to be an unflattering depiction of a dactyl dwarf. The other stood upon a dragon, compressed awkwardly into a square shape. Karn and Thianna each studied a column.

"Nothing that I can see," said the giantess.

"Me neither," admitted Karn. He gazed upward to where the columns' shafts disappeared into darkness. "Nothing we can *see*," he reflected, thinking about Thianna's choice of words. "These columns are shorter than the others. How do we know they're tall enough to reach the ceiling?"

Thianna's expression said she thought Karn was on the right track. She swam to the twisted column on the dwarf base. It was the farthest from the waterfall. The spiral curve could make for hand and footholds, if one was daring.

"This is going to be slippery," she said. Then she began to climb. When she got to the edge of their circle of illumination, she called down, "How about some light here, Norrønboy? Climbing in the dark's not my thing."

Karn grinned. Being called Norrønboy used to irritate him. Now it was a reminder of their bond. He propped his wooden shield upon the plinth, where it wouldn't float away, and followed. As he brought the light with him, Thianna resumed climbing and shortly reached the top. The column ended in a flat-topped plinth. Karn was right. It stopped well short of the ceiling. She moved over to allow Karn room beside her. They stood together in the darkness, the plinth of the next column over just visible.

"At least there's water below," Thianna said. She leapt and landed perfectly atop the dragon column. "Your turn."

Karn braced himself and jumped. He crashed into Thianna, who steadied him and kept them both from falling. With Karn's phosphorescent stone, they could now see the waterfall clearly. Here, it was running down a rock wall, the bottom of which ended level with the two columns' plinths. Where the rock stopped, the water continued in free fall.

"There's nowhere to go," said Karn.

"It can't be a coincidence that the columns line up with that wall," said Thianna. She flexed her calves, readying her legs for a jump.

"You can't be serious!" Karn exclaimed. "Thianna, you'll bounce right off that stone. There's nothing to grab on to. The water's worn it smooth as glass. And you won't fall in the water below. You'll break your back on the stone dais."

"Not if I'm right," said Thianna. And leapt.

Karn held his breath as Thianna soared across the empty space. Then he gasped as she disappeared into the waterfall.

"Thianna?" he called.

A few seconds later, her head poked back through the curtain of water. She was beaming with pleasure at her cleverness.

"There's a passageway cut into the rock," she called. "Come on over."

They were in another tunnel, one carved through a long slab of rock suspended from the ceiling. Unseen in the darkness, its entrance was hidden by a waterfall, and all of it buried in a cistern lost to time.

"Without the riddle, no one would ever find this place," Karn said. "Even if they did find the cistern. Do you think the horn is here?"

"I'm sure of it," said Thianna. "Besides, we're running out of verses."

"'When snake and cockerel sundering, seek ye then the Marble King,'" quoted Karn. That was it. All that was left of the riddle penned by the Order of the Oak in ages past. "After you," he said. It felt right to let his friend see the horn first. Her mother had fled her homeland to prevent one of the horns from being used by her enemies. Thianna had risked everything to do the same. They walked down the corridor together. The only sound was the receding roar of the water behind them.

The corridor ended in a door. It was carved with the cockatrice insignia they had seen about the city. Thianna looked for Karn's approval, then put a hand on the door and pushed it ajar.

The room beyond blazed with light.

They saw a hexagonal chamber. Each wall apart from the door was set floor to ceiling with a mirror of polished silver. The mirrors were catching Karn's phosphorescent stone and magnifying its illumination. Set in the middle of the room was a raised altar. Something crescent-shaped was placed atop. The Horn of Osius?

Or something else?

Thianna rushed forward. Then she stopped.

"It isn't here!" exclaimed Thianna. "Where's the horn? It isn't here!"

"But what's that thing?" said Karn.

Something very strange was set on the altar. Light seemed to play across its surface, flickering like a sputtering torch. Karn approached for a closer look.

It was a carving—or not a carving—of another cockatrice. Only at the end of its tail, this one had a snake-like head. Both the cock's head and the snake's head were held in clamps, which forced them to face each other. A small, round half mirror was set upright in a groove beside them.

"Come see this," said Karn.

"I can't believe it isn't here. After everything—"

"Thianna, this isn't a statue."

That got her attention. The frost giant joined him by the altar.

Karn and Thianna saw what was causing the flickering

effect with the light. The creature was alive. Or almost alive. Its body was alternating between stone and flesh in a rapid cycle of never-ending transformation. As they watched, it would grow warm and alive and then cold and stone over and over again.

"What's going on?" said Thianna. "What's wrong with it?"

"It's magical," said Karn.

"Well, yeah. Obviously something magical."

"No, I mean the creature is magical. Its eyes. I think the gaze of the rooster head turns creatures to stone. But the gaze of the serpent head turns them back to flesh. It's been forced to look at itself. It's trapped between being in one state and the other."

"That's horrible," said Thianna. She saw how the creature would squirm in the instances when it was flesh, trying to free itself from the clamps.

"It is," agreed Karn. "It's been stuck like this for a millennium. It's how they kept it preserved in case they needed it again."

"They?"

"The Gordion Empire. They used this as their ultimate weapon, and then they stored it down here."

"The Order of the Oak knew all about this."

"They knew once. They composed the riddle in case they forgot."

"And they didn't do anything about it," said Thianna

grimly. "They just left this bird-thing down here in this horrible state."

"Cockatrice," Karn said.

"I don't have to know what it's called to feel sorry for it," Thianna replied.

"Agreed. If we meet the Order again, I'm going to have a talk about the way they 'take the long view' of things."

"I'll help with that," said Thianna. "But you said the Gordion Empire used this as a weapon. Weapon against who? And what did they do with the horn?"

"Don't you see?" said Karn. Thianna didn't. "'When snake and cockerel sundering, seek ye then the Marble King.' 'Sundering.' Pulling apart. Obviously we have to separate these two."

"And then we find the horn?"

"Just you wait." Karn picked up the mirror. "Now, the trick is to place this right, so that the flesh gaze is bounced back into the creature's eyes and the stone gaze is blocked. The reverse would turn it to stone permanently."

"You're sure you got the heads right?" asked Thianna.

"No," Karn admitted. "But you can sort of see where the transformation starts." The flesh did seem to start with the rooster's head, the stone with the serpent's. It all happened so fast it was hard to be certain.

"Also," Karn continued, "we're going to need something to keep it blinded once we free it. Otherwise we might become permanent residents of the Sunken Palace."

Thianna thought about that, then she pulled her boots off. She held up her socks.

"We can put these over its heads," she said.

Karn looked at the worn, wet, smelly fabric. He wouldn't envy anyone taking their first breath in centuries through a frost giant's only pair.

"Might be kinder to turn it to stone," he said.

"My feet smell like roses," she said. "Besides, I think a little appreciation is in order. This is the second time I've used footwear to save the day."

"Oh, I appreciate it," said Karn. "I appreciate that's not going over my head."

"It may if you keep this up," growled Thianna.

Laughing, Karn positioned the mirror so that the reflective side would face the serpent head.

"Ready?" he said.

"Been ready a long time," she replied.

Quickly, he slipped the mirror between the creature's two heads.

Instantly, a wave of flesh flowed around the creature's body, away from the mirror and moving to the rooster head.

"Now," said Karn.

Thianna brought the socks down over the animal.

Karn grabbed it by each neck, clasping the socks on tightly. The animal was sluggish at first, then it began to struggle, beating its wings furiously. Using her bootlaces, Thianna bound the improvised hoods tightly while Karn held it still.

What is that gods-awful smell? said a voice in Thianna's mind.

"Karn," she said. "I can hear it. In my head. At least I can hear the tail end of it. It's a reptile."

Take this bag off my head, the creature thought to her.

"Can't do that," said Thianna. "My friend and I don't fancy the idea of being statues."

That's the other end. My gaze restores the flesh.

"Can you tell your other head to close its eyes?"

We aren't exactly on speaking terms right now. It's bird-head's fault we've been in this mess.

"Well then, I'm afraid the socks stay on. At least until you two can work out your differences."

That may take some time. Then again, this stench is some strong motivation.

"Hey, my feet smell like roses!"

Dead ones maybe. Planted in manure.

"Never mind you. How do we find the horn?"

What horn?

"Karn, it doesn't know anything about the horn. I thought this creature was supposed to lead us to it."

"Not exactly. But we need it."

"Then how—"

"Don't worry," Karn cut her off. "I know exactly where

the horn is, and I know where the King and Dragon are too. And so do you if you think about it."

Thianna's eyes slowly widened, but not with comprehension. With alarm. Her hand felt for the slender dart protruding from her neck.

"Thianna!" Karn cried, grasping for his friend. The frost giant's eyes rolled up in her head, and she fell heavily to the floor.

"So you know exactly where the horn is?" said Tanthal, strolling into the room with Desstra behind him. "Good. Then it's time to 'Seek ye then the Marble King.'"

"What did you do to her?"

Karn knelt by Thianna. He clutched the cockatrice's two necks in one grip and held his friend's hand in the other. The giantess was turning pale, and her breathing was coming in short bursts. Tanthal stood over them, mace prepared to come down heavy on Karn's head if he rose or made any move to draw his sword. Desstra stood behind him, a dart ready to render him immobile.

"Karn," Thianna gasped, "I can't feel my legs. Why can't I feel my legs?"

He knew instantly what had happened.

"You used your paralysis venom, didn't you?" he spat at Desstra accusingly.

"An extra-heavy dose," gloated Tanthal. "We didn't

want to take any chances with such a big brute. Of course, if we used too much, there's a danger it could stop her heart."

"Thianna!" Karn shouted.

The frost giantess didn't look frightened. Instead, her eyes burned with anger.

"Going to knock that smile off your face, elf," she said. "Along with most of your teeth."

Tanthal leaned over, dangling his chin tantalizingly close.

"Take your best shot," he mocked.

Thianna struggled to raise her fist, but her arm was stiff and the best she could manage was a floppy jerk.

"I didn't think so," the dark elf said. "Now," he said to Desstra, "you cover the Norrønur while I see to the prize."

Karn started to rise and felt Desstra stir behind him, ready to put him down. Would she really do it? He had no doubt she would.

"Ah, yes, the cockatrice," said Tanthal, relieving Karn of the animal. "It's quite rare. Two-headed ones even more so. No wonder the empire wanted it preserved."

"They picked a pretty terrible way to do it," said Desstra.

"Oh, there you go again," sneered Tanthal. "Sympathy for the lesser creatures. Every time I think there's hope for you, your weakness pops up. But taking out that big lug of a half giant counts for a lot."

"Compassion isn't a weakness," said Karn. "Neither is friendship."

"You're quite tedious, you know," said Tanthal, heading for the exit. "Come along, Desstra. Let's leave these two friends together. Karn can see just how strong his friendship makes him as he watches Thianna die."

CHAPTER TWENTY

Shadows of Doubt

Tanthal was whistling. So close to his victory, he could barely contain himself.

Creatures of the underground, the dark elves didn't require any additional light to see in the Sunken Palace. They made their way easily from column to column— Tanthal practically skipping—then climbed swiftly down the spiraled shaft. Karn's wooden shield still rested at the base. It had certainly made following the human easy. Slipping into the water, they followed the tunnel that led to the Hippodrome. Climbing up onto the pier, Tanthal turned to Desstra.

"Find me when you've finished here," he said.

"What are you talking about?" she replied. She assumed they were done and would be going together to recover the horn.

"Karn will have to come out eventually," Tanthal said. "You will wait for him. Then you will do what needs to be done."

Desstra's ears drooped in growing dread.

"We have what we came for," she protested. "We can leave." Tanthal shook his head and tutted at her.

"*I* have what *I* came for," he corrected her. "Or I will shortly when I put this to use." He patted the pack on his shoulder, where he had stuffed the protesting cockatrice. Desstra hoped it hadn't drowned in their short swim. "You are here for a different reason. You came here to complete your education. Something, you remember, that requires my approval. My say-so. You've performed well, I admit it, but I need proof you've overcome that weak heart of yours. Strong as the rock of our home, Desstra. Be strong and finish the Norrønur boy off for me. Then consider yourself graduated."

Smug as ever, Tanthal didn't wait for an answer. He knew she only had one course of action. He whistled as he left her there, alone in the cold and dark.

"You have to go after them."

Thianna gripped Karn's hand tightly. She didn't appear able to move anything below her neck now. He wasn't sure if she was really squeezing his hand, or if hers was simply growing rigid. He squeezed back, hoping she could feel it.

"I'm not leaving you," he said.

"You have to," she insisted.

"Thianna, I came all this way for you. You're the reason—I can't—"

"Karn, listen to me. I know you care about me."

"I do."

"If you really care about me, then you have to care about what's important to me. Forget about saving me. Finish what I came here to do. I don't like bullies. I want them stopped. I want that horn destroyed."

"I can't—"

"Yes, you can. You can do anything. You found me, didn't you?" She smiled encouragingly at him. "Whatever you did to get this far, do it to go the rest of the way. Now, go."

Karn stared at his friend. Could he really leave her? Her eyes told him she would never forgive him if he didn't. He couldn't leave her alone in the dark. But if these were her last moments, how could he let her down here at the end?

"Goodbye," he said.

"Be healthy," she replied.

Karn burst through the waterfall. Anger and sorrow drove him as he jumped across the columns. He was reckless as he scurried down the shaft.

He recovered his shield, swinging it onto his back, and dove into the water. He swam hard for the stone pier. He hauled himself onto it and stepped into the tunnel beyond. He was ready to vent his anger on the world, woe be to anyone who got in his way.

Karn felt a dart brush the hairs on his neck. He froze. Behind him, Desstra was perfectly still. The tip of her dart was so close to his skin it would be hard to slide a playing card between them. Karn waited for the point to stab home. He wondered why it didn't.

Graduation, Desstra was thinking, considering what the word meant to her. Her whole life leading to this point. They had won, and she would graduate. She and Tanthal would return together to Deep Shadow. He would be the triumphant hero, and she would be a full member of the Underhand. They would both be famous. There was no telling how far they could rise together after that. Never mind that she despised him. All it would cost her was the life of one human boy. A boy so naive he had trusted her. Trusted her to be someone decent, who understood what friendship was, who would die for their friends, not stab them in the back.

"Go ahead," said Karn bitterly. "It's everything you want."

"Karn." She shouldn't say his name. First names were

something for friends to call each other. She had no right. "This isn't how—"

"Just do it. What are you waiting for? Get it over with and go be a happy little elf with all your nasty friends."

"They aren't my friends," she said. "Friendship makes you weak."

"Do you think I'm weak, Desstra?" said Karn. "Do you think Thianna is weak?"

She didn't. She'd heard the legends, and she'd seen them in action. The two of them had fought undead, fought a dragon, fought trolls, fought the tatzelwurm, outfoxed the dark elves' wings, found the Sunken Palace . . .

"I don't think you're weak at all," she said. It was true. "Not when you're together."

Karn felt the dart withdraw from his neck. He didn't dare move.

"I can still save her," she said.

Karn turned slowly. "Why would you do that?"

"You have to stop Tanthal. I don't think I can face him. But I'll save Thianna. I promise."

"But why?" Karn stepped away from Desstra, but he didn't draw his blade. Desstra turned from him, hiding her face.

"Because you two don't deserve to end like this," she said.

"I don't understand."

"I don't need you to." Desstra turned and shoved him forward. "Go."

"Still breathing. Good." The elf knelt by the frost giant, digging in her satchel. "Can't believe it. We should have used a bigger dose."

"Back—to give me—more poison?" gasped Thianna.

"Not poison, no," said Desstra, holding up a vial. "Antidote."

She tipped the liquid in the small glass into Thianna's mouth, massaged the frost giant's throat to help her swallow. After a moment, Thianna's breathing became more regular. Remembering she was the only one who could see in this darkness, Desstra activated a phosphorescent stone for Thianna's benefit.

"Why?" said Thianna.

"It works fast," said Desstra. "You'll be back on your feet in—"

Thianna's huge hand shot up and grabbed Desstra by her skinny neck. The frost giant climbed to her feet, lifting the little elf off the ground. Thianna's eyes narrowed as her fingers tightened. Desstra dangled in the air, fighting to breathe.

"Thianna, stop!" Desstra coughed out the words, struggling to break Thianna's grip. "We—have to help—Karn."

For an instant, it didn't look like Thianna was going to listen. Then she set Desstra down on her feet and relaxed her grip.

"Karn?"

"He's gone after Tanthal."

Thianna's anger gave way to alarm.

"Don't think this gets you off the hook," she said.

"I didn't do it for your forgiveness," the elf replied.

"What did you do it for?" asked Thianna.

"For Karn. For your friendship."

"You and I are never going to be friends," Thianna spat.

"That's not what I mean. I mean for *your* friendship. The two of you." Desstra turned her eyes away, looking at the deep shadows of the tunnel, where Karn and Tanthal had gone. "I thought being a member of the Underhand was the best that life could offer. But Karn came all the way here, thousands of miles, for you. You've each risked your life over and over for the other. Something like that—it outweighs any dream I could have. If it's my path versus your path, you two deserve to win, and I deserve to lose."

"We haven't won yet," said Thianna.

"No," said Desstra. "We haven't." She looked imploringly into Thianna's eyes. "You don't have to like me, but you could use my help stopping Tanthal. I owe you that."

"Fine," said Thianna. "But I'm the one who gets to knock the grin off that smug elf's face."

❖

Karn expected to encounter at least a few Gordashan soldiers on the journey back, but he was alone in the Sunken Palace. If the dark elves had dispatched them, where were the bodies? It was puzzling, but he was glad of it. Then he reached the end of the tunnel and stood in the pool of light from the hole that Thianna had kicked open. The ceiling was a long way up. He didn't see any convenient handholds. There was a loop of rope hanging down from the lip of the hole. Obviously, Tanthal had used the rope to ascend, then pulled it up behind him. It spoke volumes about the dark elf that he'd left Desstra down here to fend for herself. Karn doubted that Tanthal was testing her resourcefulness.

But how was Karn to reach the exit? If only he had a way of catching that bit of dangling cord. He thought about it. Maybe he did.

Karn drew Whitestorm from its sheath. He held the blade hilt upward and readied his toss. Then he threw it as high as he could. It struck the ceiling but missed the line. He caught the sword as it fell. He tried to calm down and concentrate, not throw wild.

He lined up the throw again, heaved the sword high in the air. This time its hilt passed through the loop and Whitestorm snagged the rope. It hung precariously.

"Whitestorm!" Karn called.

The sword jerked downward. It strained for an instant, then Whitestorm raced to his hand, dragging one end of the line with it.

Karn sheathed his sword and tested the rope. Thankfully, it was still secured at the top. Then he began to climb.

CHAPTER TWENTY-ONE

The Marble King

Karn didn't know what to expect when he climbed out onto the sands of the Hippodrome. There were no city guards waiting for him. The spectators had mostly left the arena. The space was vast and empty. But from beyond the high walls of its tiered seating, Karn heard a roar like the thundering waves of the ocean.

A dactyl lay on the ground. He stirred, moaning, and Karn helped him to his feet.

"What happened?" Karn asked.

"Palest elf I ever saw," the dwarf replied. "Knocked me out and took—" His voice took on a note of alarm. "My horn!"

That's when Karn noticed that the statue was gone.

"You're him! You're the Marble King!"

"I am king," the dactyl said. "But I don't know anything about marble. Your speech is strange, son. What are you doing in my city, and why are we in the Hippodrome?"

"Your city?" Karn felt a pang of sympathy. The dwarf didn't know what had happened to him. Didn't realize that Gordasha hadn't been "his city" in over a thousand years.

"Are you a foreigner? Who are you not to know of Acmon the Anvil: former soldier of the empire until I threw off their yoke and freed Ambracia from their chains?"

"I think you better sit down," said Karn. "A lot has changed since your time."

"My time? What are you talking about?"

"For starters, the city isn't called Ambracia anymore. It's called Gordasha. And the empire you fought is long gone."

Acmon the Anvil glared at Karn.

"Kid, I think maybe you have a touch of heatstroke. You look a little pale for this climate."

"I'm fine," snapped Karn. "But you've been stone for almost fourteen hundred years. Like her."

Karn pointed at the other statue set on the spina.

"My dragon!" screamed Acmon, eyes wide with shock. "What have they done to my dragon?" He grabbed Karn's shirt. "Who did this? Tell me. I'll rip them apart!"

"Will you listen to me?" said Karn. "Your enemies are long gone. But your horn has been stolen by a new villain, that pale elf who attacked you. His name is Tanthal, and he has the horn and he has the creature that turned you and the dragon to stone. And I am going to get them both back."

Karn left Acmon and ran to the stables.

"Where are you going?" the Marble King demanded, chasing after Karn.

"Tanthal has a head start. But I know how to fix that."

The streets of the city were in pure pandemonium. Desstra and Thianna struggled to wade through the crowds. People were fleeing south, away from the land wall and northern seawall. The elf and the half giant were heading against the surge.

"What's going on?" Thianna shouted above the noise.

"The Uskirians have broken the walls," a man yelled back, not pausing in his rush. "They've smashed a gate and are pouring into the city."

Karn had been right about the capabilities of the huge cannon, Thianna reflected. Shambok was on his way to being spectacular. As bad as things had been since she arrived in this strange metropolis, they had just gotten a lot worse. But nothing would be as bad as the idea of dark elves in control of dragons.

"This is taking too long," she said. "We need to move faster."

"How?" asked Desstra. "Unless you have some magic way to clear the streets."

"I'm surprised at you, elf," said Thianna. "Thinking like a city dweller." She pointed up. "Those rooftops are wide open. Running across them shouldn't be a problem for two daughters of the mountains, now, should they?"

"Technically, I live under a mountain," said Desstra. "But I can climb as well as anyone."

"Anyone?" said Thianna, an edge of challenge in her voice.

"You're on," replied the elf.

Karn drove the chariot hard through the streets. The manticore was enjoying the relative freedom. Having been shut up in a stable for years, only allowed to run when it was let out onto the race course, it was loving this run through the city.

There was one advantage to having your chariot pulled by a man-eater, Karn thought. People tended to get out of your way rather quickly.

Unfortunately, Tanthal was proving very easy to follow. He left a trail of people turned to stone in his wake. They were disturbing bread crumbs marking the dark elf's passage.

Riding in the chariot beside Karn, Acmon had been

subdued since Karn had filled him in on events. He spoke up now.

"So who rules my city?" he asked.

"An imperator," replied Karn.

"And it's the supremacy, not the empire?"

"Correct."

"And they are fighting who?"

"The Uskirian Empire."

"Empire? The Uskiri are just a bunch of rustic nomads up north. Nobody pays them much attention."

"Not anymore."

"I hardly know which side I'm on."

"I've met both rulers," said Karn. "I'm not really impressed with either."

"I only want my city to be free," said Acmon. "I had my taste of slavery fighting in the empire's army."

The dactyl sounded sincere. But Karn had his doubts about the legendary king.

"If you like freedom so much, why did you enslave a dragon?"

"What?" said Acmon. "Enslave? No, you've got that wrong."

Karn was about to ask what Acmon meant, but a shout went up from people on the streets.

"It's the Marble King!" they cried. Karn saw that the excited folk were mostly dwarves. "The Marble King! The Marble King!" they chanted.

Acmon brightened at this.

"To me, my dactyls!" he cried.

Soon, they had a small army running in their wake.

"I don't want to sound ungrateful for the support," said Karn, "but half of your newfound followers aren't armed with anything more than fishing poles."

"A fine weapon in the right hands." Acmon smiled. "We have numbers now."

"Just make sure everyone stays behind us," said Karn. "If they get ahead of the chariot, I'm not sure I can keep the manticore from snacking."

"Swift as the great wolf," Tanthal chanted to himself as he ran through the streets. He gripped the horn in one hand and the cockatrice in the other. This left him unable to hold his mace, but it didn't matter. He had a more powerful weapon now. When he brought it, and the horn, back to Deep Shadow, he would be the most revered Underhand in the city's history. In fact, he thought, with the cockatrice in his grasp, he could own the city if he wanted. Why bow to another's orders when he could be the one giving them? There would be no stopping him.

He was heading for the subterranean ingress of the River Lux. His plan was to leave Gordasha the same way he entered it. He wouldn't wait for Desstra. Not worth the risk now that he had the prize. If his underling couldn't fight her way out on her own, then she really didn't deserve to escape. He hoped that she would make it. She was weak and annoying, true, but she had skills he could exploit. Hopefully killing that Norrønur boy had hardened her heart. If she could be toughened up, she'd make a good lieutenant in the new order he would bring to the Underhand. Or, if she didn't fall in line, she might make a nice statue for his throne room. There would be a delicious irony in hardening her heart along with the rest of her.

Tanthal was so caught up in his dreams of glory and conquest that he almost didn't notice the figure that blocked his path to the ingress.

"You!" he snarled. "What are you doing here?"

The cloaked figure he had fought on the rooftops of Castlebriar stood between him and the entrance to the subterranean river.

"Aren't you a little far from home?" Tanthal asked.

"Actually, I'm quite close," the stranger replied. "You're the one who's far from home. And you're never going back. Not with the horn."

Tanthal laughed at the stranger's arrogance. He lifted the cockatrice in his satchel, prepared to reach in and unveil its head.

The cloaked figure's staff shot a searing burst of flame. Tanthal shrieked and dodged aside, losing his hold on the cockatrice. His salamander-skin armor held up under the blast, but he felt his hair singed.

Scowling, he drew his mace and leapt forward. The staff wasn't a close-quarter weapon. His best chance lay in the offense.

From the folds of the cloak, the stranger raised a sword. The fight was on.

Tanthal and the stranger dueled ferociously. Whoever was under those robes, he was a trained fighter. Sword clashed with mace, while the stranger wielded the staff like a shield. Whatever was bound up in those leather wrappings, it was metal, not a wooden walking stick.

Tanthal knew he only had to reach the ingress, but he couldn't put too much distance between himself and his opponent or he would burn. His armor could resist heat, but he'd seen the flames coming off that staff. He couldn't withstand a direct blow.

The stranger knew it too and was driving him away from the river's ingress. He was losing ground. It might be time to think of a Plan B. Then the fight got really interesting.

Uskirian warriors, riding their ugly war pigs, came charging up the city streets. A troop of Gordashan militia came from the other direction.

The two forces clashed, with Tanthal and the stranger right in the middle.

"This isn't my war," he screamed in frustration as an Uskirian jabbed a spear at him. "I don't care about any of you."

Then he was too busy to talk, fighting for his life.

The rooftops were getting crowded. Thianna saw the Uskirian forces swarming through the streets below. But the Gordashan citizens were giving them a real fight. They had climbed their houses and were prying up the red clay roofing tiles. They hurled these at the Uskirians, and many an invader was knocked stunned from the saddle of his war pig.

Thianna couldn't help herself. She pried up a piece of tile and lobbed it at a soldier. It struck him right in the forehead, and he toppled to the pavement.

"Hey," said the giantess in response to Desstra's raised eyebrow. "I never liked bullies."

"You know what?" said the little elf. "Neither did I." She snatched up a tile and flung it at an Uskirian. Her shot connected with a solid *thunk*.

"Nice arm," said Thianna. Then she saw something even more impressive.

"Karn!" she exclaimed.

Karn took in the battle at a glance as his chariot drove into the fray, Acmon's dactyl army pouring in behind them. Uskirian soldiers clashed with Gordashan forces. Tanthal was fighting for his life against several invaders. And near him, the cloaked stranger from Castlebriar— the wizard, if wizard he was—was keeping opponents back with the flames from their staff. Everything was mayhem.

"Pig," warned Acmon, pointing.

An Uskiri armed with a spear and riding one of the great beasts bore down on them. Karn dropped the reins and unslung his shield. The hard Norrønir wood took the spear point, but the blow carried him out of the vehicle. He landed in the dust, the wind driven from his lungs.

He felt a hand under his arm, helping him to this feet. "Ynarr?"

The big blond Norrønur nodded.

"Shouldn't you be defending the imperator with the rest of the Sworn?" Karn asked.

"The imperator has fled the city," Ynarr replied. "He boarded his ship and left by his private dock the instant word came that the land wall had been breached."

"You can really pick them, can't you?" said Karn.

"I don't have good luck with employers, no," the man agreed. "Maybe I am not the best judge of character." Ynarr saw that the Uskirian who had knocked Karn down was bringing his war pig around for another pass. Ynarr drew his ax. "But perhaps there is honor to be had in fighting with you now, Karn Korlundsson."

Even on foot against mounted opponents, Tanthal was holding his own. He was fast and small compared with the giant pigs. He dodged in and out of their spears' range, though his mace was little use against the pigs' tough hide.

"Is this the best you can do?" he taunted. "Isn't there anyone here who can put up a real fight?"

"I can," said a voice behind him.

Tanthal turned just in time to see the frost giant's fist as it collided with his jaw. He distinctly felt a tooth crack. Then he was shaking the ringing from his ears as he lay in the mud of the riverbank.

"You?" he said incredulously.

"Told you I'd knock your smile off," Thianna said. She bent and picked up the horn where it lay beside him.

Tanthal scrambled backward, coming to his feet and raising his mace.

"Think you can beat me in a fair fight?" he asked.

"I do," said the giantess, her arming sword poised for his attack.

"Then it's too bad I don't fight fair," Tanthal replied.

Behind him, dropping out of the sky, a dozen dark elves leapt from the saddles of their wings to land in a half circle around Tanthal. There was an extra, riderless bat among the flock.

"I sent my mount for reinforcements before I even entered the city," Tanthal explained. "The Underhand has agents everywhere. You were never going to win this, you understand." He called back over his shoulder at the dark elves. "Kill her. Kill them all."

 CHAPTER TWENTY-TWO

The Fall of Gordasha

"You ever played Knattleikr?" Thianna asked the dark elf.

"What? You mean your silly frost-giant game?" sneered Tanthal.

"Didn't think so," said Thianna. She hurled the Horn of Osius, tossing it far over the heads of the dark elves. Tanthal's head turned to follow its trajectory. All their heads turned.

The frost giant charged.

She barreled into them like she was an Uskirian war pig. Like a bull. Like the littlest giant suddenly enjoying being the largest person on the playing field. Elves were knocked aside as easily as bowling pins.

She cleared them, leaving battered Svartálfar in her

wake. Then a mounted Uskirian turned his spear on her. Thianna grabbed the shaft and shoved backward, pushing the warrior right off his hog. She knocked Uskiri aside right and left, until she broke the shaft on the tusk of another boar. She scooped up the Horn of Osius from the ground where it had fallen. Then it was time to draw her sword.

"There's your companion," said Ynarr, elsewhere on the battlefield.

"Where?" said Karn, his face a mixture of excitement and relief.

"Right in the heart of the action," replied the man.

Karn looked and saw Thianna towering above dark elves, city militia, fishing pole–wielding dactyls, and dismounted Uskiri. She seemed to be enjoying herself.

"Why am I not surprised?" he said.

Karn fought his way toward his larger-than-life best friend.

"Norrønboy!" She beamed with excitement when she saw him. "I've got the horn!" she said. "So that's good. But I don't think this city is having its best day."

Karn looked around at the chaos. He knew the scene here was being repeated in quarters all over Gordasha.

"I know this isn't our fight . . . ," said the frost giant.

"But can we do something, you mean?" said Karn.

Thianna nodded.

"I don't know what," she said. "But a lot of people are going to die here today. It all seems so pointless."

Karn noticed a small bag, flopping strangely by the banks of the river. It took a minute to realize he was seeing the cockatrice. It was struggling to climb out of a dark elf's satchel.

"I think I know how to stop this," he said. "At least I think I do. It's a bit of a gamble, but . . ."

"Tell me what we have to do," Thianna replied.

"First, we need that," he said, pointing at the cockatrice. "And then we need to get back to the Hippodrome."

Tanthal had lost the horn and the cockatrice. He was mired in a battle that had nothing to do with him. Who cared who won, Uskirian or Gordashan? Both powers would fall beneath dragon fire if only he could get the Horn of Osius to the caverns of Deep Shadow. His small squad of dark elves fought anyone who came near them as they strove to get to the boy and the giantess. Then he noticed another elf in their number. His face tightened with suspicion.

"Karn isn't dead. Thianna isn't dead. So why are *you* still breathing?"

"I'd say it isn't what it looks like," Desstra said, drawing two darts from her leg sheath, "but I'm afraid it is."

"I don't understand," he said. "You would throw away

your place in the greatest society in the world for two enemies who aren't even your species?"

"You'd stab any one of us in the back if it served your purpose," said Desstra.

"For the good of Deep Shadow."

"For the good of yourself."

"It's the same thing," Tanthal spat. "When we make ourselves strong, we strengthen the whole of the Svar-tálfar."

"That's a lonely kind of strength. There are better kinds."

"Then show me how strong you are." Tanthal swung his mace.

Desstra was prepared but still the blow missed her only by inches. "Outcast!" Tanthal yelled, and swung again, driving her back. "Weakling! Freak! Traitor!"

Tanthal rained blow after blow down on her. Desstra leapt and dodged like she had never moved before. Her former superior officer and classmate's fury fueled his rage. She hurled a dart at him, but he swept it aside. She flung her remaining egg sacs, but he ducked and kicked her savagely in the stomach. For all his willingness to exploit his teammates, he knew how to fight when he had to. He pressed her hard, wearing her down.

She was running out of ammunition, out of breath, and out of time.

"You're sure about this?"

Karn and Thianna were back in the Hippodrome, having fought their way through the streets. Ynarr had covered their retreat, as had several of Acmon's makeshift dactyl army, though the dwarves weren't clear whom they were helping or why.

"Reasonably," replied Karn.

"Okay," said Thianna. "Sure, why not? What's the worst thing that could happen?"

"We get roasted alive five seconds from now by an angry monster," replied Karn.

"There is that. Okay, here goes nothing."

She held up the cockatrice and pulled her sock off the serpent head.

Oh thank goodness, said the snake voice in her mind. *Fresh air. You know, it isn't really necessary to put a sock over both our heads. Just the cock's. I don't turn anyone to stone.*

"Really? Well, I didn't want to play favorites. You two work out your differences?"

We're getting there. Let us go if we do?

"We've got some people to free if we live through this, but yeah. But we've got work to do here now." She held the snake head up before the colossal statue. "Do your stuff."

The serpent's eyes gazed upon the statue of the dragon on the spina. The marble seemed to warm and soften. A beautiful reddish-gold color bloomed on the leathery scales of the great beast. The dragon unfurled its enormous wings and shook out its neck, flexing muscles not used in over a thousand years.

Karn saw confusion in the huge eyes. The dragon looked left and right, taking in the Hippodrome, wondering how it got there. Like the Marble King, the dragon didn't realize it had been stone. It roared, and they covered their ears at the sound. Then the dragon's attention fell on Karn and Thianna.

"Where is Acmon?" The voice was thunderous, angry, and, as Karn had guessed, distinctly female.

"Acmon is fighting for the city," said Karn. "But he's outnumbered and people are going to die. Lots of people. We need your help."

"Why should I help you? Why—" the dragon leaned down, her enormous snout so close they could feel the hot, stinking breath. "Why should I not devour you both now, when you carry Acmon's horn?"

"Because we aren't using it," said Thianna. "We're asking, not commanding."

"And because your brother sent us," said Karn.

"What do you mean, 'brother'?" exclaimed Thianna, turning to Karn with a stunned expression. "You mean this is—that she's—Orm's sister?"

Desstra was tiring. Tanthal's blows were getting harder to deflect. Around her, other elves battled dwarves, humans, and Uskiri. Bats swooped and dove, clawing at any unprotected heads they could find. Shards of roofing tiles still rained down upon the Uskirians, and one or two struck a Svartálfar.

Tanthal's mace caught Desstra in the shoulder. The blow sent her spinning off balance. A second attack collided painfully with her ribs.

He was driving her away from any allies. Not that she had allies. They splashed in the shallows now. The grill to the underground river was behind her.

"There's one body down there already," Tanthal said. "Let's send it some company." He kicked at her savagely, catching her knee. The move unbalanced him as well, though, and she flung her last dart. For an instant she thought she had him. Then he brought his mace up. The dart sank into the shaft and stuck. He glanced at the dart and gave an exaggerated expression of shock, mocking her.

"No more weapons, underling."

Tanthal advanced on her slowly. He was savoring her final moments.

"You could have had it all," he said. "We would have been heroes. Conquerors. The greatest elves in all of Deep Shadow. In history. All you had to do was obey me and you could have been anything. But you let me down and now you're nothing. You're less than nothing. You're soft, compassionate, and weak."

Tanthal brought his mace up for a killing strike.

"Time for your final lesson, Desstra."

In desperation, Desstra's hand slipped into her satchel,

searching for anything that could help her. It was empty, barren of egg sacs and weapons. All expended on this fruitless quest. Empty but for—her fingers closed on a hard, round object.

She smashed Tanthal in the side of his head as hard as she could.

He dropped to his knees.

"What?" he stammered.

"Strong as the rock of our home," she said as his eyes turned up.

Tanthal collapsed into the water, felled by the small rock he had given her as a reminder of the values of Deep Shadow.

Desstra dropped to her knees in the river waters, exhausted. Beside her, the currents carried Tanthal's still form away. She reached for him, but she was out of energy. His unconscious body spilled through the grates, disappearing belowground.

The stone slipped from her fingers and fell into the river. It didn't matter anymore. She didn't need it. She was never going back. She didn't belong there. Or anywhere. She glanced at her orange-patterned leather armor. The mark of an outcast. All the reminder she would ever need.

War pigs ran squealing before the descending dragon.

The dragon was swooping over the Uskirian forces.

Orma, as they learned the dragon was called, bore Karn and Thianna on her back. Without any kind of saddle, they clung tightly to her ridged scales and to each other. They were passing parallel to the land wall, using the dragon's intimidating presence to drive the Uskirian forces away.

"How did you know?" the giantess asked.

"I didn't. I guessed," said Karn.

"Good guess."

"Well, I knew Orm was fleeing something when he came to Norrøngard. Something happened, but he wouldn't talk about it. And he really hated the Gordion Empire. He must have suffered a loss that really unbalanced him. Then I saw the family resemblance."

"So when Orm's sister was turned to stone, Orm was so scared—"

"My little brother does *not* get scared," rumbled Orma. Thianna hadn't realized she was listening. She thought the dragon was having too much fun chasing pigs.

"Rattled? Ruffled? Disconcerted?" offered Thianna.

"Angered," said Orma.

"Okay," conceded Thianna. "He was so *angered* that he *fled*."

Orma growled menacingly at this but didn't say anything.

"All the way to Norrøngard," Thianna finished. "He found Gordions already there in the city of Sardeth and freaked out."

"My little brother does not 'freak out.'"

"Your, um, 'little brother' isn't so little anymore," said Karn. "You do know how long you were stuck in the marble, right? He's sort of your bigger, older brother now."

This shut Orma up. She flew over the Somber Sea, ready to give the naval forces the same treatment as the army.

"Anyway," said Karn. "That's basically how things happened. But what I don't understand is how you and Acmon got together."

"When the Anvil first found the horn," Orma explained, pausing to shoot a blast of fire at a ship that had wandered too close to the seawalls, "he did not know what it was for. He tried to play music on it. But his ancestry called to me."

"He was a Thican," said Thianna. "Must be from a family that could use the horn originally."

"Also," said Orma, "I liked his music."

"Watch it," said Karn. Cannon shot was starting to be aimed their way. The dragon banked, rose, and dove, avoiding the shells.

"When I asked Acmon how I could repay him for his song, he said, 'Free my people,'" explained the dragon. "It was more than I bargained for, but I didn't have any plans that century anyway."

"Speaking of plans," said Karn, "time for the next stage of ours. You see that big tent palace in the midst of their land forces?"

"Yes," said Orma.

"Head for that."

The dragon beat her wings and made a beeline for the grand pavilion. The Uskirians observed their trajectory. They turned their enormous boar-shaped cannon on their new adversary.

"Incoming," yelled Thianna as a cannonball the size of a large boulder roared their way.

Orma waited until the last minute, then she soared upward. The cannonball almost grazed her belly.

"You cut that close," said Thianna. She thought the dragon was enjoying herself.

Orma spat a glob of flame. Uskiri leapt aside of the fireball. It struck the enormous artillery weapon, the pride of their army, and left it a puddle of molten metal. There was little in the world that could stand up to dragon fire.

"Now comes the tricky bit," said Karn.

Shambok Who Borders on Spectacular was on his throne, wondering if it was worth it to call himself Shambok the About to Be Spectacular Any Minute Now just for today or wait for confirmation that the city had fallen and go the whole hog. He was looking forward to being Shambok the Spectacular and considering the celebration he would throw when that was the case.

One of his commanders, Lagra Shathmir, burst into

the room in a most unseemly fashion, hollering and waving his arms.

"What's that man on about?" he asked his advisor Dargan Urgul, Speaker to Barbarians.

Dargan bowed and went to see about the commander. Shambok heard a lot of unintelligible shouting, more waving of arms, and generally more panic than a hardened Uskirian warrior should ever display. He was quite irritated when Dargan returned to him.

"'What does he say?' Shambok Who Is So Close to Spectacular He Can Taste It and Won't Stand for Any Delays asks."

"He said," replied Dargan, with something less than his usual confidence, "that begging your pardon, but the invasion has run into a slight snag."

"A snag? What snag?"

"Quite a big one, I'm afraid. Lagra says it's a dragon."

That surprised Shambok.

"But there haven't been any dragons seen in this part of the world for ages," Shambok said. "What dragon is he talking about?"

At that moment, the entire tent palace was ripped away above them. It simply rose into the air, all the beautiful silks and rough canvas rising straight up, ropes snapping and tentpoles yanked right out of the ground. All eyes followed the tent as it soared across the battlefield to land with a crash in the fields beyond the army's camp.

Several hundred palace officials, servants, and other

attendants, who until a moment ago had all been in different chambers inside the huge pavilion, were suddenly standing without walls or ceiling in the middle of the field.

Hovering over them was an enormous creature, its gargantuan wings beating the air to keep it in place. Two children clung to its back. The suspected spies who had escaped.

"I believe it would be *that* dragon," said Dargan.

 CHAPTER TWENTY-THREE

An Empire Unchained

They were in the Basilica of Mensis. It was the largest space in the city, the only one in which the dragon could fit comfortably. The Hippodrome had been suggested, but they wanted something roofed so they wouldn't be inconvenienced by stray fire. The fighting had mostly stopped, however, except for sporadic bursts from sections of the city that still hadn't heard the news. With the imperator fled and the Uskirian leader the guest or prisoner of an enormous fire-breathing dragon, both sides were confused as to what they should be doing. Soldiers throughout and outside the city stood around awkwardly, gaping at each other and awaiting orders.

Thianna had been the one to suggest the basilica.

"No one is living in there right now," she had said.

Then, in response to the surprised looks, she had added, "What? If the god had wanted it, he shouldn't'a left."

Everyone agreed that made sense, and so in the absence of any better ideas, they were gathered in the basilica's large nave under the great dome of its roof. In this case, everyone was Karn; Thianna; Acmon the Anvil; several Gordashan city officials and ministers; Idas the Street Fisher; Desstra, whom they had rescued when they grabbed Acmon; Shambok Who Wasn't Sure If He Was Spectacular Yet or Not; Dargan Urgul, Speaker to Barbarians; and, of course, one very large and hard-to-miss dragon.

"Now that we're all here," said Karn, "make peace."

"What?" said several voices at once.

"Make peace," Karn said again. "We'll wait."

"But not very long," boomed the dragon.

"But—" said Shambok with a nervous glance at Orma. He hadn't enjoyed being plucked into the air by dragon claws, but he was still coming to grips with his relief that he was alive and unroasted, and he wanted to stay that way. "But my ancestors charged me with conquering the city. That isn't something I can just sweep under the rug, as it were. It's my hereditary duty."

"And we can't make any treaties in the absence of the imperator," said one of the officials.

"Your imperator is long gone," said Thianna. "I think he abdicated when he fled the battle."

"One thing at a time," said Karn. He addressed Shambok, "What exactly is your charge?"

"That I have to open up the Gordashan Strait so that the glories of the Uskiri can move into the Sparkle Sea and beyond."

"Okay. Now, the imperator's gone, but do we have any other royalty present?"

Acmon the Anvil grinned at this. He could see where it was going.

"I might fit that bill," he said.

"You?" asked Shambok.

"We ruled this city centuries before the imperator was born. Orma and I together." Acmon reached out an affectionate hand to stroke the dragon's snout. Orma rubbed against his palm. Theirs was an odd friendship.

"And don't forget that dactyls founded this city," said Idas, "before any Gordions ever came and conquered it."

"There you go," said Karn. "The King and"—he glanced at the dragon—"er, Queen, of Gordasha. Your Majesties, would you be willing to drop the Great Chain and allow the Uskirian fleet to head south?"

"Drop the chain?" several people exclaimed at once.

"Not for war," said Karn. "For trade. Diplomatic vessels. Merchant vessels." He looked at Shambok and Dargan. "See? There are other ways to spread your culture."

Dargan smiled at this. Shambok looked confused.

"Could we, perhaps, hold a dance to celebrate?"

"I don't see why not," said Karn.

All present thought that was a very good idea.

In the end, it was called the "Dragon Accord," the peace that was brokered by Karn Korlundsson at the end of the "Siege of Gordasha." The new King Acmon would take up residence in the palace while his coregent, Orma, would live in the basilica. The Great Chain would lower for any Uskirian merchant vessel that wanted to go south, provided their intentions were peaceful. Acmon's first act was to issue a decree legalizing street fishing. And there was talk of replacing manticores with horses at future races in the Hippodrome.

The dark elves were rounded up, though Tanthal's body was never recovered. And two men formed an un-likely bond—Dargan Urgul and Ynarr Ulfrsson both thought it was time to leave their employment. Ynarr wanted to find the remainder of his honor and Dar-gan wanted to see the western world before it was "civi-lized." And so the barbarian and the speaker to same set off together. Some wanted to rename the city New Ambracia to celebrate what everyone hailed as a coming era of peace and prosperity. Others said it was wiser to "wait and see," but everyone agreed that it was better to not have a war than have it. Whatever the outcome, Gordasha had been saved, though it clearly would never be the same.

Karn and Thianna stood on the upper northern peninsula, near a dwarven district, where the Great Chain was anchored to a tower in the seawall. The enormous barrier shone in the setting sun with the same reddish-golden glint as Whitestorm.

"Both forged by dwarves," said Thianna. "I was right about that."

"It's a special sword, we always knew," said Karn.

"Not as special as its owner," said the frost giant, punching his arm affectionately. "Thanks for coming after me, Short Stuff. I couldn't have made it without you."

"No," said Karn, rubbing his arm and grinning. "No, you couldn't."

"You'll take the horn back to Orm, then?" Thianna asked. There was a husky note in her voice.

"He'll want to eat it like he did the other, I'm sure," said Karn. He patted his satchel, where the horn was safely tucked away. "What about you?"

For answer, Thianna gazed across the strait. The chain was being slowly lowered, disappearing under the water. New courses were being opened up for everyone.

"Thica?" asked Karn. "I know you want to, but are you sure that's wise?"

"I have to go." It was true. "Don't worry," she said. "I'll try to keep my head down."

"As much as that's possible." Karn laughed.

"Yes, well . . ." Thianna dropped her gaze to where

waves broke upon the rocks at the seawall's base, then she stepped back from the edge of the drop.

The giantess gripped Karn in a tight hug.

"I don't really look forward to going alone," she said softly.

Someone coughed behind them.

"I could, maybe, help with that," said Desstra.

"How do you keep sneaking up on me like that?" marveled Karn.

Desstra shrugged. Karn saw that the dark elf still wore the orange-patterned skin of the fire salamander. She had explained what it meant. He wasn't sure if she wore it as a badge of shame or a mark of honor.

"I can't go back to the Svartálfaheim Mountains," Desstra said. "I probably shouldn't go anywhere near Norrøngard."

"So what are you saying?" asked Thianna, her eyes narrowing.

"I could come with you," said Desstra hopefully.

"With me?" said Thianna. Her tone wasn't very inviting.

"Any company is better than none, right?"

"I'll think about it." Clearly, Thianna wasn't ready to trust the little elf, even though she had switched sides when it counted. Karn hoped the frost giantess would give Desstra a chance. Forgiveness might not come quickly, but he knew his large friend had a soft spot for underdogs.

"Hey," he said, suddenly noticing Desstra's eyewear. "What are those?"

"You like?" said the elf. She was wearing round lenses of smoked quartz. "I got them from a merchant's stall while I was re-equipping my gear. He said they come from LongGuo or somewhere. Anyway, all this sunlight is hard on my eyes. Figured I'd need them if I'm going to be a surface dweller."

"They look good," said Karn. He was pleased by the transformation that had come over the elf. "They must have been expensive, though. How much did they cost?"

"Don't know." Desstra shrugged. "I gave myself a five-finger discount."

Karn groaned and Thianna snorted. There was apparently only so far a dark elf could change so fast.

"You have to take her with you, Thianna," said Karn. "She needs someone to straighten her out."

"I said I'd think about it," replied Thianna.

Desstra smiled in gratitude. She didn't expect the giantess's forgiveness anytime soon, if ever. But at least neither Thianna nor Karn were trying to kill her. It was better than she deserved. And more than she had hoped. Then her ears twitched. Desstra looked for the cause and noticed someone over the friends' shoulders, approaching them along the wall.

"You!" she said.

The cloaked figure with the staff nodded in greeting.

"Who's this?" asked Thianna. She noticed the others' consternation and tensed.

"He—or she—followed me in Castlebriar," said Desstra.

"But helped us there too," explained Karn. "When Desstra was Nesstra."

"And you were at the battle on the shores of the River Lux," the elf said to the stranger.

"I prevented the dark one from leaving the city," replied the newcomer. "At least until other forces arrived."

"Who you are, then?" asked Thianna. "Friend or foe?"

"I am someone who wanted to see you succeed in your quest," said the stranger. "I knew the two of you could find the horn. What you accomplish together is truly remarkable." The figure held a hand out. "May I see it?"

"No," said Thianna.

"No?" said the stranger, surprised.

"We've been through too much to get this thing. We're not handing it over to anyone but the dragon who asked for it."

"Very well," the cloaked figure replied. "I understand. Now let me show you something."

"Watch out," yelled Karn as the staff was brought to bear. A jet of flame shot from its tip, forcing them to leap aside. Karn and Thianna were separated. Another burst of flame kept them that way.

"You're not going to melt the horn if you want it so badly," said Karn.

"No, I'm not," said the stranger. "But I can burn one of you."

The staff swung back and forth between Karn and Thianna.

"But which one of us has it?" said Karn. "You can't take that risk, not when you're so close . . . to home."

The stranger laughed.

"So you guess!" A free hand tore the cloak away, revealing a woman in finely sculpted bronze armor with black leather straps. What Karn had first taken for a wizard's magic staff was a Thican fire lance wrapped in leather. Her armor had seen better days. It was scuffed and dented, and her face was scarred.

"You?" Thianna gasped, recognizing a former enemy. "You were one of Sydia's soldiers! You survived!"

"I survived," said the woman. "But only barely. Without the horn, I couldn't go home. Not in disgrace. Not a failure. I lived only for revenge. But when I followed you, I learned about your quest. I saw a chance for redemption."

"You were helping us just so we'd lead you to it," said Karn.

"Don't be so angry," said the soldier. "You could say I appreciated your talent. I knew the two of you together could find the horn."

"Still doesn't mean we're giving it to you," said Thianna. "And you don't know which one of us has it."

"The way I see it, I have a fifty-fifty chance." The

fire lance continued to move back and forth between Karn and Thianna. The soldier thumbed the trigger. "And nothing more to lose. So, which of you gets to burn?"

"That's not the question you should be asking," said Karn.

"No?" said the soldier.

"No," replied the boy. "You should be asking, 'Where's Desstra?'"

The woman screamed as her weapon was suddenly yanked from her grasp. Desstra was atop one of the crenellations of the wall, where she had cast a long, thin, and apparently sticky line that fastened on the fire lance. A jerk of her wrist sent the weapon soaring over the wall to fall into the sea below.

The soldier snarled and drew her sword.

"Three against one aren't good odds," said Karn.

"Then let's even them."

Behind Desstra, a wyvern suddenly rose into the air. Just as the elf realized something was there, its claws snatched and lifted her straight up into the sky. She kicked and struggled helplessly in its grip.

"The horn," said the soldier, holding a hand out.

Thianna took a menacing step forward.

"The horn," the woman repeated, "or we'll pull her arms off."

Karn looked to Thianna. In the air above them, Desstra stilled her kicks and watched them. She had no expectation they would give up the horn for her.

Thianna's head sagged. There was really only one choice.

"Give it to her," she told Karn.

Desstra looked on, stunned, as Karn handed the Horn of Osius over to the Thican soldier. The woman backed away rapidly, and the wyvern dipped suddenly. The soldier leapt from the wall, and the wyvern caught her on its back. Then it rose again. She hovered in the air before them, the dark elf still dangling below the beast.

"Let her go," Karn called.

"Why not?" The soldier smirked. "I have what I came for."

The wyvern opened its claws and Desstra fell.

"The rocks," yelled Karn in warning. Desstra wasn't far enough out from the wall to avoid the rocks at its base. She would be smashed to bits.

Thianna moved as fast as she ever had.

Leaping from the seawall, the frost giantess slammed into the little elf as she dropped. Thianna's momentum carried them both outward.

Karn reached the edge of the battlements and looked down. He saw with relief the two girls splashing into the water. They had narrowly missed the rocks below, but they had missed. Then he glared at the wyvern as it sped away over the intersection of the Somber Sea and the

Sparkle Sea, heading for Thica. They had lost the horn but saved the dark elf.

In the waters below, Desstra broke the surface and gasped for breath.

"Why?" she asked, disentangling herself from the larger girl's embrace.

"I'm as surprised as you are," Thianna replied. Then she began to swim for the docks.

Karn met them at the Grand Harbor as they came out of the water. Thianna was fuming.

"Stupid, stupid, stupid," she said, kicking several cargo barrels unfortunate enough to be in her way. "We've lost it. We've lost it!"

"You did save a city," Desstra said. "You stopped two enormous armies from slaughtering each other. That's got to be some consolation."

"There is that," said Karn. "All the people here. We stopped a war."

"And that's not all," said the elf. "You saved me. Both of you did. From more than just the fall."

Thianna looked first at the dark elf and then at Karn.

"We won here, Thianna," Karn said.

"I know that," she said grudgingly. "And I'll get the horn back."

"We'll get it back," said Karn.

"We?" said Thianna. "You're not going back to Nor-røngard?"

"To face Orm without a horn?" he replied. "You're the

crazy one. Besides, I can't have you rushing off again and getting into trouble. I've already rescued you once. You need me, and I need you."

"Thanks, Norrønboy," said Thianna, already brightening. "I don't think there's anything the two of us can't handle."

"The three of us," said Desstra.

Karn and Thianna looked at the dark elf.

"I feel responsible," she explained. "I've got nowhere else to be. And, face it, you two are going to need someone a lot sneakier if you're going to pull this off."

"Fair enough," said Thianna. "You can come." She drew her sword and pointed it at her mother's homeland. "A half giant, a barbarian, and a devious little elf. Are you ready for us, Thica? Because here we come!"

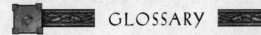

Acmon the Anvil (ACK-mahn): A dwarf of Thican ancestry, Acmon proclaimed himself king of Ambracia
but was deposed a few short years later. Legend has
it that when the city (now called Gordasha) faces its
greatest threat, Acmon will return. But who believes
legends?

Ambracia (am-BRAY-see-uh): A city on the eastern
coast of Gordasha founded by dactyl dwarves. It was
rechristened as Nova Gordion in 137 EE by Emperor
Gordas after he successfully reunited the Gordion
Empire. However, locals preferred the name Gordasha and Nova Gordion fell out of use. (See: Gordasha)

Blackfire Forest: A large forest northeast of the city of
Castlebriar in the country of Nelenia. The forest
takes its name from a terrible fire that nearly burned
it to the ground over a millennium ago.

Castlebriar: A former Gordion outpost, now an independent city in the country of Nelenia. Once called
Castrusentis (kass-troo-SEN-tiss), it was originally
the site of a military border keep of the Gordion
Empire. After the collapse of the empire, the town
became an important trade center. These days Castlebriar is a city of around four thousand individuals,

home to mostly humans, wood elves, gnomes, and murids.

cockatrice (KOK-uh-triss): Said to be born from an egg laid by a chicken and incubated by a toad, the cockatrice is a strange animal with the head and legs of a rooster but the body of a dragon. Reportedly, the gaze of a cockatrice can turn a person to stone, though, not surprisingly, there are few eyewitness reports. Very rarely, a cockatrice is born with two heads, the second head being a serpent head on the end of its long tail.

Cybelle (SIH-buh-lee): A deity of the fallen Gordion Empire still worshiped in parts of Katernia today. Cybelle is also called the Mountain Mother and is often depicted with a lion beside her. She is the goddess of wild animals, town and city walls, fertility, and corn. Yes, corn has a deity. Who knew?

dactyl (DAK-tull): A type of seafaring dwarf native to the warmer climates of Thica and the Sacred Gordion Supremacy. Dactyls resemble other dwarves in stature but are darker-skinned, have curlier hair and more aquiline noses, and like to fish.

Dargan Urgul (DAR-gahn UR-gull): Called the Speaker to Barbarians, Dargan Urgul is a diplomatic aide in the Uskirian royal court. It is his job to communicate with outsiders on behalf of his emperor. Dargan is intrigued by the "barbarian" countries of the west and longs to see the world before the Uskirians "civilize" it. He thinks it will be a shame when all the untamed places are brought to heel, but he knows that, really, it's for their own good.

Deep Shadow: The major underground city of the dark elves, located in caverns under the Svartálfaheim Mountains. Deep Shadow is the greatest city on earth, a place of incredible wonder and achievement. At least, they'll kill anyone who says otherwise.

Desstra (DESS-truh): An elf in training to join the Underhand, she excels at stealth, strategy, and setting traps. Despite this, her superiors question if she truly fits in with her own people.

Fairshadow: A city of wood elves deep in the Blackfire Forest, within a few days' journey from Castlebriar. Visitors are welcome there, as long as they don't bring an ax.

Flittermouse: A giant bat that is one of a colony used by the dark elves of the Underhand as flying mounts.

Fosco Pertfingers (FOSS-koh): A gnome in the city of Castlebriar and owner of the tavern Fosco's Folly, which caters to wee folk such as gnomes, dwarves, and murids. All are welcome at Fosco's, but if you stand taller than five feet, you'd better watch your head!

gnome: A small humanoid creature that is very fond of gardens and flowers. Gnomes are native to Nelenia and the neighboring country of Tho Bovo. They can appear similar to dwarves, but they are smaller and more slender, and not as fond of rocks and jewels. Also, not quite so particular about beards.

Gordasha (gohr-DAH-shuh): Founded by dactyl dwarves from the country of Thica, this city was renamed Gordasha during the days of the Gordion Empire and was later made the capital of the Sacred Gordion Supremacy. It now has a population of around five hundred thousand people. Gordasha is located in an area of strategic importance, as it controls access to a strait between the Somber Sea and the Sparkle Sea. The city is protected by a formidable double wall on all sides. It has withstood many sieges in its history. Surely, it always will.

Hippodrome (HIH-puh-drohm): An enormous, U-shaped race course in the city of Gordasha, the Hippodrome is roughly 1,500 feet long and 500 feet wide. It was intended for horse-drawn chariot racing, but these days the chariots are pulled by deadly manticores, to make things more "interesting," you understand.

hörgr (HURR-gurr): A heap of stones erected as a shrine to a Norrønir god or guardian spirit. Hörgar dot the landscape of Norrøngard, and one is found in the city of Bense in Trickster's Market.

Horn of Osius (OH-see-us): Actually three magical horns crafted by Osius of Talsathia (tal-SAH-thee-uh) more than a thousand years ago. The horns offer mastery over serpents, wyverns, and other reptiles. Would-be wielders are cautioned, however, that their use has a tendency to annoy large dragons.

imperator (im-PAIR-uh-tohr): His Highness Adrius the Fourth, Ruler of the Sacred Gordion Supremacy, Monarch of the City of Gordasha, First Among Equals. The ruler of Gordasha and (ostensibly) the Sacred Gordion Supremacy. He likes to order people around, but he's not much good when the going gets tough.

Katernia (kuh-TUR-nee-uh): The continent of Katernia is one of the five major landmasses on the planet Qualth. It is home to a diverse range of cultures and races from many countries, from the Norrønir of the far northwest to the catfolk of Neteru in the south to the Uskirians of the northeast.

Leflin Greenroot (LEFF-lin): Ostensibly a historian living in the city of Castlebriar, the wood elf named Leflin Greenroot enjoys gambling and is often found at the Windy Willows, listening to music and playing Charioteers.

Malos Underfoot (MAL-ohs): Patron of Dark Elves, one of five sacred elders of the elfin race, Malos is an ancestor spirit venerated by all Svartálfar. If you want inspiration for the perfect dirty trick, Malos is your patron. But don't count on him for much that isn't deceitful, dangerous, or deadly.

manticore (MAN-ti-kohr): Nasty creature with the body of a lion, the face of a man, and the tail of a scorpion. Manticores are known for swallowing people whole and for having rather crude senses of humor.

Mensis (MEN-siss): A deity of the fallen Gordion Empire still worshiped in parts of Katernia today, especially in the city of Gordasha. He is often depicted with crescent-like horns protruding from his shoulders.

murids (MYOO-rids): A race of rodent-people. Murids are one of the smallest races in the world, and they face the most prejudice from other races. Despite this, or perhaps because of it, they are a resourceful people. There are four types of murids. Each resembles a different rodent. Mousekin are the most timid of the murids. Hamustros (HAM-oo-strohs) may be small, but you'd never know it from their hair. The Jird (jurd) are desert dwellers fond of arid environments. Ratkins, city dwellers by nature, are the most universally disliked of all murids. They never do anything to deserve this unsavory reputation. Never.

Nasthia Greenmother (NAHS-thee-uh): Patroness of Wood Elves, one of five sacred elders of the elfin race. Nasthia is an ancestor spirit venerated by all wood elves. She is the protector of forests and nature, loved by all who love growing things.

Nelenia (nuh-LEH-nee-uh): A country at the center of the continent of Katernia, Nelenia controls a major east-west passage between two mountain ranges, making it one of the most cosmopolitan countries on the continent, with a diverse population of humans, elves, gnomes, and murids.

Order of the Oak: A centuries-old secret society dedicated to finding lost magical artifacts and then hiding them away where they can never be used to tip the balance of power in the world. Or so they say.

Orysa (oh-RISS-uh): Senior instructor of the Underhand. Students find Orysa to be as stern as they come. You really don't want to get on her bad side. Unfortunately, that's the only side there is.

Sacred Gordion Supremacy: A small country that formed in the wake of the collapse of the Gordion Empire. The Sacred Gordion Supremacy proclaims itself as the legitimate heirs of the Gordions, but not many people believe that. Still, the Supremacy holds power because of its control of the strait between the Somber Sea and the Sparkle Sea. The Uskirians say it is an apple waiting to be plucked, but what do they know?

scutum (SKYOO-tuhm): A type of shield carried by soldiers in the long-vanished Gordion Empire. The scutum was a rectangular, curved shield. It was made of wood and covered with canvas and leather, and had a small metal boss in the center to protect the hand.

Shambok Who Borders on Spectacular (SHAM-bahk): The current leader of the Uskirian Empire, Shambok would rather dance than wage war. But life isn't all fun and games.

Svartálfar (SVAR-tahl-fahr): The dark elves of Norrøngard, who live under the Svartálfaheim Mountains (SVAR-tahl-fuh-hime). Once great wars were fought between the elves and the Norrønir. Now the Svartálfar mostly keep to themselves underground, but who knows what they are plotting?

Tanthal (TAN-thall): A dark elf from the city of Dark Shadow, Tanthal is snide, superior, and convinced of his own genius.

tatzelwurm (TAHT-zull-wurm): A creature native to the woods of Nelenia. It has the head and forelegs of a cat and the hind end of a serpent. Tatzelwurms are also called springwurms (SPRING-wurmz) because of their ability to leap great distances. They can be quite deadly, so be sure to carry your catswort (KATS-wohrt).

Ti-Emur (TY EE-mur): The Uskirian god of war. Ti-Emur is the trailblazer who must subdue the world so that Umalgen (oo-MAHL-gun), god of benevolence, and Karshan (KAHR-shawn), god of wisdom and knowledge, can follow in his wake. Ti-Emur is an impatient god, for only when all peoples are brought together under the banner of the Uskiri can he rest.

Underhand: An elite organization of the city of Deep Shadow dedicated to the protection of the city and the gathering of intelligence. The Underhand always has your best interest at heart. Honest.

Uskiri (USS-keer-ee): A group of once nomadic people who came together under the leadership of Yarak Uskir to form the Uskirian Empire. Now it is one of the largest and most sophisticated empires on the continent. In addition to being great warriors, the Uskiri are advanced in philosophy, mathematics, astronomy, floral arrangements, and dance.

wood elves: A subspecies of the elfin race who live in or near forests. Their skin color ranges across a variety of hues, similar to shades of tree bark and living wood.

Wyrdwood (WEIRD-wood): A forest in a valley in Norrøngard entirely surrounded by the Svartálfaheim Mountains. Humans avoid the Wyrdwood, which is home to many strange and dangerous creatures. *Wyrd* is the Norrønir word for "an individual's fate or destiny." However, any human out walking in the Wyrdwood at night might find that destiny cut short.

Yarak Uskir the Bone Breaker (YAH-rock USS-keer): The founder of the Uskirian Empire, in the year 832 AG, Yarak organized the warring nomadic bands of Uskiri into a formidable army, then proceeded to conquer several of his neighbors. At the time of his death, he charged his successors with expanding his empire southward through the Gordashan Strait. And so, for over a century, Uskirian armies periodically hurl themselves at the double walls of Gordasha.

Yelor (YAY-lohr): A dark elf and officer in the Underhand. Yelor has been assigned to the city of Castlebriar, which he dislikes, although he learns that he dislikes half giants even more.

Ynarr Ulfrsson (EE-nahr OOL-furrs-sun): A Norrønur who fought in the battle of Dragon's Dance, Ynarr left Norrøngard after a stain on his honor. He now serves as one of four members of the Sworn, the elite private guard for the imperator of the Sacred Gordion Supremacy. Unfortunately, he seems to have bad luck with employers.

THE RIDDLE OF THE
SOUNDLESS HORN

First to a Castle in the Briars,
Where ends all of life's desires.
Over Oak and under Corn,
There to seek the soundless Horn.

A little finger holds the fate,
Where a crescent commands a straight.
Upon the arc where shatters wheel,
Alter course and come to heel.

In Sunken Palace waters reign,
King and Dragon find their bane.
When snake and cockerel sundering,
Seek ye then the Marble King.

"WHEN YOU'RE AN USKIRIAN"

As sung by Shambok Who Borders on Spectacular
to Karn Korlundsson and Thianna Frostborn*

When I was young,
Just a wee lad,
My father said, "Shambok,
All your siblings are bad.
Kill them all
Or they'll get you.
There's room for only one at the top.
There's no place for number two.
It's a firm hand
You must have to lead a nation.
You'll lose your head
If you're not committed to this vocation."

When you're an Uskirian,
There's more to life than fun.
You have to take the whole wide world
With saber, scimitar, and cannon gun.
The civilization that we bring
Is such a fine and worthwhile thing.

---

* Translated from the Uskirian

Libraries, schools, centers of philosophy.
War is a classroom, and the teacher would be me.

When I was young,
Just a wee boy,
My father told me,
"The world is more than just your toy.
You have a job,
A task you must fulfill.
Conquer the world.
Only then can you sit still.
It's your quest.
Bringing peace to everyone.
It isn't pretty,
But it's a thing that must be done."

When you're Uskiri,
You have to travel every sea.
You have to conquer every land
For the empire's glory.
You've got to break the strait
To fulfill your legacy.
So you hammer at the walls
Of the Sacred Gordion Supremacy.

When I was young,
Just a wee one,
My father told me,

To take my place in the sun,
I must succeed
Where everyone has bent the knee.
"Conquer Gordasha.
Open up the Sparkle Sea.
You will be great."
And here Dad got a bit oracular.
"When you do this thing,
They'll call you Shambok the Spectacular!"

THE RULES OF CHARIOTEERS™

A GAME OF THE LOST GORDION EMPIRE

Charioteers is a game that dates all the way back to the Gordion Empire, but it is still played today in many countries across the continent of Katernia. The game is typically played by two to four players on a board where squares are used to approximate the shape of the famous Hippodrome of Gordasha, a racetrack for chariot racing. As in the Hippodrome, four starting lanes converge into only two racing lanes. This makes some starting positions more desirable than others.

OBJECT OF THE GAME

The object of the game is to race around the board. The first player to get any two of his or her four pieces to the finish line wins first place. Game play continues to determine second, third, and last place.

STARTING THE GAME

Each player controls four playing pieces, designated by the colors red, green, black, and gold. The turn sequence occurs in this same order, red first to gold last.

At the start of play, everyone rolls one six-sided die.

The player with the highest roll takes the gold team, second-highest the black team, third-highest the green team, and lowest the red team. Ties are resolved by rolling again.

The red player begins first, and turn sequence progresses from left to right: red, green, black, gold.

RED   GREEN   BLACK   GOLD

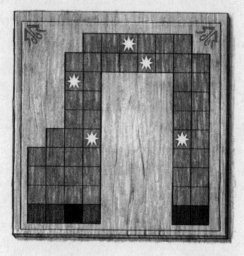

PLAYING THE GAME

To move, a player rolls four six-sided dice and counts the number of dice that show an even number (a 2, 4, or 6, as opposed to a 1, 3, or 5). The player can move the number of spaces equal to the number of evens in his or her roll. For example, a roll of 1, 2, 5, and 6 has two even numbers in it (2 and 6), and that player may move two spaces.

Pieces must move either in the direction of the course toward the finish line or side to side, but they may not reverse toward the starting gate. Diagonal moves are not allowed. A player may not occupy another player's starting square.

An even number of moves may be divided between more than one playing piece. In other words, two moves can be split 1/1, and four moves may be split 2/2, 2/1/1, or 1/1/1/1. Odd moves may not be divided and must be executed by a single playing piece only. (A roll resulting in three moves, for instance, cannot be divided between playing pieces.)

SMASHING AND CRASHING

Landing on an opponent represents smashing your chariot into him or her and sends your opponent back to the start. Passing over an opponent does not.

SMASHING

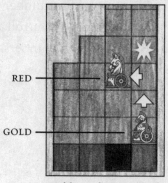

Gold smashes into Red.   Red returns to the start.

PASSING

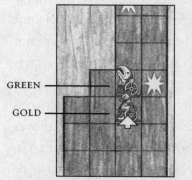

Gold passes over Green.   Green is not sent back.

If a playing piece is returned to the start, it is possible that a player might have more than one piece at the starting gate, and this is permissible.

Getting a result of 0 (no evens in a roll) is a crash, and the piece returns to the start. If a player has more than one piece on the board at the time he or she rolls a 0, the piece nearest to the finish line is the piece that crashes.

Star Squares

Star squares provide protection. A playing piece occupying a star square cannot be returned to the start either by another player or by a crash. Two opposing pieces can occupy a square at the same time, but only one per color and no more than two pieces total.

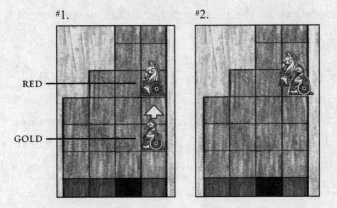

Winning the Game

The game is won by the first player to get any two of his or her four pieces across the finish line. Game play does not end when a player takes first place, but continues to determine second, third, and last place. Once a piece crosses the finish line, it is removed from play. However, a player may continue to play the game after he or she has won, using the remaining two playing pieces to affect the outcome of the remaining contestants.

Players may find that Charioteers encourages both cooperation and backstabbing, just like the chariot races in the Hippodrome!

Optional Rules

Over the centuries, variations of Charioteers have sprung up in different cities and countries around Katernia. Here are two of the most popular variations, presented as optional rules.

Fast Play: To speed up the game, players may roll six dice instead of four.

Long Play: Players wishing for a longer game can stipulate that all four of a player's pieces must cross the finish line in order to win, rather than two.

A HISTORY OF THE CONTINENT OF KATERNIA

(FROM *THE BOOK OF THE WORLD*,
AS RECORDED BY ALENYA CLOUDSPELL)

Twice upon a time the world began. First came the Dawn Age, a timeless era when gods, monsters, spirits, and other things for which there are no names wandered the lands and moved under the seas. From this chaos the elves arose. The Ljósálfar, whom men call the High Elves, ruled the world for centuries unchallenged. This period came to be known as the Era of Empires, and great things were accomplished that had not been done before and would not be done again. Theirs was the Light Empire, and humans existed only in the shadows of that light.

But Osius of Talsathia (an island that once existed off the southern coast of Thica) wanted more for his kind. From the dactyls, Osius learned the secrets of crafting and enchanting metals. Using a magical forge, Osius made three horns that gave him mastery over serpents. Using these horns, he gathered and enslaved the Great Dragons. The war of the Dragon King versus the Light Elves was fought for many years, and though not destroyed, the Light Empire was crippled.

But then the Great Dragons rebelled.

The dragons sank Talsathia beneath the sea; the forge and its secret knowledge were lost. But various human tribes on the continent were now free of Talsathian dominance. They picked at the remains of the Light Elf Empire, and from the scraps they snatched, they grew into what would become the Gordion Empire, the second great power of the age.

But what of the horns? Rumors of the powerful objects from Talsathia abounded.

One horn traveled to Thica. It was used there for a time. Lost and found again.*

One horn remained submerged. Legends of sunken Talsathia have lured many adventurers to their death beneath the waves.

One horn traveled to the Gordion outpost of Castrusentis, but its bearer died without successfully mastering it. Recognizing that the horn was valuable and dangerous, a secret society known as the Order of the Oak hid the horn in a special tomb. The Order recorded these events in the form of a cryptic riddle. It chose this method to both preserve the riddle's meaning across the centuries and ensure that only society members could decipher it.

One day, the tomb was robbed by a Gordion soldier, an auxiliary conscript and dactyl dwarf of Thican ancestry. He came from the city of Ambracia, and he was known as Acmon the Anvil.

Acmon used the horn to enslave the dragon Orma (or

---

* And finally destroyed, as per the events of the novel *Frostborn*.

so it was believed) and led a rebellion against the Gordion Empire in Ambracia. There, he ruled as king for a brief time, but Acmon and his dragon were overthrown by the Gordion Empire. Seeing his sister's downfall, the great dragon Orm fled across Katernia to the land of Norrøngard. When the dragon arrived in the city of Sardeth and found Gordions, his displeasure was terrible.

Meanwhile, the Order of the Oak added two more verses to their riddle, this time hidden on Acmon's lost shield, which he had left in the tomb in Castrusentis.

Years later, Ambracia was renamed Nova Gordion (New Gordion) by Emperor Gordas, but the name was not popular and the people called the city Gordasha instead.

When the Gordion Empire collapsed, marking the end of the Era of Empires, the Sacred Gordion Supremacy arose, a tiny remnant clinging to past glories. The Supremacy chose Gordasha as its capital and drew its meager power from the control of the Gordashan Strait.

Farther north, the once-wild Uskiri nomads united under the leadership of Yarak Uskir, Yarak the Bone-Breaker, who fashioned his people into a formidable power. Then Yarak turned his eyes southward to Gordasha. Ever after, Uskirian rulers hurled themselves against the city's walls. Those walls have always held, but it is said that one day they will fall.

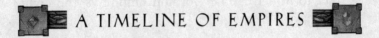

A TIMELINE OF EMPIRES

DA: The Dawn Age
EE: Era of Empires
AG: After Gordion

- ❖ **? to 4000 DA:** Gods and monsters roam the world.

- ❖ **4000s to 2000s EE:** The earliest human cultures start to emerge. On the mainland of Katernia, the Light Elf Empire arises and rules much of the continent.

- ❖ **1967 EE:** The great Dragon King civilization is founded when Osius of Talsathia forges the three horns (and many other legendary artifacts).

- ❖ **1912 to 1565 EE:** The War of the Dragon King vs. the Light Elves.

- ❖ **1565 EE:** The destruction of Talsathia. Many Talsathian refugees—particularly dactyl dwarves—immigrate to Thica.

- ❖ **1220 EE:** Gordion is founded by Gordius and Gordilla.

- ❖ **1138 EE:** Ambracia is founded by dactyl dwarves in a period of Thican colonial expansion.

❖ 942 to 808 EE: The Gordion Empire vs. the Light Empire.

❖ 739 EE: All free Thican colonies on Katernia, including Ambracia, surrender to the Gordion Empire.

❖ 731 EE: The Gordion Empire destroys the last vestiges of the Light Empire. Ljósálfaria falls under Gordion control.

❖ 645 EE: The Gordion Empire establishes an outpost in Norrøngard, which becomes the city of Sardeth.

❖ 616 EE: The Gordion Empire conquers Thica after winning the Battle of Pymonia.

❖ 389 EE: A tomb in Castlebriar, Nelenia, is robbed by a Gordion soldier, an auxiliary conscript and a Thican from Ambracia (who claims royal Thican lineage). He inadvertently leaves clues—a shield that is left propping open a stone slab—that identifies his origins in the city of Ambracia.

This soldier, named Acmon the Anvil, uses the horn to enslave the dragon Orma and lead a rebellion against the Gordion Empire in Ambracia.

❖ 386 EE: Acmon and Orma are turned to stone by the Gordion Empire. The great dragon Orm flees to Sardeth, upset at the empire. When he arrives, he burns the city to the ground.

- 172 EE: The Gordion Empire is divided into the Northern Empire and the Southern Empire.

- 137 EE: After he conquers the north and reunites the Gordion Empire, Emperor Gordas rechristens the city of Ambracia as Nova Gordion (but the name is not popular, and the locals call the city Gordasha instead).

- 3 AG: The official end of the Gordion Empire. Many new kingdoms are founded, and many old ones throw off the Gordion yoke. Collectively, they are sometimes called the Ember Kingdoms because they sprang from the ashes of the Gordion Empire. A remnant of the empire survives as the Sacred Gordion Supremacy, which makes its capital at Gordasha.

- 832 AG: Yarak Uskir forms the Uskirian Empire. He charges his successors with seizing Gordasha.

- 876 AG: Failed Siege of Gordasha by Kagrak the Nearly Great.

- 920 AG: The Thican Strait falls fully under the rule of the Sacred Gordion Supremacy, but non-Thicans are expelled from Thica. The Great Chain between Gordasha and the Fortress of Atros is covered by treaty.

- 923 AG: Failed Siege of Gordasha by Orzob the Almost Magnificent.

- 928 AG: Failed Siege of Gordasha by Shunk the Reasonably Impressive.

- 929 AG: Herzeria is conquered by Shunk the Now More Than Reasonably Impressive. Galdachian, Herzerian, Rosnian, and Turman forces, combined with forces from the Sacred Gordion Supremacy and a few troops drawn from Escoraine and Nelenia, undertake a grand crusade. 16,000 Crusaders meet 15,000 Uskirians. Herzeria falls, and the Uskirians slaughter almost 3,000 captured soldiers, while ransoming captured nobles. The scale of the defeat discourages further crusades. Rosnia, Galdachia, and the Sacred Gordion Supremacy are now the major impediment to Uskirian expansion (although the undesirable Rosnia climate forces most expansion attempts to be directed southward, while the Muspilli mountain range, home to fire giants and volcanoes, proves its own effective barrier).

- 985 AG: The events of the novel *Frostborn*.

- 986 AG: Under the leadership of Shambok Yargul, known as Shambok Who Borders on Spectacular, the Uskirians lay siege to the city of Gordasha.

ACKNOWLEDGMENTS

Thanks to my beta readers this round: Justin Anders, Judith Anderson, Logan Ertel, Howard Andrew Jones, Janet Lewis, J. F. Lewis, Jay Requard, and Cindi Stehr. Thanks to Jonathan Anders for insightful comments about the rules of Charioteers™ and help with the play-testing. Additional thanks are also due to Jay Requard for his expert opinion on swords and their classifications and merits. Thanks to James Enge for helping me to clarify some elements of Greek mythology. Thanks again to Trond-Atle Farestveit for help with my Norrønian pronunciation.

Thanks to my agent, Barry Goldblatt of Barry Goldblatt Literary. Thanks to my editor at Crown Books for Young Readers, Phoebe Yeh, and to Random House Children's Books publisher Barbara Marcus. Thanks to Rachel Weinick, editorial assistant; Cassie McGinty, associate publicist; Alison Kolani, director of copyediting; Isabel Warren-Lynch, executive art director; and Ken Crossland, senior designer. Thanks to Julianna N. Wilson, my audiobook producer at Penguin Random House Audio's Listening Library; to my audiobook director, Christina Rooney; and to my fabulous narrator, Fabio Tassone. Thanks to Dominique Cimina, director, publicity and corporate communication. And to everyone who worked on the incredible ThronesandBones.com site.

Once again, thanks to Justin Gerard for his awe-inspiring artwork, to Robert Lazzaretti for his marvelous maps, and to Andrew Bosley for the wonderful work that appears on the Thrones and Bones website.

Finally, and always, thanks to my wonderful family for their love and support.

For Thianna, Karn, and Desstra,
all roads converge in Thica.
Continue the quest for the
Horn of Osius in . . .

SKYBORN

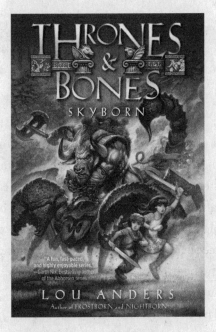

CHAPTER ONE

The One Truth

The javelin flew with lethal speed. A long, thin messenger of death in an otherwise blue sky. It was fast, but Sirena struck even faster. The young girl's blade sliced the wooden shaft in half. The two pieces clattered on the polished marble squares of the courtyard. Then everything was still except for the noise of waves crashing on rocks far below, the beating of hearts, and the rushing of blood.

"Well done," her opponent said.

Sirena narrowed her brown eyes.

"Of course it was," she replied. "Compliments are a waste of breath. You tell me nothing I don't already know."

Her opponent nodded grimly and drew her sword. She was close to Sirena in size and age. Both wore bronze breastplates molded to the contours of their torsos above tunics hung with strips of black leather. Both carried shields, while their heads were protected by bronze helmets with proud black plumes.

"Is your mind as sharp as your weapon?" Sirena's opponent charged as she spoke, sandals pounding on the smooth stone of the courtyard. "What is the One Truth?" the soldier asked.

Sirena shifted her own stance to meet the assault.

"War is the mother of all," she replied, catching the blade on her own. With a twist of the wrist, Sirena opened the soldier's guard, driving her shield hard into the armored breastplate.

Stunned by the blow, the soldier fell to the ground. Sirena pointed the tip of her sword at the girl's throat.

"I yield," her opponent said.

Sirena hesitated before withdrawing her blade.

"You *yield*," she said. The word was like dung in her mouth. She would never speak it herself.

Sirena didn't spare the fallen girl another glance. She adjusted her grip on her pelta, the distinctive crescent-shaped half shield of Calderan soldiers. The hot sun beat down on her as she squared her small but muscled shoulders. She gazed for a moment at the bright stone columns of the Twin Palaces where they gleamed in the noonday sun, but she didn't look to the stands where her audience of one watched. Then Sirena advanced to the next challenge.

"What is Damnameneus's theorem?" A harder question from a tougher warrior. This opponent was taller than Sirena and older than her own twelve years. She would not be so easily bested.

"The square of the hypotenuse," replied Sirena as she swung her blade at the patch of bare neck between the woman's helmet and armored torso, "matches the total of the squares of the other two sides."

"Correct," the woman said, stepping out of Sirena's reach and bringing her own sword around in a sweeping arc.

Sirena dropped to the ground and rolled under the woman's attack. Then she came to one knee and drove her sword between the black leather straps of the soldier's tunic and into her thigh.

"I know it's correct," Sirena said. "I don't need you to tell me that. I only require that you fall."

Admirably the woman did not cry out as her leg collapsed. Better yet she did not waste words spinning flattery or admitting defeat. She lay still, appraising Sirena with hard eyes.

Good, Sirena thought. She is a proper soldier. I shall remember this one when I am a queen. She should be promoted. But not too high.

"Describe Metarchus's thoughts on justice?" the third opponent asked.

Sirena turned just in time to avoid a searing bolt of flame. She leapt aside, landing in a crouch.

"Nothing is straighter than that which is straight. Nothing is juster than that which is just."

Sirena stayed low, racing under the long fire lance and tackling the soldier around the legs. They went down together, but only Sirena stood up. She could not deny that she was proud of her performance. Philosophy, mathematics, combat—she had mastered them all. But the day was not yet won. Almost.

The cliffside courtyard was laid out in a grid of eight-by-eight squares, with opponents waiting on alternating rows. It was a giant game board for deadly play. Sirena had advanced past the midpoint now and had only one challenge remaining.

"Who said, 'There is nothing eternal except for change'?" the last soldier asked.

"Lanera the Playwright, in her first tragedy," Sirena replied. She disarmed the woman in two moves, stabbed her through the shoulder with a third.

"But she was a fool." Sirena looked to the stands now, to her single observer. She called across the intervening space, "Caldera is eternal. Thica is eternal. We make it so."

The sound of clapping rang out over the hilltop.

"Bravo!" Queen Melantha shouted. "Bravo!"

Sirena sheathed her sword, then removed her helmet and shook out her long black hair. She moved to join her aunt, the Land Queen of Caldera.

"Your mind and your body are in top form," Melantha

said. "You will make a fine champion this day. And a finer queen when the time comes. Your mother would have been proud."

Sirena nodded, her cheeks reddening from something other than the hot sun. She might refuse compliments from an inferior, but the praise of her aunt she would accept.

"We will crown you champion properly tonight, then," she said. "But let's take refreshment together now."

Sirena smiled. So much that she had always wanted was hers now. But her pleasure was to prove short-lived.

"Perhaps I will join you in that celebration," said a newcomer. "Though we'll raise our cups to something other than what you have in mind."

Queen Xalthea, the Sky Queen, stepped out from between marble columns. Together, Xalthea the Sky Queen and Melantha the Land Queen ruled the island-continent of Thica. One commanded the forces of the ground and the other the forces of the air.

"Good fortune to you, Xalthea," said Melantha. "If you had come just five minutes earlier, you wouldn't have missed my niece's performance."

"It hardly matters," said the Sky Queen dismissively. "Something far more important has occurred."

Sirena glared at the co-monarch. What could be more important than her life's goal? Ever since her own mother's death, her aunt had groomed her for this day and all the days to follow.

Ignoring the angry eyes of the young girl, Xalthea turned to the Land Queen.

"They've found it," she said.

Melantha didn't understand what the Sky Queen meant at first. But Sirena did. She knew exactly what "it" was. The knowledge descended on her like a boulder dropped from a tower.

"The Horn of Osius," she whispered.

"Yes," said Xalthea. "The Horn of Osius has been recovered. Our empire is secure." She turned to Sirena. "Or it will be. If you do your part correctly."

"My part?"

"You are the closest in blood," the Sky Queen said.

"I don't know anything about the horn," Sirena protested. "I'm a soldier. I'm the Queen's Champion. I'm going to be—"

"Not anymore," interrupted Xalthea. "My needs—our needs—are more important. You will leave your aunt's side and take your place by mine."

"No!" protested Sirena.

"No?" said Xalthea softly. Sirena froze. When the Sky Queen spoke so calmly she was at her most dangerous.

"Perhaps there is another way," interjected Melantha. But her voice was tentative, hesitant. She lacked the determination of the Sky Queen. She lacked the fire.

"You know there isn't," said Xalthea. "Or are you challenging me?"

Sirena looked at her aunt, daring to hope. The two

queens of Caldera rarely disagreed, but there was a precedent for resolving disputes when they arose. A deadly precedent.

Melantha dropped her eyes.

"No," she said. "No, of course not."

Sirena felt cold despite the midday sun. How could she stand by her aunt if her aunt would not stand by her?

"But—but—" she stammered. "But this is everything."

"Thica is everything," said Xalthea. "Caldera is everything."

Sirena's aunt laid a hand on her shoulder.

"Remember the words of Lanera the Playwright," said Melantha. "Take some comfort in her advice: 'A ship should not be secured by a single anchor; a life should not be tethered to a single hope.'"

"I already told you Lanera was a fool," said Sirena. She met the Land Queen's gaze. "Go to the crows."

Watching the hurt swell in her aunt's eyes, Sirena almost took back her words. But what was said was said. She allowed Xalthea to take her arm above the elbow and lead her away from everything she had always wanted to whatever her new life would be.

It was a treasonous thought, but she wished the horn had never been found. Wished it had stayed lost on the other side of the world. But how had this come about? She wanted to know who was responsible for undoing her happiness.

"Tell me," asked Sirena as she entered Xalthea's wing

of the Twin Palaces, "how was the horn recovered? Has Talaria finally been captured?"

"That traitor died long ago," said the Sky Queen. "But apparently she had a child. A girl of mixed race who blew the horn and alerted us to its presence. My soldiers have been after it for some months, and it's finally come back to us."

A girl. A child of Talaria.

"This girl," asked Sirena, "what's she called?"

Sirena wanted to know her name, this half-breed who had inadvertently ruined her life.

"Her name isn't important," replied Queen Xalthea. "Though you might find it amusing—Thican and barbarian names cobbled together." The queen chuckled. "I'm told she is called Thianna Frostborn."

"Sweet Ymir's feet," said Thianna Frostborn with a whistle as she slid from the wyvern's back.

"I don't know how sweet *his* feet are," Karn Korlundsson said from where he still sat atop the reptile. "But if yours are any indication of what frost giants' feet smell like, I think I'd choose a different word. Now move over and let me down."

Thianna chuckled as she stepped aside, then reached a large hand up to help her best friend dismount. They stood together on the hillside and looked at the lights of the coastal city before them, though, as a half giant, Thianna stood a head and a half taller than Karn.

"Thica is a big land to find one horn," Thianna observed. "I wish we'd had time to learn a bit more about what we're in for."

"You're not tackling it alone this time," Karn replied.

"Don't think I could?" Her eyes had that glint in them that they always got when she contemplated a challenge. "Don't worry," she said, breaking into a chuckle. "I've learned my lesson."

Thianna was referring to their recent adventures in which they had fought dark elves and other dangers in a race to find the lost Horn of Osius, a powerful weapon now in the hands of their enemies in Thica. She had set off alone on a quest to find the horn at the behest of the dragon Orm. Then Karn had been sent to rescue her. Now, together, they were going to get it back.

"No more adventuring without my trusty Norrønboy," she continued. Karn was from Norrøngard, the source of the nickname. It was better than Short Stuff, her other name for him.

"Good," he answered. "But it's not just me coming with you. Don't forget; we've got Desstra's help now too."

Thianna's dark eyes clouded.

"I don't know how much help she's going to be," the giantess grumbled.

"You don't mean that," said Karn. "She's already proven herself."

"To you maybe."

Karn winced. True, the dark elf had opposed them for most of their quest, even tricked and betrayed Karn to her superiors in the sinister organization known as the Underhand, but when she had switched sides at the end, she had sacrificed everything to save them.

Karn thought to say more, but then the shadow of a giant bat swooped low overhead. Desstra's mount, Flittermouse, glided to a nearby tree, where it grasped a branch and hung upside down. Karn watched as Desstra somersaulted from her saddle to land nimbly on the ground. He wondered how much of their conversation the elf's keen ears had picked up.

Despite Thianna's feelings, Desstra had proved very helpful getting here. Choosing a night when both the moon and her satellite were invisible, her giant bat had guided them in the dark to this coastal city. But now that they were in Thica, they couldn't risk traveling overland in the sky where the only fliers would be Thican soldiers wielding deadly fire lances. Not that the surly wyvern would carry them any closer to the home of its once-masters. And Flittermouse wasn't large enough to carry anything heavier than one small elf. They'd have to make their own way from here on out.

The elf ran a hand through the fur of her upside-down mount's cheek.

"I'm sorry to say goodbye to you again, boy," she told the bat. "I wish I could take you with me."

Flittermouse squeaked sadly, as though it understood. Probably it did.

Desstra stood on tiptoes to hug the animal around its neck.

"Don't go back to Deep Shadow," she whispered, speaking of the underground city of dark elves. "There's nothing for either of us there. I hope you find a new home where you fit in, one where they treat you nicely."

The bat's eyes said it hoped the same thing for her. Desstra sighed. Then she let go of her mount and approached Thianna and Karn.

"Sun's coming up soon," she said. "We'd better get inside the city before it does."

"Yeah, we already know that," said Thianna. "So not very helpful."

"Good thinking, though," said Karn, glaring at the giantess. Thianna shrugged. Beside her, the wyvern hissed.

"I guess this is goodbye to you too," Thianna said.

If you expect me to shed any tears at our parting, it spoke into her mind, *you're going to be sadly disappointed.*

"I know you're really crying inside," Thianna said with a chuckle. Then she surprised the reptile by hugging it around its long neck.

Get off! Get off! Get off! its thoughts screamed. It tugged its neck in a useless attempt to dislodge the frost giantess, but when Thianna released it, the wyvern added, *For what it's worth, I hope you succeed at your mad scheme.*

"Sure you won't come?"

Bringing you here to the coast was risk enough. I'm leaving now, before the dawn arrives. Live well or die well, Thianna Frostborn.

Then, without another word, it flapped its wings and rose into the night. Flittermouse squeaked once, then the bat too flew away into the darkness.

"A tearful farewell?" asked Karn. Lacking Thianna's ability to communicate with reptiles, he had only heard the frost giantess's half of the conversation.

"What do you think?" she replied. "Still, I think that wyvern was as sentimental as they get." She chuckled. "I must be growing on it."

"Kind of like mold on cheese?" teased Karn.

Thianna punched his shoulder playfully, then guided by Desstra's night vision the three companions began making their way down the hill.

They knew from Karn's experience studying maps of the world that the city was called Ithonea. Choosing it as their point of entry into Thica had been a compromise between avoiding the most obvious, direct route while not wanting to detour too far out of their way. They slipped into the city just as it was waking up. There were no guards or gates to impede their progress. Non-Thican boats were kept at bay by the Death Ray of Damnameneus, a large parabolic mirror that harnessed the sun's rays to project a beam of light that set ships afire. Similar mirrors were erected around the entire Thican coast.

Thianna had visited a half-dozen cities since she'd left her mountaintop last year. Each was as different from the other as it was from a frost giant's village. Ithonea was no exception. It was a city of twisting, narrow streets that wound between white-painted houses roofed with large terra-cotta tiles. It stretched up a hillside, broken into districts by ancient walls and crumbling fortifications that still stood from the era of Gordion conquest. Paved steps that ascended narrow passageways were painted an aquamarine blue. At a glance they looked like tumbling fountains spilling over rocks. As Ithonea came to life, so did Thianna's enthusiasm.

"My mother's homeland," she pronounced in awe. "I never imagined that I'd see it, but here we are."

Although the half giant was taller than anyone else, the people around her all shared her dark olive complexion and dark hair. Even the nonhumans she saw amid the crowd looked more like her kin than the frost giants she had grown up with. This was indeed her mother's country, and she drank it all in. Beside her, her companions had donned cloaks and hoods to hide their pale skin and, in Karn's case, fair hair. Desstra also wore quartz lenses to protect her eyes from the sun.

Thianna's nostrils quivered at the smell of grilled lamb.

"Food!" she said enthusiastically. "Hey, what do they use for money here?"

"Drachmas," Karn replied. "I'd be surprised if they took our foreign coin." He fingered the silver ring on his left hand. The face was cast to look like the rings of a tree stump. It was the symbol of the secret society known as the Order of the Oak. "I wonder what this is worth."

"You're thinking of pawning it?" Thianna was surprised. "Didn't Greenroot say it would mark you as a friend of the Order, maybe open doors for you?"

"Surely not here," said Karn, but he left the ring on his finger.

They followed the market as it wound uphill. Thianna observed that the shops became more expensive the higher they rose. She also noticed that they had begun to draw stares from the Ithoneans, some of them unfriendly. Despite her height, however, most of the looks were directed downward, toward their legs.

She stopped walking when a little boy blocked her way, gaping at her with his mouth open. Thianna frowned at him, a rude retort taking shape on her tongue.

"Awesome!" he said, and his face lit with admiration.

"What?" said Thianna, taken aback.

The boy pointed.

"My legs?" she asked. "What is it about my legs?"

The child reached out tentatively to poke the fabric of her woolen breeches.

Suddenly the boy's mother was beside him, her face pinched with disapproval.

"Come away from her, Pogos," she said, ushering her son back from Thianna.

"We were just talking," said the giantess.

"I don't care if it's all the rage among you young people to dress like barbarians," said the child's mother. "Your parents would be ashamed."

"What are you on about?" replied the frost giant, her face flushing in anger.

"Your pants!" the woman spat. "Look at you, parading around like a savage in pants!"

With that she hurried her child away.

It was then that Thianna realized they were the only ones in the city sporting leg wear. Everyone else was dressed in robes or, as a concession to the heat, knee-length tunics bound at the waist. No one besides herself, Karn, and Desstra had anything on their legs. Thinking of Desstra, Thianna realized the girl had vanished.

"Where's the elf?" she asked Karn.

He looked around and shrugged. "I don't know."

"Maybe she had a change of heart after all," Thianna said.

"Or maybe she got you breakfast," said Desstra, surprising them by appearing in their midst. She passed Karn and Thianna wraps of grilled lamb in pita bread.

"How did you get these?" asked Karn.

"Drachmas," replied the elf, jingling a newly stolen coin purse affixed to her belt. Karn winced at her casual thievery, though he knew the need was great. And unlike other dark elves he had met, she wouldn't have harmed anyone for it.

"Thank you," he said, glaring at Thianna to do the same.

"We need to find the Thican Empire's local garrison," she replied, ignoring him.

"Already taken care of," said Desstra. "Yes, I'm that perfect," she added when Thianna raised an eyebrow. "There's an old keep midway up the hill." She indicated the way. "Just far enough away you'll be able to eat your breakfast before we get there."

Sure enough, by the time Thianna and Karn had finished eating and Thianna had purchased and wolfed down a second breakfast, Desstra had led them to the garrison. They saw several soldiers lounging about before the gate.

"This looks like the place," said the frost giant.

"Yes," said Karn, who recognized the distinctive bronze and black leather armor. "But are *all* Thican soldiers women?"

Sure enough, the soldiers out front were exclusively female. As had been all the Thican soldiers they had encountered on their adventures.

"I guess we'll find out," said Thianna. "Are we ready to do this?"

"If you're certain," said Karn.

"The only way out is through," she replied. "Let's go

make some new friends." Then she marched forward to the gate, her height and her strange companions drawing looks from the soldiers.

"Looks like we've got their attention," Karn observed.

"One way to be sure," his friend replied.

Thianna slid the arming sword from her sheath. Beside her, Karn drew his sword, Whitestorm, and Desstra readied a pair of slender darts. Now the soldiers became alert, readying swords, spears, and the deadly fire lances. They shouted for backup and rushed into defensive positions.

Thianna let them assemble, then walked straight up to their line of menacing weapons.

"I'm Thianna Frostborn," she said. "And these are my companions." She held her sword ready. Then she dropped it on the ground at her feet, where it clattered loudly on the paving stone.

"We yield," said Thianna.

"You what?" asked a confused soldier.

"Are you deaf?" replied the giantess. "We *yield*. So what are you waiting for? Capture us and take us to your leader, already. We surrender."